SAS
OPERATION

Gambian Bluff

DAVID MONNERY

HARPER

Though many of the events depicted in this novel actually took place in
The Gambia in the summer of 1981, it should be considered entirely a work of
fiction. The names, characters and incidents portrayed in it are the work
of the author's imagination. Any resemblance to actual persons,
living or dead, events or localities is entirely coincidental.

Harper
An imprint of HarperCollins*Publishers*
1 London Bridge Street,
London SE1 9GF
www.harpercollins.co.uk

This paperback edition 2016
1

First published by 22 Books/Bloomsbury Publishing plc 1994

David Monnery asserts the moral right to
be identified as the author of this work

A catalogue record for this book
is available from the British Library

ISBN: 978 0 00 815518 6

Set in Sabon by Born Group using Atomik ePublisher from Easypress

Printed and bound in Great Britain

MIX
Paper from
responsible sources
FSC™ C007454
FSC
www.fsc.org

FSC is a non-profit international organisation established
to promote the responsible management of the world's forests.
Products carrying the FSC label are independently certified
to assure consumers that they come from forests that are managed
to meet the social, economic and ecological needs
of present and future generations.

Find out more about HarperCollins and the environment at
www.harpercollins.co.uk/green

1

'This town is 'coming like a ghost town . . .'

The song seemed to float ominously out of every open door and window as Worrell Franklin walked slowly down Acre Lane.

'Do you remember the good old days before the ghost town?'

No, not really, he thought, although only a fool would deny that things were getting worse.

A Rasta walked past him, going up the hill, and the look he flashed Franklin was for his uniform, not his face. Or, to be precise, the combination of the two. The oppressor's uniform, the face of the oppressed. A black soldier in a white man's army.

Franklin was used to looks like that, and to the more subtle ones that blended hostility with respect, contempt with envy. He was someone who had got out, escaped. He was someone with a job, which these days felt more and more like a privilege in itself.

Normally he did not wear his uniform around Brixton – it was just easier not to – but this morning he had it on for a reason. The only reason around here. For impressing Whitey.

He turned left onto the High Road and walked north. A crowd of youths were outside the tube station, doing nothing, just waiting for something to ignite their interest. On his side of the road a crowd were gathered round a TV shop, watching the Royal Wedding on the dozen or so sets in the window. When Franklin had left his mum in their living room Lady Diana had been setting out from Clarence House in the ceremonial Glass Coach, looking like an upmarket Cinderella. Now she was walking up the steps of St Paul's, trailing an ivory-coloured dress which looked long enough to play cricket on.

The camera followed her into the cathedral, dwelling on a few famous faces in passing: Mrs T in a blue pillbox hat, Nancy Reagan in a nauseating pink, the Queen in aquamarine, looking like she usually did, as if she was trying hard not to notice that someone had farted nearby.

And then there was the King of Tonga, whose specially reinforced chair had been featured on the news that morning. It would hardly do to have the great fat git crashing through his pew in the middle of the ceremony.

Franklin tore himself away from the glorious nuptials and walked on under the railway bridges. The police station was another two hundred yards down on the right, across from the junction with Stockwell Road. Even from a distance it looked like a fortress, with its windows protected by wire mesh, and the building itself by iron railings.

He wove his way through the stopped traffic at the lights and walked in through the front door. The desk sergeant's face went through that series of expressions which Franklin could have painted from memory. First there was the instinctive mixture of contempt and hostility accorded any black face, second the unpleasant element of surprise which went with putting that face above the authority of a uniform. Then the observer's brain engaged, realized that it was a British Army uniform, and spread relief back through the limbs.

Finally the question of a reason for his presence intruded, creating a wariness which was usually expressed through mock aggression.

It all took about five seconds.

'What can we do for you, John?' the sergeant asked. Behind him, from somewhere deep within the recesses of the station, the sounds of the Royal Wedding could be heard. Another two policemen were watching the exchange, both of them white. Where are the black policemen? Franklin wondered. Probably 'out in the community', trying to explain themselves.

This was why he had joined up, to get away from all this.

'My name is Worrell Franklin,' he said formally. 'I believe my brother Everton Franklin is in custody here.'

The desk sergeant's face went through another sequence, culminating in brisk correctness. He opened one of the ledgers in front of him and ran his finger down a list. 'That is correct, sir,' he said. 'He was remanded by the magistrates this morning.'

'I'd like to talk to someone about the circumstances of the arrest, and to see my brother if that's possible.'

'I don't know . . .'

'I only have a twenty-four-hour leave,' Franklin lied, 'so I would appreciate it if something could be arranged.' He wondered if anyone had recognized the winged-dagger badge, or whether he would have to spell out his membership of the SAS.

The desk sergeant glanced round at his two comrades, who stared blankly back at him. 'I'll see what I can do,' he said, adding 'have a seat, sir' as he disappeared through a door. The other two resumed their paperwork.

Franklin sat down on the long bench and picked up the copy of the *Sun* which someone had left behind. Opposite the tits on page three he read that the identity of the Toxteth hit-and-run policeman had still not been established. Surprise, surprise, he thought. And the constable who had been brained by the TV thrown from the high-rise walkway was still in critical condition. There were victims wherever you looked.

Too much fighting on the dance floor . . . The bloody song would not leave him alone.

The sergeant returned with a plain-clothes officer, who introduced himself as Detective-Sergeant Wilson. 'Like in *Dad's Army*,' he explained, most likely out of habit. 'Not often we see the SAS in Brixton,' he said. 'We could have used you a few times this year,' he added with a smile.

Someone had recognized the beret badge, then. Franklin politely returned the smile. 'Can you tell me the circumstances of my brother's arrest?' he asked.

'I can.' He opened the file he was carrying, and extracted a typed sheet. 'I'm afraid he's facing four charges – possession of an offensive weapon, assault, damaging a police vehicle and using threatening behaviour. This is the arresting officer's report,' he said, handing it across.

It was not exactly a literary masterpiece. Nor did it seem particularly precise where it needed to be. The gist of it was that two officers had been inside one of the small businesses in Spenser Road when someone had thought fit to roll a petrol bomb under their car. Several arrests had followed, including that of Everton Franklin. He had apparently put up rather more than token resistance, setting about a policeman with a cricket bat.

'There's nothing here to connect my brother with the torching of the vehicle,' Franklin murmured. Indeed there was nothing to suggest why the police had tried to arrest him in the first place.

4

'He was probably carrying the bat,' Wilson said, when confronted with this apparent oversight. 'More evidence must have been offered to the magistrates, or they wouldn't have remanded him.'

It didn't seem the time or place to push the issue. 'Can I see my brother?' he asked.

'If you wish, sir.' The detective waited for a reply, as if hoping for a change of mind.

'Yes, I would like to,' Franklin said patiently. He was depressingly aware that if he had not been wearing his uniform his chances of getting even this far would have been less than zero.

'Then come this way, sir.'

He was led down two corridors and ushered into what looked like an interview room. There was just a single table, with one chair either side of it, and two more against a wall. The two windows to the outside world were high enough to reveal only sky, the one in the door was small enough to remind Franklin of depressing prison films.

'It'll be a few minutes, sir,' Wilson said, and disappeared, closing the door behind him. Franklin could hear the TV coverage of the Royal Wedding through the ceiling.

The minutes stretched out. How long could it take to bring someone up from the cells? Franklin had a sudden sinking sensation in his stomach – what if Everton was one of the unlucky few who went into a police station and never came out again? It did not happen often, but it did happen. It would kill their mum. Except that she would kill him first. He had always been expected to look out for his younger brother, and he had, at least until he had left home for the Army. He could scarcely watch over him from Germany or Northern Ireland. Or even from Hereford. And Everton was nineteen now. He should be able to look after himself.

But try telling his mum that.

He was about to go looking for Wilson when the door opened to reveal Everton. 'Fifteen minutes, sir,' Wilson said from behind him, before closing the door on the two brothers.

'What you doin' here?' Everton asked wearily, sitting down at the table.

'It's good to see you, too,' Franklin said, holding up a palm in greeting.

Everton gave it a half-hearted slap with his own. His face, Franklin noticed, bore a couple of angry-looking bruises. 'How d'ya get those?' he asked.

'How d'ya think? I assaulted a policeman's boot with my head.'

Franklin said nothing.

'Don't you worry 'bout me, bro,' Everton said, more to break the silence than for any other reason. 'There's some Rastas here who pulled their own dreadlocks out to scourge the poor policemen with. By the roots,' he added.

'I read your arrest sheet,' Franklin said.

'Yeah? I bet that was a fine piece of fiction. They probably write poetry in their spare time, like that dickhead detective on telly.'

'What did happen?'

'You have to ask?'

'Yeah, I have to ask. If the police report is a fine piece of fiction then I need someone else to tell me some fine fact, right?'

Everton breathed out noisily. 'OK. I got no call to take it out on you.' He sighed. 'What happened was what always happens. Someone gives the police reason to freak, and they freak. Arrest anyone they can who's the right colour, fill up the cells, then retire to their easy chairs upstairs to square their stories . . .'

'What happened? Did a police car get petrol-bombed?'

Everton smiled. 'Yeah. It was a couple of dumb kids. They's probably halfway to Jamaica by now. They just roll this Coke can full of petrol with a bit of rag in it under the car. There's no one inside it – the cops are inside Dr Dread's, looking for some reason to bust him again. And the bomb goes off, but only like a firework – the car don't go up or nothing. I was right there, talking to Benjy, when it all happens, and we see these kids in the garden next door playing cricket so we run in and try and get 'em to move in case there's an explosion, right, but they ignore us, so we have to steal their bat. They come running after us, and the next thing I know about five policemen are jumping on top of me and throwing me in the back of a van. And they bring me here. And they make up a nice story for the magistrates, who all look at me like I should be grateful for not having been shot already.' He looked at his brother. 'That's the whole story,' he said.

'And they beat you up?'

'Not really. Just a couple of playful punches in the van. It was nothing much. I was lucky. Like I say, some of the Rastas really got treated bad.'

Franklin looked at the floor. Somewhere deep inside him, in that place he had learned to shut it away, his anger was straining for release. He suppressed the urge – where could it take him that he had not already been? He asked if Benjy had also been arrested.

'No. He must have picked the right road to run down. Or maybe he just not carrying a cricket bat . . .'

'So he can be a witness. Where's he live?'

'He won't want to make himself that conspicuous. He knows what happens if he does.'

7

'What happens?'

'You've been away too long, bro. His car gets stopped every time he goes out, his social security gets delayed, the sniffer dogs take a liking to his house . . . you know.'

'I'll talk to him anyway. And there must have been other witnesses.'

'Hundreds. And they all know they're on a hiding to nothing. Even if they speak out the judges take the word of the policeman. So why speak out?'

Franklin had no answer. 'You still looking for a job?' he asked Everton.

'Me and the rest of Brixton.'

'I'll get you out of here,' Franklin said.

'Oh yeah? Then I'll keep my eyes on the windows for when the big black man comes abseiling in.'

Franklin refused to be provoked. 'I'll talk to some people,' he said.

'Worrell,' his brother said, 'one thing I like to know. The next time Brixton goes up, and they need the Army to put out the fire, whose side you be on?'

'I go where my conscience say I should go,' Franklin said. 'I not on anyone's side,' he added, noticing that it only needed a few minutes with Everton and the old anger to have him talking like a Rasta again.

'Then I hope your conscience is in good shape, man,' Everton said, 'cos I think you're gonna need it to be.'

'Yeah. You worry about your own future,' Franklin said, getting up. 'And don't go assaulting no more policeman's boots with your head.'

'I'll try real hard to restrain myself.'

'Any message for Mum?'

'Tell her I'm OK. Not to worry.'

'OK. I'll be back.'

As if on cue, Detective-Sergeant Wilson opened the door. 'We're done,' Franklin said. He had already decided to make no complaint about the beating his brother had been given. It would serve no purpose, and it might conceivably get in the way of getting Everton released. 'I appreciate your help,' he told Wilson, catching a glimpse of his brother's disapproving face over the detective's shoulder.

Out on Brixton Road once more, he took a deep breath of fresh air and walked slowly back in the direction he had come. The crowd was still clustered around the bank of televisions, watching the now-married twosome leaving St Paul's. They looked happy enough, Franklin thought, but who could really tell? He wondered if they had made love yet, or if the royal dick was yet to be unveiled. Maybe the Queen Mother would cut a ribbon or something.

He remembered his own mother had asked him to pick up some chicken wings in the market. Her younger son might be in custody, but the older one still had to be fed. Franklin recrossed the road and walked down Electric Avenue to their usual butcher. A street party seemed to be getting under way, apparently in celebration of the royal event. Prince Charles was the most popular establishment figure in Brixton – in fact, he was the only popular establishment figure. People thought he cared, which in the summer of '81 was enough to make anyone look like a revolutionary.

The only big difference between this and a thousand other British neighbourhoods was the colour scheme – the flags and balloons were all red, yellow and green rather than red, white and blue. Even the kids milling on the street corners seemed to have smiles on their faces this morning, Franklin noticed. For a couple of hours it was just possible to believe there was only one Britain.

Unless, of course, you were locked up in one of the Brixton Police Station's remand cells for no better reason than being the wrong colour in the wrong place at the wrong time.

2

One of the many heads of state attending the Royal Wedding was Sir Dawda Jawara, President of the small West African state of The Gambia. In the colonial twilight of the early 1960s Jawara had led his nascent country's pro-independence movement, and ever since that heady, flag-exchanging day in 1965 he had presided over the government of the independent state. The Gambia was not exactly a huge pond – its population had only recently passed the half-million mark and its earnings were mostly derived from groundnuts and tourism – but there was no doubting who was the biggest fish.

The Wedding over, the embassy limousine swished President Jawara out of London and south down the M23 towards Haywards Heath, where he planned to spend a long weekend with an old college friend. With him he had one of his younger wives; the senior wife, Lady Chilel Jawara, had stayed at home to preside over the household and the well-being of his eight children.

That evening he watched reruns of the Wedding, and talked with his host about the next day's test match. It had always been one of Jawara's great disappointments that his country, unlike, say, Guyana, had not taken the Empire's game to its

11

collective heart. The occasional unofficial test matches against Sierra Leone in the early 1960s had by now almost faded from the national memory.

Lately, though, there had been more serious causes for Gambian concern. The previous November a Libyan-backed coup had been foiled only with Senegalese help, and in the meantime the poor performance of the economy had led to food shortages, particularly in the volatile townships in and around the capital. That evening, sitting in his friend's living room, a pleasant night breeze wafting through the open French windows, Jawara might have felt momentarily at peace with the world, but not so his countrymen.

As *Newsnight* drew to a close in the Sussex living room, two lorry-loads of armed men were drawing up in front of The Gambia's only airport, at Yundum, some ten miles as the crow flies to the south-west of the capital, Banjul. The forty or so men, some in plain clothes, some in the uniform of the country's paramilitary Field Force – The Gambia had no Army as such – jumped down from the lorries and headed off in a variety of directions, in clear accordance with a previously decided plan. Those few members of the Field Force actually on duty at the airport had received no advance warning of any exercise, and were at first surprised and then alarmed, but the appearance of Colonel Junaidi Taal, the 500-strong Field Force's second in command, was enough to set their minds at rest, at least for the moment. Clearly this was official business.

Taal did not stop to explain matters. As his men fanned out to occupy all the relevant aircraft, offices and communication points, he headed straight through the departure area and into the office of the airport controller.

The last plane of the day – the 21.30 flight to Dakar – had long since departed, but the controller was still in his office, catching up on paperwork. As his door burst open he looked up in surprise. 'What is this . . .' he started to say in Mandinka, his voice trailing away at the sight of the guns in the hands of the civilians flanking the Field Force officer.

'There has been a change of government,' Taal said bluntly in English.

The controller's mouth opened and closed, like a fish's.

'The airport will remain closed until you hear to the contrary,' Taal said. 'No planes will take off, and no planes will land. The runway is being blocked. You will inform all the necessary authorities that this is the case. Understood?'

The controller nodded vigorously. 'Yes, of course,' he said, wondering, but not daring to ask, how much more of the country these people – whoever they were – had under their control. 'What reason should I give the international authorities for the closure of the airport?'

'You don't need to give a reason. They will know soon enough.' He turned to one of the two men in civilian clothes. 'Bunja, you are in command here. I'll call you from the radio station.'

Banjul lies on the south-western side of the River Gambia's mouth and is separated from the rest of the southern half of the country – the major tourist beaches of Bakau and Fajara, the large township of Serekunda and the airport at Yundum – by a large area of mangrove swamp, which is itself intersected by numerous small watercourses and the much larger Oyster Creek. Anyone leaving or entering Banjul had to cross the creek by the Denton Bridge, a two-lane concrete structure two hundred yards long. At around two a.m. Taal and twenty rebels arrived to secure the bridge, left half a dozen of their number to set up checkpoints at either end, and roared on into Banjul.

13

The lorry drew up outside the darkened building in Buckle Street which was home to Radio Gambia. No one answered the thunderous knock on the door, so two Field Force men broke it down, and the rebels surged into the building. They found only three people inside, one man in the small studio, sorting through records for the next day's playlist, and one of the engineers undressed and halfway to paradise with his equally naked girlfriend on the roof. The engineer was bustled downstairs, while the two remaining rebels handed his girlfriend her clothing bit by bit, snickering with pleasure at her embarrassment, and fighting the urge to succumb to their own lust. It was fortunate for the girl that the coup leaders had stressed the need for self-discipline – and the punishments reserved for those who fell short of this – to all of their men. The girl, tears streaming down her face, was eventually escorted downstairs, and left sitting in a room full of records.

The radio station now secure, Taal called Bunja at the airport and checked that nothing had gone amiss. Nothing had. Further calls confirmed that the Banjul ferry terminal and the main crossroads in Serekunda had been seized. Taal called the main Field Force depot in Bakau where the coup leader, Mamadou Jabang, was waiting for news.

'Yes?' Jabang asked, his voice almost humming with tension. 'Everything has gone according to plan?'

'So far,' Taal said. 'We'll move on to the Presidential Palace now. Are our men in position around the hotels yet?'

'They should be,' Jabang replied. 'The tourists never leave their hotels anyway,' he added sourly, 'so it hardly seems necessary to use our men to keep them in.'

'We don't want any of them wandering out and getting shot,' Taal reminded him. Their chances of success were thin

14

enough, he thought, without bringing the wrath of the white world down on their heads.

'No, we don't,' Jabang agreed without much conviction. 'We're on our way, then. I'll see you at the radio station.'

Dr Sibou Cham yawned and rubbed her eyes, then sat for a moment with her hands held, as if in prayer, over her nose. You should pray for a decent hospital, she told herself, one with all the luxuries, like beds and medicines. She looked down at the pile of patients' records on her desk, and wondered if it was all worth it.

There was a muffled crack, like a gun being fired some way off. She got wearily to her feet and walked through the treatment room to the empty reception area, grateful for the excuse to leave her paperwork behind. The heavyweight concertina door, which would have seemed more at home in a loading dock than a hospital, was locked, as she had requested. Ever since the incident the previous May this had been done. Her attacker might be in prison, but there were others.

She put the chain on the door before unlocking it, then pulled it open a foot, letting in the balmy night air. Almost immediately there was another sound like gunfire, but then silence. It was a shot, she was sure of it. Perhaps a gang battle. She might be bandaging the victims before the night was over.

She closed the door again and sat down at the receptionist's desk. All the drawer knobs were missing, which seemed to sum up the state of the place. It was all of a piece with the peeling cream paint on the walls, the concrete-block partition which had been half-finished for six months, the gaping holes in the mosquito screens, and the maddening flicker of the fluorescent light. It went with a pharmacy which had fewer drugs than the sellers in the marketplace.

What was she doing here? Why did she stay? One person could not make all that much difference, and maybe the very fact that she was there, working herself into the ground day after day, took away any urgency the authorities might feel about improving the situation.

But where else could she go? Into private practice, of course. It would be easier, more lucrative. She might even get some sleep once in a while. But she could not do it. In The Gambia it was the poor who needed more doctors, not the rich. If money and an easy life was what she wanted, she could have stayed in England, got a job in a hospital there, even become a GP.

Most of the other Africans and Asians she had known at medical school had done just that. They had escaped from the Third World, so why on earth would they want to go back? They would bitch about the English weather, bitch about the racism, but they liked being able to shop at Sainsburys, watch the TV, give their children a good education. And she could hardly blame them. Their countries needed them back, but to go back would be a sacrifice for them, and why should they be the ones to pick up the tab for a world that was not fair?

She could hardly pretend it had been a sacrifice for her, because she had never been able to separate her feelings about the practice of medicine from the unfathomable desire she had always felt to serve humanity. A doctor went where a doctor was most needed, and it was hard to imagine a more needy country in this respect than her own.

But – lately there always seemed to be a 'but'. Since the attack on her there had been a sense of . . . loneliness, she supposed. She felt alone, there was no doubt about it. Her family lived in New York, and in any case could not understand why she had not used her obvious gifts to make more of her life. More, that is, in terms of houses, cars and clothes.

The people she worked with were the usual mixed bunch – some nice, some not so nice – but she had little in common with any of them. There were no other women doctors at the Royal Victoria Hospital, and the male doctors all wished they were somewhere else.

The Englishman who had saved her that night had become almost a friend. Or something like that. He flirted a lot, and she supposed he would take any sexual favours that were offered, but he had a wife in England, and she guessed that he too was more than a little lonely. And he was at that age, around forty, when men started wondering whether they had made the right life for themselves, and whether it was too late to do something about it.

She was nearly thirty herself, and there seemed little chance of finding a husband in Banjul, even if she had wanted one. She was not sure what she did want. Not to be alone, she supposed. Just that.

It was a funny thing to be thinking in an empty hospital reception area in the middle of the night. She sighed. In the morning it would all look so . . .

The burst of gunfire seemed to explode all around her, almost making her jump out of her skin. For a moment she thought it had to be inside the room, but then a shadowy figure went racing past in the street outside, then another, and another. They were probably heading for the Presidential Palace, whose gates were only a hundred yards away, around the next corner.

It had to be another coup.

There was a loud series of knocks on the concertina door and shouts of 'open up'. She took a deep breath and went to unlock it. As she pulled it back a man half fell through the opening, wiping the blood from his head on her white coat

17

as he did so. Behind him another man was holding a bloody side. 'We need help,' he groaned, somewhat unnecessarily.

Taal had walked down the radio station's stairs, and was just emerging onto Buckle Street when a distant burst of automatic fire crackled above the sound of the lorry's engine. It seemed to be coming from the direction of the Presidential Palace, half a mile or so to the north.

'Fuck,' he murmured to himself. He had hoped against hope that this could be a bloodless night, but the chances had always been slim. The men guarding the Palace had received enough personal perks from their employer over the last year to guarantee at least a few hours of stubborn resistance.

The last few bars of 'Don't Explain' faded into silence, or rather into the distant sound of the waves tugging at the beach beneath the Bakau cliffs. Lady Chilel Jawara had discovered Billie Holiday on a trip to New York several years before. Her husband had been attending the UN, and she had decided, on the spur of the moment, to visit an exhibition of photographs of Afro-American music stars. It was the singer's face she had first fallen in love with, before she'd heard a single note of her music. It was like her mother's, but that was not the only reason. It was the face of someone who knew what it was like to be a woman.

Not that Billie Holiday had ever been the senior wife of the president of a small African state. Lady Jawara had a lot to be thankful for, and she knew it. Her children were sleeping between sheets, went to the best school, and ate when they were hungry. If they got ill a doctor was sent for.

As for herself, she enjoyed the role of senior wife. Her husband might rule the country but she ruled the household, and of the two administrations she suspected hers was both the more efficient and the less stressful. She hoped he had enjoyed the wedding in London, though she doubted it. Generally he was as bored by European ceremonies as she was.

She yawned and stretched her arms, wondering whether to listen to the other side of the record or go to bed. At that moment she heard the sound of a vehicle approaching.

Whoever it was, they were coming to the Presidential bungalow, for the road led nowhere else. She felt suddenly anxious. 'Bojang!' she called, walking to the living-room door.

'Yes, Lady,' he said, emerging from the kitchen just as a hammering started on the compound gate.

They both stood there listening, she uncertain what to do, he waiting for instructions. 'See who it is,' she said at last.

He let himself out, and she went in search of the gun she knew her husband kept somewhere in the house. The drawers of his desk in the study seemed the best bet, but two of them yielded no gun and the other two were locked. She was still looking for the key when an armed man appeared in the study doorway.

'Who are you? And what do you want in my house?' she asked.

'You are under arrest,' he said.

She laughed. 'By whose authority?'

'And your children,' the man added, looking round with interest at the President's study. 'By the authority of the Revolutionary Council.'

'The what?'

Her contempt stung the man. 'Your days are over, bitch,' he said.

* * *

The firefight which began at the gates of the Presidential Palace soon after four a.m., and which continued intermittently across its gardens, up Marina Parade and down to the beach, for the next two hours, woke up most of those sleeping within a quarter of a mile of the Palace.

Opposite the new Atlantic Hotel in Marina Parade, Mustapha Diop was happily snoring his way through it all until his wife's anxiety forced her to wake him. The two of them sat up in bed listening to the gunfire, then went together to the window, where all they could see was a distant view of the moon on the surf and any number of palm fronds swaying gently in the night breeze.

Diop and his family were from Senegal, and had been in Banjul only a few weeks, since his appointment as secretary to the committee overseeing the proposed union between the two countries. Since a treaty already existed whereby either government would intervene to save the other from an armed take-over, Diop was already aware that he might prove an important bargaining card for any Gambian rebels. The sudden violent knocking on the door downstairs made it clear that the same thought had occurred to them.

Half a mile to the west, the gunfire was only audible, and barely so, when the breeze shifted in the right direction. Moussa Diba and Lamin Konko shared a north-east-facing cell in Banjul Prison, and Diba, prevented from sleeping as usual by the vengeful thoughts which circled his brain, was at first uncertain of what it was he could hear. The sound of lorries rolling past, headed into Banjul from the direction of the Denton Bridge, offered him another clue. Either there was a mother of an exercise going on – which seemed about as likely as an edible breakfast – or someone was trying to topple that little bastard Jawara. Diba smiled to himself in the gloom, and woke Konko with a jab of his foot.

His cellmate groaned. 'What is it?' he said sleepily.

'Listen.'

Konko listened. 'Gunfire,' he said. 'So what?'

'So nothing. I thought you'd enjoy some excitement.'

'I was having plenty in my sleep. There's this girl I used to know in my village. I'd forgotten all about her . . .'

He rambled on, making Diba think of Anja, and of what she was doubtless doing. The woman could not say no. Unfortunately, he could not say no for her, not while he was locked up in this cell.

Another burst of gunfire sounded, this time closer. So what? Diba's thoughts echoed his cellmate's. Whatever was happening out there was unlikely to help him in here.

Simon McGrath, awoken in his room on the fourth floor of the Carlton Hotel, thought for a moment he was back on the Jebel Dhofar in Oman, listening to the *firqats* firing off their rifles in jubilation at the successful capture of Sudh. The illusion was brief-lived. He had never had a bed in Oman, not even one as uncomfortable as the Carlton's. And it had been more than ten years since the men he had helped to train had taken Sudh and started rolling back the tide of the Dhofari rebels.

This was Banjul, The Gambia, and he was no longer in the SAS. Still, he thought, swinging his legs to the floor and striding across to the window, the gunfire he was listening to was coming out of Kalashnikov barrels, and they were not standard issue with the Gambian Field Force. Out there on the capital's mean streets something not quite kosher seemed to be taking place.

21

The view from his window, which faced south across the shanty compounds towards the Great Mosque, was uninstructive. Nothing was lit, nothing moving. He tried the light switch, but as usual at this time of night, the hotel's electricity was off.

McGrath dressed in the dark, wondering what would be the prudent thing to do. Stay in bed, probably.

To hell with that.

He delved into his bag and extracted the holster and semi-automatic 9mm Browning High Power handgun which he had brought with him from England. Since McGrath was in The Gambia in a civilian capacity, seconded from the Royal Engineers to head a technical assistance team engaged in bridge-building and pipe-laying, his possession of the Browning was strictly illicit, but that hardly concerned him. The Third World, as he was fond of telling people who lived in more comfortable places, was like an overpopulated Wild West, and he had no intention of ending up with an arrow through his head. A little string-pulling among old contacts at Heathrow had eased the gun's passage onto the plane, and at Yundum no one had dreamed of checking his baggage.

He threaded the cross-draw holster to his belt, slipped on the lightweight jacket to hide the gun, and left his room. At first it seemed as if the rest of the hotel remained blissfully unaware of whatever it was that was happening outside, but as he went down the corridor he caught the murmur of whispered conversations.

He was about to start down the stairs when the benefits of a visit to the roof occurred to him. He walked up the two flights to the fifth floor, then one more to the flat roof. With the city showing its usual lack of illumination and the moon hiding behind clouds, it was little lighter outside than in, and for almost a minute McGrath waited in the open doorway, searching the shadows for anyone who had chosen to spend the night in the open air. Once satisfied the roof was empty, he threaded his way through the washing lines to the side overlooking Independence Drive.

As he reached this vantage point a lorry full of men swept past, heading down towards the centre of town. Several men were standing on the pavement opposite the hotel, outside the building housing the Legislative Assembly. A yellow glow came from inside the latter, as if from gas lamps or candles.

It looked like a coup, McGrath thought, and at that moment a fresh volley of shots resounded away to his right, from the direction of the Palace. There was a hint of lights through the trees – headlights, perhaps – but he could see nothing for certain, either in that direction or any other. Banjul might be surrounded on its three sides by river, sea and swamp, but at four in the morning they all looked like so many pieces of gloom.

The Royal Victoria Hospital, whose main entrance was little more than a hundred yards from the Palace gates, showed no more lights than anywhere else. McGrath wondered if Sibou was sleeping there that night, as she often did, or whether she had gone home for some of that rest she always seemed to need and never seemed to get.

He would go and have a look, he decided, one part of his mind commending him for his thoughtfulness, the other thanking his lucky stars that he had come up with a good excuse to go out in search of adventure.

It was almost six-thirty before Colonel Taal felt confident enough of the outcome of the fighting around the Presidential Palace to delegate its direction, and to head back down Buckle Street to the radio station for the prearranged meeting.

Mamadou Jabang and his deputy, Sharif Sallah, had arrived in their commandeered taxi more than half an hour earlier, and the subsequent wait had done little to soothe their nerves.

'What is happening?' Jabang asked, when Taal was only halfway through the door. He and Sallah were sitting at either end of a table in the station's hospitality room. 'Has anything gone wrong?'

'Nothing.'

'The Palace is taken?' Sallah asked.

'The Palace is cordoned off,' Taal answered. 'Some of the guards have escaped, either down the beach or into the town, but that was expected.' He sat down and looked at the two of them: the wiry Jabang with his hooded eyes and heavy brow, Sallah with the face that always seemed to be smiling, even when it was not. Both men were sweating heavily, which perhaps owed something to the humidity, but was mostly nerves. Jabang in particular seemed exhausted by the combination of stress and tiredness, which did not exactly bode well for the new government's decision-making process. Nothing perverted the exercise of judgement like lack of sleep, and somehow or other all three of them would have to make sure they got enough in the days to come.

'It will be light in half an hour,' Jabang said.

'And the country will wake to a better government,' Sallah said, almost smugly.

Taal supposed he meant it. For some reason he could never quite put his finger on, he had always doubted Sallah's sincerity. Whereas Jabang was transparently honest and idealistic almost to a fault, Sallah's words and deeds invariably seemed to carry a taint of opportunism.

Maybe he was wrong, Taal thought. He hoped he was. Jabang trusted the man and there had to be easier ways to glory than taking part in the mounting of a coup like this one. Everyone knew their chances of lasting success were no better than even, and in the sanctum of his own thoughts Taal thought the odds considerably longer. Seizing control was one thing, holding on to it something else entirely.

McGrath had decided that even in the dark a stroll along Independence Drive might not prove wise, and had opted for the long way round, making use of Marina Parade. On this road there was less likely to be traffic or headlights, and the overarching trees made the darkness even more impenetrable. He worked his way along the southern side, ears alert for the sound of unwelcome company, and was almost level with the Atlantic Hotel when two headlights sprang to life some two hundred yards ahead of him, and rapidly started closing the distance. There was no time to run for better cover, and McGrath flattened himself against the wall, hoping to fall outside the vehicle's cone of illumination.

He need not have bothered. The lights swerved to the left, disappearing, as he immediately realized, into the forecourt of the Atlantic Hotel. He wondered what the rebels had in store for the hundred or so guests, most of them Brits, and all of whom had come to The Gambia on package tours in search of a sunny beach, not the wrong end of a Kalashnikov.

He would worry about that later. For the moment he wanted to make sure Sibou was all right. Hurrying on past the Atlantic, he came to the doors of the Royal Victoria's Maternity Wing, and decided that it might be better to use them than attempt the front entrance. Ten minutes later, having threaded his way through the labyrinth of one-storey buildings and courtyards, he found himself looking across at the lit windows of the emergency department some twenty yards away. Several men were standing around inside, some of them bending down to talk to those who were presumably lying, out of sight, on the cubicle beds and waiting-room benches. One man was moaning continuously, almost forlornly, but otherwise there was virtual silence.

Then he saw Sibou, rising wearily into view after treating one of the prone casualties. Her dark eyes seemed even darker, the skin stretched a little tighter across the high cheekbones, the usually generous mouth pursed with tension and tiredness. McGrath worked his way round the perimeter of the yard to the open window of her private office and clambered over the sill. He opened the door a quarter of an inch and looked out through the crack. The corridor was empty.

Sooner or later she would come, and he settled down to wait, thinking about the first time they had met, a couple of months earlier, soon after he had arrived on his secondment. The circumstances could hardly have been more propitious for an intending Galahad. He had come to the Royal Victoria looking for the tetanus shot he should have had before leaving home, and found himself face to face with a room full of terrified Gambians, her half-naked on the floor and a man about to rape her at knife-point in full view of everyone else. All the old training had come instantly into use, and before he had had time to ponder the risks McGrath had used the man's neck for a chopping board and his genitals for a football.

The damsel in distress had been grateful enough to have dinner with him, but he had foolishly allowed himself to be a little too honest with her, and she had declined to be anything more than a friend. That had not been as difficult as he had expected, though he still dreamed of covering her ebony body with his kisses, not to mention her covering his with hers. But Sibou was great company even fully clothed, and he had even found himself wishing his wife and children could meet her.

He could not remember being so impressed by someone's dedication – in the face of such awe-inspiring odds – for a long, long time. She could have had a doctor's job, and a doctor's ample rewards, anywhere in the world, but here she was, in this ramshackle office, struggling to stretch always inadequate resources in the service of the ordinary people who came in off the street, and offering every one of them a smile almost beautiful enough to die for.

McGrath looked at his watch. In twenty minutes it would begin to get light: where did he want to be when that happened? At the Atlantic, he decided, where there would probably be a working telephone and some chance of finding out what was happening. After all, now he had found out that Sibou was all right, there had to be more pressing things to do than watch her smile.

He was halfway out of the window when she came in through the door. She jumped with surprise, then burst out laughing. 'What are you doing, you crazy Englishman?' she asked.

He pulled himself back into the room, wondering how anyone could look so sexy in a white coat and stethoscope. 'I've come to take you away from all this,' he said grandly.

'Through the window?'

'Well . . .'

'And anyway, I like all this. And I'm busy,' she added, rummaging around in her desk drawer for something.

'I just came to check you were OK,' he said.

She turned and smiled at him. 'Thank you.'

'What's happening out there?' he asked.

'Out in the city? Oh, another bunch of fools have decided to overthrow the government.'

27

'And are they succeeding?'

She shrugged. 'Who knows? Who cares?'

'I thought you didn't like Papa Jawara.'

'I don't. But playing musical chairs at the Palace is not going to get me the medicines I need. In fact I'm having to use the little I've got to patch up those toy soldiers in there.'

'How many of them?'

'About a dozen or so. We're already running out of blood. Look, I have to go . . .' She suddenly noticed the holstered gun inside his jacket. 'What are you wearing that for?' she demanded to know.

'Self-defence.'

'It will give them a reason to shoot you.'

'Yeah, well . . .'

She threw up her hands in disgust. 'You play what games you want,' she said, adding over her shoulder, 'and take care of yourself.'

'I'll come back later,' he called after her, although he was not sure if she had heard. 'What a woman,' he muttered to himself, and worked his body back out through the window. He retraced his steps through the sprawling grounds to the Maternity Wing entrance, crossed over the still-dark Marina Parade and scaled the wall of the grounds opposite. Five minutes and another wall later he was standing on the beach. Away to his right, over the far bank of the river mouth, the sky was beginning to lighten. He turned the other way, and walked a couple of hundred yards along the deserted sand to the hotel's beach entrance.

The kidney-shaped pool shone black in the artificial light, but its only occupant was an inflatable plastic monkey. McGrath walked through into the hotel building, hands in pockets to disguise the bulge of the Browning. In the lobby

28

he could hear voices, and after a moment's thought decided to simply take a seat within earshot, and pretend he was just one more innocent tourist.

It was a fruitful decision. For five minutes he listened to two voices trying to explain to several others – the latter presumably the hotel's management – that there was a new government, that the foreign guests would not be allowed out of their hotels for at least a day, but that there was nothing to stop them enjoying the sun and the hotel beach and the swimming pool. It was up to the management to make these rules clear to the guests. And to point out that anyone attempting to leave the hotel grounds risked being shot.

3

'All authority now rests in the Revolutionary Council,' said the voice coming out of the speakers. Someone on the hotel staff had channelled the radio through the outdoor hi-fi system, and around a hundred staff and guests were sitting around the hotel pool, listening to the first proclamation of the new government.

'The Socialist and Revolutionary Labour Party, which was illegally suppressed during the regime of the tyrant Jawara, has contributed nine members to the new ruling Council. The other three members have been supplied by the Field Force, which has already proved itself overwhelmingly in support of the new government.'

Oh yeah? McGrath thought to himself. Some of the bastards must have been in on it, but he doubted if it had been a majority.

'The Jawara regime,' the voice went on, 'has always been a backward-looking regime. Nepotism has flourished, corruption has been rife, tribal differences have been exacerbated rather than healed. Economic incompetence has gone hand in hand with social injustice, and for the ordinary man the last few years have been an endless struggle. The recent severe food shortages offered proof that, if unchecked, the situation would only have grown worse. That is why the Council has now assumed control, so that all the necessary steps to reverse this trend can at once be taken.'

The voice paused for breath, or for inspiration. What was the magic panacea going to be this time round, McGrath asked himself.

'A dictatorship of the proletariat . . .'

McGrath burst out laughing.

'. . . a government of working people, led by the Socialist and Revolutionary Labour Party, will now be established to promote socialism and true democracy. This will, of course, take time, and the process itself will doubtless provoke opposition from the forces of reaction, particularly those remnants of the old regime who still occupy positions of authority throughout the country. In order to accelerate the process of national recovery certain short-term measures must be taken. Accordingly, the Council declares Parliament dissolved and the constitution temporarily suspended. The banks and courts will remain closed until further notice. All political parties are banned. A dusk-to-dawn curfew will be in force from this evening.

'Guests in our country are requested, for their own safety, not to leave their hotel compounds. The Council regrets the need for this temporary restriction, which has been taken with our guests' best interests in mind.'

McGrath looked round at the assembled holidaymakers, most of whom seemed more amused than upset by the news. There were a few nervous giggles, but no sign of any real fear.

'Oh well, we'll be going home the day after tomorrow,' one Lancastrian voice said a few yards away.

Maybe they would be, McGrath thought, but he would not bet on it. It all depended on how secure the new boys' control was. If it was either really firm or really shaky, then there was probably little to worry about. But if they were strong enough to keep some control yet not strong enough to make it stick, then these people around the pool might well become unwilling pawns in the struggle. Hostages, even. It could get nasty.

The voice was sinking deeper into generalities: '. . . their wholehearted support in the building of a fair and prosperous society. It wishes to stress that the change of government is an internal affair, and of practical concern only to the people of The Gambia. Any attempt at interference from outside the country's borders will be considered a hostile act. The Council hopes and expects a comradely response from our neighbours, particularly the people and government of Senegal, with whom we wish to pursue a policy of growing cooperation in all spheres . . .'

So that was it, McGrath thought. They were expecting Senegalese intervention. In which case, it should be all over in a few days. He did not know much about the Senegalese Army, but he had little doubt that they could roll over this bunch. And then it was just a matter of everyone keeping their heads down while the storm blew itself out.

'How did it sound?' Jabang asked as they settled into the back seat of the commandeered taxi. A few minutes earlier two Party members had arrived from Yundum with Jawara's personal limousine, assuming that Jabang would wish to use it. He had sent them packing with a lecture on the perils of the personality cult.

Which was all to the good, Taal thought. And maybe riding round Banjul in a rusty Peugeot behind a pair of furry dice was a suitably proletarian image for the new government. At least no one could accuse them of élitism.

'Junaidi, how did it sound?' Jabang repeated.

'Good, Mamadou, good,' Taal replied. Jabang looked feverish, he thought. 'We all need some sleep,' he said, 'or we won't know what we're doing.'

Jabang laughed. 'I could sleep for a week,' he said, 'but when will I get the chance?'

'After you've addressed the Council,' Taal said.

'Just take a few hours. We'll wake you if necessary.'

'And when will you sleep?' Jabang asked.

'Whenever I can.' But probably not for the rest of the day, he thought. Whatever. He should get his second wind soon.

The driver arrived with Sallah, who joined him in the front. The street seemed virtually empty, but that was not surprising. Today, Taal both hoped and expected, most people would stay home and listen to the radio.

'I must talk to the Senegalese envoy after the Council,' Jabang remembered out loud. 'Where is he at the moment?'

'In the house where he is staying,' Sallah said over his shoulder. 'He has only been told he cannot go out.'

'You will bring him to the Legislative Assembly?'

'Yes.'

'Good.' Jabang sat back as the taxi swung through the roundabout at McCarthy Square, his eyes darting this way and that as if searching for something to rest on.

Watching him, Taal felt a sudden sense of emptiness. He had known Mamadou Jabang for almost twenty-five years, since he was fourteen and the other man was seven. They had grown up in adjoining houses in Bakau, both sons of families well off by Gambian standards. Both had flirted with the religious vocation, both had been educated abroad, though on different sides of the Iron Curtain.

Taal had graduated from Sandhurst in England, while Jabang had received one of the many scholarships offered by

33

Soviet embassies in Africa during the early 1970s. The former had worked his way effortlessly to his position in the Field Force, and only Jawara's unspoken but justified suspicion of Taal's political sympathies had prevented him holding the top job before he was forty.

Jabang, on the other hand, had become mired in politics, and had foolishly – as he himself admitted – allowed himself to overestimate Jawara's instinct for self-preservation. The SRLP had become too popular too quickly, particularly among the township youths and the younger members of the Field Force, and in the early summer of 1980 Jawara had seized on the random shooting of a policeman to ban the Party. With all the democratic channels closed, the SRLP had spent the succeeding year planning Jawara's overthrow by force.

And here they were, driving to the parliament building behind a pair of pink furry dice, the new leaders of their country, at least for today. Taal felt the enormity of it all – like burning bridges, as the English would say. If the Council could endure, then he and Mamadou would have the chance to transform their country, to do all the things they had dreamed of doing, to truly make a difference in the lives of their countrymen. If they failed, then Jawara would have them hanged.

The stakes could hardly be higher.

'Junaidi, we've arrived,' Jabang said, pulling him out of his reverie. Mamadou had a smile on his face – the first one Taal had seen that day. And why not, he thought, climbing out of the taxi in the forecourt of the Legislative Assembly. They had succeeded. For the moment at least, they had succeeded.

He followed Jabang in through the outer doors, across the anteroom and into the chamber, where the forty or fifty men who had been waiting for them burst into spontaneous applause.

Jabang raised a fist in salute, beamed at the assembly, and took a seat on the platform. Taal sat beside him and looked out across the faces, every one of which he knew. He had the sudden sinking feeling that this would be the high point, and that from this moment on things would only get worse.

Jabang was now on his feet, motioning for silence. 'Comrades,' he began, 'I will not take up much of your time – we all have duties to perform,' adding with a smile: 'And a country to run. I can tell you that we are in firm control of Banjul, Bakau, Fajara, Serekunda, Yundum and Soma. Three-quarters of the Field Force has joined us. I do not think we have anything to fear from inside the country. The main threat, as we all knew from the beginning, will come from outside, from the Senegalese. They have the treaty with Jawara, and if they judge it in their interests to uphold it then it is possible they will send troops. I still think it more likely that they will wait to judge the situation here, and act accordingly.

'So it is important that we offer no provocations, no excuse for intervention. At the moment we have no news of their intentions, but I will be asking their envoy here to talk to his government in Dakar this morning. And of course we shall be making the most of the friends we have in the inter-national community.

'The Senegalese will not act without French approval, so we must also make sure that nothing tarnishes our image in the West. The last thing we need now is a dead white tourist.' He grinned owlishly.

'The Council will be in more or less permanent session from now on – and when any of us will get any sleep is anyone's guess. All security matters should be channelled through Junaidi here.'

Taal smiled at them all, reflecting that it was going to be a long day.

The British High Commission was situated on the road between Bakau and Fajara, some eight miles to the west of Banjul. McGrath finally got through on the phone around ten o'clock. The line had been jammed for the previous two hours, presumably with holiday-makers wondering what the British Government intended to do about the situation. As if there was anything they could do.

He asked to talk to Bill Myers, the all-purpose undersecretary whose roles included that of military attaché. Myers had helped smooth the path for McGrath on the ex-SAS man's arrival, and they had met several times since, mostly at gatherings of the expatriate community: Danes running an agricultural research station, Germans working on a solar-energy project, Brits like McGrath involved in infrastructural improvements. It was a small community, and depressingly male.

'Where are you?' was Myers's first question.

'At the Atlantic'

'How are things there? No panic?'

'Well, there was one outbreak when someone claimed the hotel was running out of gin . . .'

'Ha ha . . .'

'No, no problems here. People are just vaguely pissed off that they can't go out. Not that many of them wanted to anyway, but they liked the idea that they could.'

Myers grunted. 'What about the town? Any idea what's going on?'

'Hey, I called you to find out what was going on – not the other way round.'

'Stuck out here we haven't got a clue,' Myers said equably. 'There seems to be a group of armed men outside each of the main hotels, but there haven't been any incidents involving Europeans that we know of. There was some gunfire in Bakau last night, but we've no idea who got shot. And we listened to Chummy on the radio this morning. And that's about it. What about you?'

McGrath told him what he had heard and seen from the Carlton roof, and at the hospital. 'It seems quiet enough for now,' he concluded. 'Looks like they made it stick, at least for the moment.'

'If you can find out anymore, we'd appreciate it,' Myers said. 'It's hard to give London any advice when we don't know any more than they do.'

'Right,' McGrath agreed. 'In exchange, can you let my wife know I'm OK?'

Myers took down the London number. 'But don't go taking any mad risks,' he said. 'I'm not taking a day trip to Banjul, not even for your funeral.'

'You're all heart,' McGrath said, and hung up. For a moment he stood in the hotel lobby, wondering what to do. The new government had only restricted the movement of 'guests', by which they presumably meant the three hundred or so lucky souls currently visiting The Gambia on package holidays. McGrath was not on holiday and not a guest, so the restrictions could hardly apply to him.

He wondered if the guards at the hotel gates would appreciate the distinction.

Probably not. He decided discretion was the better part of valour, and after moving the holstered Browning round into the small of his back, left the hotel the way he had come, through the beach entrance. Already twenty or so guests were

37

sunning themselves as if nothing had happened, a couple of the women displaying bare breasts. McGrath supposed they were nice ones, and wondered why he always found topless beaches such a turn-off.

Better not to know, probably. At least there were no armed men guarding the beach: the new regime was either short on manpower or short on brains. He headed west, reckoning it was best to avoid the area of the Palace and cut back through to Independence Drive just above the Carlton. There was a heavy armed presence outside the Legislative Assembly, but no one challenged him as he walked down the opposite pavement and ducked into the Carlton's terrace.

The hotel seemed half-deserted. There were no messages for him and the telephone was dead. He decided to visit the office he had been given in Wellington Street, in the heart of town. If he was stopped, he was stopped; there was no point in behaving like a prisoner before he got caught.

Outside he tried hailing a taxi, more out of curiosity than because he really wanted one. The driver slowed, noticed the colour of his face, and accelerated away. McGrath started walking down Independence Drive, conscious of being stared at by those few Gambians who were out on the street. It was all a bit unnerving, and recognition of this added a swagger to his walk. He was damned if he was going to slink around the town in broad daylight.

The stares persisted, but no one spoke to him or tried to impede his passage. Once on Wellington Street he noticed that the Barra ferry was anchored in midstream: no one could escape in it, and no one could use it to launch an attack on Banjul. McGrath found himself admiring that piece of military logic. The rebel forces were obviously not entirely composed of fools, even if they did include the last person on earth who could use the phrase 'dictatorship of the proletariat' with a straight face.

The offices of the Ministry of Development, where he had been allotted a room, had obviously not been deemed of sufficient importance to warrant a rebel presence. McGrath simply walked through the front door and up to his room, which he half-expected to find as empty as the rest of the building. Instead he found the smiling face of Jobo Camara, the twenty-four-year-old Gambian who had been appointed his deputy.

'Mr McGrath!' Camara called out to him. 'What are you doing here?'

'I've come to work,' McGrath answered mildly.

'But . . . there is a revolution going on!'

'There's nothing happening at the moment. Why are you here?'

'I only live down the street. I thought I would make certain no one has come to the office who shouldn't have.'

'And has anyone?' McGrath asked, going over to the window and checking out the street.

'No . . .'

'Jobo, what's happening out there? I'm a foreigner – it's hard to read the signs in someone else's country. I mean, do these people have any support among the population?'

The young man considered the question. 'Some,' he said at last. 'It's hard to say how much. Today, I think, many people are still waiting to see how these people behave. They will give them the benefit of the doubt for a few days, maybe.' He shrugged. 'The government – the old government – was not popular. Not in Banjul, anyway.' He stopped and looked questioningly at McGrath, as if wanting to know if he had said too much.

'People don't like Jawara?' McGrath asked.

'He is just a little man with a big limousine, who gives all the good jobs to his family and friends. He is not a *bad* man. People don't hate him. But I don't think they will fight for him, either.'

'You think most people will just wait and see?'

'Of course. It is easier. As long as the new men don't behave too badly . . .'

'They seem to have the Field Force on their side.'

'Some of them. Maybe half. My uncle is in the Field Force in Fajara, and my mother wanted me to check on him, make sure he's all right. That was another reason I came to the office: to borrow the jeep,' he added, hopefully.

'Fine, I'll come with you,' McGrath said.

Franklin had been woken early by his mother setting off for the dawn shift at the South Western Hospital in Clapham, and then again by his sister leaving for school. When he finally surfaced it was gone eleven, and he ate a large bowl of cornflakes in front of the TV, watching the opening hour of the Third Test between England and Australia. The play hardly came up to West Indian standards, but the England batting did remind him of the last time they had faced Roberts and Holding. Boycott and Gower were both gone before he had finished his second cup of coffee.

With some reluctance he turned off the television, got dressed and left the house. He was wearing jeans and a T-shirt – the people he meant to see today would not be impressed by his uniform. In fact, they would probably use it for target practice if they thought they could get away with it.

The weather was much the same as it had been for the Royal Wedding, but the mood on the streets seemed less sunny, more like its usual sullen self. Franklin's first port of call was the address for Benjy which Everton had given him – a sixth-floor flat on a big estate in nearby Angell Town. Benjy, a thin young man with spiky hair and gold-rimmed glasses, was alone, watching the cricket.

'You know why I've come?' Franklin started.

'It's about Everton.'

'Yeah.'

He let Franklin in with some reluctance, but offered him a cup of tea. While he was making it Gooch was bowled out. England were doing their best to make the Australians feel at home.

'Did you see what happened?' Franklin asked, when Benjy came back with the tea.

'When?'

'When he was arrested.'

'No. I'm running too hard, you know. One moment the street is empty, the next the policemen are tripping over each other. I go straight down the alley by Dr Dread and over the wall and out through the yards. The last time I see Everton he is standing there with the cricket bat. I yelled at him to come, but he must have run the other way.'

'OK,' Franklin said. 'Did you know anyone else who was there, anyone who might have seen what happened?'

Benjy shook his head. 'They all got arrested. Or they didn't stop to watch and didn't see nothing. Like I and I. I's sorry, Worrell, but that's how it goes. Anyways, if the police all saying one thing, then nobody listen to nobody else.' He opened his palms in a gesture of resignation.

Franklin walked down the twelve flights of steps rather than face the smell of concentrated urine in the lift, and stopped for a moment on the pavement outside the building, giving the sunshine a chance to lighten his state of mind.

It did not work. He walked back towards the centre of Brixton, hyper-aware of the world around him. There were too many people on the streets, too many people not actually going anywhere. It felt like a football crowd before a game, a sense of expectation, a sense of looming catharsis. It felt ugly.

He walked up to Railton Road to the address his mum had given him, where the local councillor held surgeries on a Thursday afternoon. Franklin did not know Peter Barrett very well, but his father had always had good things to say about the man, and even Everton had given him the benefit of the doubt.

The queue of people ahead of Franklin bore testimony to Barrett's popularity in the community. Or maybe just the number of problems people were facing. Franklin took out his Walkman and plugged himself into the Test Match commentary. It was still lunch, so he switched to Radio One and let his mind float to the music.

Around two it was his turn. Peter Barrett looked tired, and a lot older than Franklin remembered, but he managed a smile in greeting. Franklin explained why he was there, knowing as he did so that none of it was news to the councillor.

It turned out that Barrett had already been contacted by half a dozen relatives of those who had been arrested in Spenser Road. He was trying to get them and any witnesses they could find to a meeting on the following evening. Then they could discuss what was possible. If anything.

'Do you still live with your parents?' Barrett asked.

'No, I'm in the Army,' Franklin said, wondering what the reaction would be.

Barrett just gave him a single glance that seemed to speak volumes, before carrying on as if nothing had happened. But something had – Franklin had failed a loyalty test.

Walking back up Acre Lane he wondered if he had doomed himself to a life in permanent limbo – for ever denied full access to one world, and with no way back into the other.

In Banjul, Mustapha Diop had not had the most relaxing of mornings. The rebel soldiers who had arrived at his front door in the hour before dawn were still there, albeit outside. He had been 'asked' not to leave the house – in the interests of his own safety, of course – and had been unable to derive any joy from the telephone. The radio broadcast had rendered his wife almost hysterical, which was unusual, and all morning the children had been driving him mad, which was not. He was lighting yet another cigarette when two men appeared in the gateway and started across the space towards his front door.

One of them was thin-faced, with dark-set eyes and hair cut to the scalp, the other had chubbier features and seemed to be smiling. Once inside they introduced themselves as Mamadou Jabang and Sharif Sallah, respectively the new President and Foreign Secretary of The Gambia.

'I will come directly to the point,' Jabang said. 'We wish you to contact your government, and to give them an accurate picture of what is happening here in Banjul . . .'

'How could I know – I have been kept a prisoner here!'

'You have not been ill-treated?' Sallah asked in a concerned voice.

'No, but . . .'

'It was merely necessary to ensure that you did not venture out while the streets were not safe,' Sallah said. 'The same precautions were taken with all the foreign embassies,' he added, less than truthfully.

'Yes, yes, I understand,' Diop said. 'But it is still the case that I know nothing of the situation outside.'

'We are here to change that,' Jabang said. 'We are going to take you on a tour of the city, so that you can see for yourself.'

'And if I refuse?'

'Why would you do that?' Jabang asked with a smile.

Diop could not think of a reason. He smiled back. 'I suppose you're right,' he said, and a few minutes later, having told his wife where he was going, he found himself seated next to the new President in the back of a taxi.

'Do you know the town well?' Jabang asked, as they set off down Marina Parade.

'Quite well.'

'Good. We will go down Wellington Street to the ferry terminal, and then back up Hagen Street. Yes?'

'Yes, of course.'

The taxi sped down the tree-lined avenue, then turned past the Royal Victoria Hospital onto Independence Drive. There seemed to be few people outdoors, though one group of youths gathered around a shop at the top of Buckle Street offered clenched-fist salutes to their passing vehicle.

'It looks peaceful, yes?' Sallah asked from the front seat.

'Yes,' Diop agreed. Actually, it looked dead. What were these people trying to prove?

'Is there anywhere in particular you'd like to see?' Sallah asked.

My home in the Rue Corniche in Dakar, Diop thought to himself. 'No, nowhere,' he answered.

They drove back up Independence Drive to the Legislative Assembly, where Diop was ushered through into a small office containing desk, chair and telephone. 'You can speak to your government from here,' Sallah told him. 'And tell them that the fighting is over and the new government in full control. Tell them what you saw on the streets.'

'I will tell them what I know,' Diop agreed.

At that moment someone else appeared and started talking excitedly to Sallah in Mandinka, in which Diop was less than fluent. The gist of what was being said, though, soon became clear. As Sallah turned back to him, Diop did his best to pretend he had not understood.

'There is a problem with the telephone connection,' the Gambian said. 'In the meantime you will be taken back to your house.'

'I . . .' Diop started to say, but Sallah had already gone, and two armed rebels were gesturing for Diop to follow them. He walked back to his house between them, pondering what he had heard – that all connections with Senegal had been cut by the Senegalese Government. That could only mean one thing as far as Diop could see – Senegal intended living up to its treaty with the ousted government, and troops would soon be on their way to dispose of this one. Where that left him and his family, Diop was afraid to think.

Moussa Diba turned away from the cell window and its unrelenting panorama of mangrove swamp. Lamin Konko was dozing fitfully on the half-shredded mattress they shared, his hand occasionally stabbing out at the fly which seemed intent on colonizing his forehead. It was the middle of the afternoon – normally the quiet time in Banjul Prison – but today was different. Today all sorts of noises seemed to be sounding elsewhere in the building: whispered conversations, hammering, even laughter. And more than that: all day there had been tension in the air. It was hard to put his finger on exactly how this had expressed itself, but Moussa Diba knew that something was happening outside his cell, or something had happened and the ripples were still spreading. He did not know why, but he had a feeling it was good news. Maybe he did have his grandmother's gifts as a future-teller, as she had always thought.

Time would tell.

His thoughts turned back to the Englishman, as they often did. The man had humiliated him, and he was still not sure how it had been done. One moment he had had the woman on the floor ready for him and enough drugs in his hand to live like a king for six months, and the next he was waking up in a police cell, on his way to this stinking cell for five years. If he ever got out of here, Anja would be his first stop, and the Englishman would be his second. And next time the boot would be on the other foot.

4

McGrath and Jobo Camara took the Bund Road route out of Banjul, to avoid the rebel activity on Independence Drive, but there was no way round the Denton Bridge. As they drove past the prison, its two watch-towers both apparently unmanned, McGrath could feel the reassuring pressure of the Browning in the centre of his back. Driving hell for leather along a tropical road in a jeep brought back more memories than he could count, most of them good ones, at least in retrospect.

They saw the first checkpoint from about a quarter of a mile away. A taxi was parked on either side of the entrance to the bridge, and four men were grouped around the one on the left. Two were leaning against the bonnet, the others standing a few yards away, silhouetted against the silver sheen of Oyster Creek. All four moved purposefully into the centre of the road as they saw the jeep approaching, rifles pointed at the ground. None of them was wearing a uniform.

McGrath pulled the jeep to a halt ten yards away from them, and got down to the ground, slowly, so as not to cause any alarm.

'Where are you going?' one man asked. He was wearing dark glasses, purple cotton trousers with a vivid batik pattern and a Def Leppard T-shirt.

'Serekunda,' McGrath said.

'Whites are confined to the hotels,' the man said.

'Not all whites,' Jobo said, standing at McGrath's shoulder. 'Only tourists.'

'I work for the Ministry of Development,' McGrath added. 'We have business in Serekunda, checking out one of the generators.'

'Do you have permission?'

'No, but I'm sure the new government will not want all the lights to go out in Serekunda on its first day in office. But why don't you check with them?' McGrath bluffed. He was pretty sure that the checkpoint had no means of communicating with the outside world.

The rebel digested the situation. 'That will not be necessary,' he said eventually. 'You may pass.'

'Thank you,' McGrath said formally.

They motored across the long bridge. A couple of yachts were anchored in the creek, and McGrath wondered where their owners were – they seemed rather conspicuous examples of wealth to flaunt in the middle of a revolution. On the far side the road veered left through the savannah, the long summer grass dotted by giant baobab trees and tall palms.

Ten minutes later they were entering the sprawling outskirts of Serekunda, which housed as many people as Banjul, but lacked its extremes of affluence and shanty-town squalor. Jobo directed McGrath left at the main crossroads, down past the main mosque and then right down a dirt street for about a hundred yards. A dozen or so children gathered around the jeep, and Jobo appointed one of them its guardian, then led McGrath through the gate of the compound.

Mansa Camara was sitting on a wooden bench in the courtyard, his back against the concrete wall, his head shaded by the overhanging corrugated roof. He was dressed in a traditional African robe, not the western uniform of the Field Force.

His nephew made the introductions, and asked him what had happened.

'I resigned,' Mansa said shortly.

'Why?'

'It seemed like the right thing to do, boy. I'll give it to Taal – he was honest enough about it. "Join us or go home," he said, "and leave your gun behind." So I came home.'

'How many others did the same?' McGrath asked him.

'I do not wish to be rude,' Mansa asked, 'but what interest is this of yours?'

McGrath decided to tell the truth. 'I work here,' he said, 'so I'm interested in whether these people can hang on to what they've taken. Plus my embassy is worried about all the tourists, and wants all the information it can get.'

'No problem there,' Camara said. 'Not as long as the leaders are in control. They know better than to anger foreign governments for no reason.'

Jobo took out his cigarettes and offered them round. Mansa puffed appreciatively at the Marlboro for a moment, and then shouted into the house for tea. 'Jobo is a good boy,' he said, turning back to McGrath, and I know he likes to work with you. So I answer the question you ask.' He took another drag, the expression on his face a cigarette advertiser's dream. 'One-third is my guess,' he said. 'One-third say no, the other two-thirds go with Taal.'

'They really think they can win?' Jobo asked.

'Who will stop them?' Mansa asked. 'There is no other armed force inside the country.'

'So you think the British will come, or the Americans?'

Mansa laughed. 'No. The Senegalese may. But Jobo, I did not walk away because I think they will lose. I just did not want any part of it. My job is to keep the law, not to decide which government the country should have.' He looked at McGrath. 'That is the civilized way, is it not? Politicians for politics, police for keeping the law, an army for defending the country.'

'That's how it's supposed to be,' McGrath agreed.

The tea arrived, strong and sweet in clay pots. Another cigarette followed, and then lunch was announced. By the time McGrath and Jobo climbed back aboard the jeep it was gone three.

'Did you like my uncle?' Jobo asked as they pulled out into Mosque Road.

'Yep, I liked him,' McGrath said.

Serekunda seemed more subdued than it had when they arrived, as if the news of the coup was finally sinking in. The road to Banjul, normally full of bush taxis and minibuses, was sparsely populated within the town and utterly empty outside it. In the three-mile approach to the Denton Bridge they met nothing and saw no one.

The personnel at the checkpoint had changed. The man in the purple batik trousers, along with his three less colourful companions, had been replaced by two men who seemed more inclined to take their work seriously. As McGrath drove slowly over the bridge they moved into the centre of the road. Both were wearing Field Force uniforms; one was holding a rifle, the other a handgun.

The one with the handgun signalled them to stop.

McGrath did so, and smiled at him. 'We're working . . .' he started to say.

'Get down,' the man growled. His partner, a younger man with a slight squint in his left eye, looked nervous.

Jobo recognized him. 'Jerry, it's me,' he said, and the man smiled briefly at him.

His partner was not impressed. 'Get down,' he repeated.

'Sure,' McGrath said, not liking the unsteadiness of the hand holding the gun. He and Jobo got out of the jeep, the latter looking angry.

'What's this for?' he angrily asked the man with the handgun.

'Give me your papers,' the man demanded. 'And your passport,' he said to McGrath.

'Papers? I have no papers,' Jobo protested. 'This is stupid. What papers?'

'Everyone leaving or entering Banjul must have a pass, by order of the Council,' the man said, as if he was reciting something memorized. 'You are under arrest,' he added, waving the gun for emphasis.

It went off, sending a bullet between Jobo's shoulder and upper chest.

For a second all four men's faces seemed frozen with shock, and then the man with the handgun, whether consciously or not, turned it towards McGrath.

The ex-soldier was not taking any chances. In what seemed like a single motion he swept the Browning from the holster behind his back, dropped to one knee, and sent two bullets through the centre of the Gambian's head.

He then whirled round in search of the other man, who was simply standing there, transfixed by shock. There was a clatter as the rifle slipped from his hands and fell to the tarmac. McGrath flicked his wrist and the man took the hint;

he covered the five yards to the edge of the bridge like a scared rabbit, and launched himself into the creek with a huge splash.

McGrath went across to where Jobo was struggling into a sitting position, looking with astonishment at the blood trickling out through his shirt and fingers. 'Let's get you to hospital,' McGrath said, and helped him into the jeep.

He then went back for the body of the man he had killed. The only obvious bullet entry hole was through the bridge of the nose; the other round had gone through the man's open mouth. Between them they had taken a lot of brain out through the back of the head. At least it had been quick. McGrath dragged the corpse across to the rail and heaved it into the creek, where it swiftly sank from sight in the muddy water.

Colonel Taal replaced the telephone and sat back in the chair, his eyes closed. He rubbed them, wondering how long he could keep going without at least a couple of hours of sleep.

He found himself thinking about Admiral Yamamoto, whose biography he had read long ago at Sandhurst. In November 1941 Yamamoto had told his Emperor that he could give the Americans hell for six months, but that thereafter there was no hope of ultimate military victory. Even knowing that, he had still attacked Pearl Harbour.

Reading the biography Taal had found such a decision hard to understand, yet here in The Gambia he seemed to have taken one that was remarkably similar. They could take over the country, he had told the Party leadership, but if any outside forces were brought to bear their military chances were non-existent. Like the Japanese, their only hope lay in the rest of the world not being bothered enough to put things back the way they had been.

But the rest of the world, as he had just learned on the telephone, did seem bothered enough.

Should he wake Jabang? he wondered. Probably. But just as he was summoning the energy to do so, Jabang appeared in the doorway, also rubbing his eyes.

'I can't sleep,' the new President said, sinking into the office's other easy chair and yawning.

'I have bad news,' Taal said wearily.

'The Senegalese?' It was hardly even a question.

'They're sending troops tomorrow morning. I managed to get a connection through Abidjan,' he added in explanation.

'Shit!' Jabang ran a hand across his stubbled hair, and exhaled noisily. 'Shit,' he repeated quietly. 'How many?' he asked. 'And where to?'

'Don't know. I doubt if they've decided yet. As to where, I'd guess they'll drop some paratroops somewhere near the airport, try and capture that, and if they succeed then they can fly in more.'

Jabang considered this. 'But how many men can they drop?' he asked. 'Not many, surely?'

Taal shrugged. 'A few hundred, maybe five, but . . .'

'And if we stop them capturing the airport they can't bring any more in, right?'

'Theoretically, but . . .'

'Surely our five hundred men can stop their five hundred, Junaidi.'

Taal shook his head. 'These will be French-trained soldiers, professionals. Our men are not trained for that sort of fighting . . .'

'Yes, but an army with political purpose will always triumph over mere mercenaries, Junaidi. History is full of examples. Castro and Guevara started with only twelve men and they beat a professional army.' Jabang's eyes were fixed on Taal's, willing him to believe.

'I know, Mamadou. I know. But the circumstances were different. And anyway,' he added, overriding a potential interruption, 'if we send all our five hundred to defend the airport who will keep order elsewhere? We just do not have enough men.'

'So what are you proposing we do – nothing? Should we head for the border, after being in power for just a few hours?'

'No.' It was tempting, Taal thought, but he would not be able to live with himself if they gave up this easily. 'No, we must resist as long as we can.'

Jabang grinned. 'Yes,' he said, 'yes!' and thumped his fist on the arm of his chair.

'What is it?' Sharif Sallah asked, coming into the room, a smile on his face.

The temptation to wipe the smile away was irresistible. 'The Senegalese are coming,' Taal said.

'What?'

'Sit down, Sharif,' Jabang said. 'And tell us how we can increase the number of our fighters in the next twelve hours.'

Sallah sat down, shaking his head. 'You are certain?' he asked, and received a nod in return. He sighed. 'Well, there is only one way to increase our numbers,' Sallah said. 'We will have to arm the men in Banjul Prison.'

It was Taal's turn to be surprised. 'You must be joking,' he said wearily.

Sallah shook his head. 'There are two hundred men in the prison, and many of them know how to use guns. If we let them out they will fight for us, because they will know that if Jawara wins he will put them back in the prison.'

'And what if they decide to use the weapons we give them to take what they want and just head for the border?' Taal asked. 'After having their revenge on whichever Field Force men put them in the prison.'

'We can keep them under control. In groups of ten or so, under twenty of our men. And in any case, they will know that Senegal offers no sanctuary for them. I tell you, they will fight for us because only we can offer them freedom.'

'And the moral question?' Taal wanted to know. 'These men are not in prison for cheating on their wives. They are murderers and thieves and . . .'

'Come on, Junaidi,' Jabang interrupted. 'There are only two murderers in Banjul Prison that I know of. But there are a lot of men who were caught stealing in order to feed themselves and their families.' He looked appealingly at Taal. 'Most crimes are political crimes – I can remember you saying so yourself.'

Yes, he had, Taal thought, but a long, long time ago. In the intervening years he had learned that not all evil could be so easily explained. 'I'm against it,' he said, 'except as a last resort.'

'You were just telling me this is the last resort,' Jabang insisted.

As soon as he could McGrath had pulled off the open road and examined Jobo's wound. It had already stopped bleeding, and seemed less serious than he had at first feared. Still, it would have to be looked at by a proper doctor, if only because there was no other obvious source of disinfectant.

He drove the jeep straight down Independence Drive, mentally daring anyone to try to stop him. No one did, and once at the hospital the two men found themselves in what looked like a scene from Florence Nightingale's life story. Somewhere or other there had been more fighting that day, because the reception area was full of reclining bodies, most of them with bullet wounds of varying degrees of seriousness. The woman receptionist, who must have weighed at least eighteen stone, and who would have looked enormous even in a country where overeating was commonplace, clambered with difficulty over the prone patients in pursuit of their names and details. Sibou Cham, who looked like grace personified in comparison, was forever moving hither and thither between the reception area and the treatment rooms as she ministered to the patients.

It was almost two hours before she got round to seeing Jobo.

'You look all in,' McGrath told her, with what he thought was a sympathetic smile.

'Yes, I know, you have a bed waiting for me.'

'I didn't mean that,' he said indignantly. 'Not that it's such a terrible idea,' he murmured, as an afterthought.

She ignored him and bent down to examine the wound. 'Did he really get shot by a sniper?' she asked.

'You don't want to know,' McGrath said. 'Is he going to be OK?'

'Yes, provided he keeps away from you for the next few days.'

'It was not Mr McGrath's fault,' Jobo blurted out. 'He saved us both . . .'

'She doesn't need to know,' McGrath interrupted.

Sibou gave him one cold, hard look and strode out of the office.

'I don't want to get her in trouble,' McGrath explained. 'The other guy – you called him Jerry – what do you think he'll do?'

Jobo thought. 'I don't know. He was always a scared kid when I knew him at school. And not very clever. He may worry that he'll get in trouble for letting his partner get shot or for running away. He may just go home and keep quiet, or even go up to the family village for a few days.'

'Or he may be telling his story to Comrade Jabang right this moment.'

'I don't think so.'

'Well, there's not a lot we can do about it if he is. Except maybe send you to your village for a few days . . .'

'I come from Serekunda,' Jobo said indignantly.

'Oh, pity.'

The doctor came back with a bowl of disinfectant and a roll of new bandage. After carefully washing the entrance and exit wounds she applied a dressing, then the bandage, and told Jobo to take it easy for a few days. 'If it starts to smell, or it throbs, come back,' she told him. 'Otherwise just let it heal.'

'I'll take him home,' McGrath said. She was already on her way back to the reception area. 'When do you get off?' he called after her.

She laughed. 'In my dreams,' she said over her shoulder, and disappeared.

Outside the jeep was still there, much to McGrath's relief and somewhat to his surprise. Darkness was falling with its usual tropical swiftness. He helped Jobo aboard, climbed into the driving seat, and started off down the road into town.

The first thing that struck him was how dark it was. Banjul's lighting would have done credit to a vampire's dining room at the best of times, but on this night every plug in the city seemed to have been pulled, and McGrath's vision was restricted to what the jeep's headlights could show him.

The sounds of the city told him more than he wanted to know. The most prominent seemed to feature a never-ending cascade of glass, as if someone was breaking a long line of windows in sequence. Some evidence to support this theory came at one corner, where the jeep's headlights picked out a tableau of three shops, each with their glass fronts smashed, and fully laden silhouettes bearing goods away into the night.

The sound of tearing wood also seemed much in evidence, offering proof, McGrath supposed, that in the Third World not many shops were fronted by glass. Banjul seemed to be in the process of being comprehensively looted.

And then there was the gunfire. Nothing steady, no long bursts, just single shots every minute or so, from wildly different directions, as if an endless series of individual murders was being committed all over the town.

It was eerie, and frightening. At Jobo's house his mother pulled him inside and shut the door almost in the same motion, as if afraid to let the contagion in. McGrath climbed back into the jeep and laid the Browning on the seat beside him, feeling the hairs rising on the nape of his neck. He engaged the gears and took off, hurtling back up the street faster than was prudent, but barely fast enough for his peace of mind.

It was only half a mile to the dim lights of McCarthy Square, only forty seconds or so, but it felt longer. At the square he slowed, wondering where to go. The Atlantic Hotel offered a whites-only haven, but there would be guards there, maybe guards who were looking for him, and he knew he would feel more restricted, more vulnerable, surrounded by fellow Europeans. Particularly if the rebels suddenly got trigger-happy with their tourist guests. No, he decided, the Carlton offered more freedom of movement, more ways out. And he could sleep on the roof.

* * *

The Party envoys, along with an armed guard of a dozen or so Field Force men, arrived at the prison soon after dark, and after a heated discussion with the warden, which ended with his being temporarily consigned to one of his own cells, they addressed the assembled prisoners in the dimly lit exercise yard. Moussa Diba and Lamin Konko listened as attentively as everyone else.

There had been a change of government, the speaker told them, and all prisoners, with the exception of the two convicted murderers, were being offered amnesty in return for a month's enlistment in the service of the new government. They would not be asked to fight against fellow Gambians or workers, only against foreigners seeking to invade the country. If they chose not to enlist, that was up to them. They would simply be returned to their cells to serve out their sentences.

'What do you think?' Konko asked Diba.

'Sounds like a way out,' Diba said with a grin. He was still inwardly laughing at the exemption of the two murderers, whom everybody in the prison knew to be among the gentlest of those incarcerated there. Both had killed their wives in a fit of jealous rage, and now spent all their time asking God for forgiveness. Some of the thieves, on the other hand, would cut a throat for five dalasi. He would himself for ten.

'I've only got two years more in here,' Konko said. 'I'd rather do them than get killed defending a bunch of politicians.'

'We won't,' Diba insisted. 'Look, if they're coming here to get us out, they must be desperate. It must be all craziness out there in Banjul. We'll have no trouble slipping away from whatever they've got planned for us, and then we hide out for a while, see how the situation is, get hold of some money and get across into Senegal when it looks good. No problem. Right, brother?'

Konko sighed. 'OK,' he said with less than total conviction. 'I guess out there must be better than being in here.'

There's women out there,' Diba said. Anja was out there. And with any luck he would have her tonight.

The two of them joined the queue of those waiting to accept the offer of amnesty. Since only three of the prison's two hundred and seventeen eligible inmates turned down the offer it was a long queue, and almost an hour had passed before the new recruits were drawn up in marching order on the road outside. They were kept standing there for several minutes, swatting at the mosquitoes drawn from the swamp by such a wealth of accessible blood in one spot, until one of the Party envoys addressed them again. They were being escorted to temporary barracks for the night, he told them. On the following morning they would be issued with their weapons.

The barracks in question turned out to be a large empty house in Marina Parade. There was no furniture, just floor space, and not enough of that. The overcrowding was worse than it had been in the prison, and, despite the protests of the guards, the sleeping quarters soon spilled out into the garden. There was no food, no entertainment, and after about an hour the sense of too much energy with nowhere to go was becoming overpowering. The guards, sensing the growing threat, started finding reasons to melt away, and with their disappearance an increasing number of the prisoners decided to go out for an evening stroll, some in search of their families, some in search of women, some simply in search of motion for its own sake.

Diba went looking for Anja.

Finding Independence Drive partially lit by a widely spaced string of log brazier fires, he slipped across the wide road and down the darker Mosque Road. It could not be much later than ten, he reckoned, but Banjul was obviously going to bed early these days. There were no shops open, no sounds of music, and few lights glowing through the compound doorways. Occasionally the sounds of conversation would drift out across a wall, and often as not lapse abruptly into silence at his footfall.

Conscious that he had no weapon, Diba kept a lookout for anything which would serve for protection, and in one small patch of reflected light noticed a two-foot length of heavy cable which someone had found surplus to requirements and discarded. It felt satisfyingly heavy in his hands.

Some fifteen minutes after leaving Marina Parade he found himself at the gate to the compound where she had her room. Her husband's family had once occupied the whole compound, but both his parents had died young, he had been killed in a road accident in Senegal, and his brothers had gone back to their Wollof village. She had fought a losing battle against other adult orphans, and the compound had become a home to assorted con men and thieves.

To Diba's surprise the gate was padlocked on the inside. He climbed over without difficulty, proud of how fit he had managed to keep himself in prison, and stood for a moment, listening for any sounds of occupation. He heard none, but as his eyes became accustomed to the gloom they picked out a pile of identical cardboard boxes stacked against a wall. They were new stereo radio-cassette players. No wonder the gate had been locked. He walked gingerly down one arm of the L-shaped courtyard, and turned the corner. The first thing he noticed was the yellow glow seeping out under Anja's door, the second was the sound of her voice, moaning softly, rhythmically, with pleasure.

Maybe it's not her, he told himself, a knot of anger forming in his stomach. He silently advanced to the door, and placed an eye up against the gap between the window shutters.

A single candle burnt on the wooden table, illuminating the two naked people on the bed. She was underneath, her back slightly arched, eyes closed, hands behind her head, gripping the cast-iron rail of the bedstead. He was above her, supporting his upper body on two rigid arms as he thrust himself slowly this way and that. The two bodies glistened in the candlelight.

Anger surged through Diba's guts, but he fought it back. He took two deep breaths before walking through the curtained doorway into the room, the length of cable loose in his hand.

Though her eyes were closed she became aware of him first. Perhaps it was a draught from the door, or perhaps they really did have a telepathic connection, as she had always claimed. Her eyes opened, widened, and snapped shut again as he swung the cable in a vicious arc at the man's head.

Blood splattered, and the man seemed to sway, as if he was held upright only by his position inside her. She cried out and twisted, and he collapsed off the bed with a crash, falling onto the already crushed back of his head. Two thin streams of blood emerged from his nose and mouth, merged on his cheek, and abruptly ceased flowing.

Diba used a foot to roll the body into the shadows. Anja was just lying there, one hand still gripping the iron rail, the other covering her mouth, palm outwards. Her eyes were wide again, wide with shock. He reached down a hand and brushed a still-erect nipple with his palm.

She reached for the sheet to cover herself, but he ripped it away from her, and threw it on the floor.

He pulled his shirt over his head, tore off his trousers and stood over her, his dick swelling towards her face. For a moment he thought of thrusting it into her mouth, but the expression on her face was still unreadable, and he did not want it bitten off.

'Moussa,' she said.

He clambered astride her, and thrust himself into the warm wetness which the dead man had so recently vacated. She moaned and closed her eyes, but Diba was not fooled. He came in a sudden rush, spilling three months of prison frustration into her, and then abruptly pulled out, and rolled over onto his back.

For several moments the two of them lay there in silence.

'How did you get out?' she asked after a while, her voice sounding strange, as if she was trying too hard to sound normal.

'They let us all out to fight for the new Government,' he told her.

She risked moving, raising herself onto one elbow. 'Is he dead?' she asked.

'Looks like it,' Diba said coldly. It was funny – he would have expected to feel something after killing a man, but he felt nothing at all. Unless he counted being aware of the need to make sure he was not caught.

But he did remember how angry he had felt. 'Who was this man you were fucking?' he asked in a threatening voice.

'Just a customer,' she lied. It was her experience that men who got it for free did not usually feel jealous of those who had paid.

She was right. 'You been prostituting yourself?' he asked, with an anger that was less than convincing.

'While you're in the prison I have to eat,' she said, risking some self-assertion for the first time.

He reached out a hand and grabbed her by the plaited hair. 'You sounded like you were enjoying it,' he said.

'Men like that need to think they're making you feel good,' she said.

He grunted and let her go. He wanted to believe her – he always had. 'OK,' he said. 'But you're all mine again now – got it? And we're getting out of this shit-hole.'

'Where to?'

'I haven't decided yet. You got anything to drink?'

'No, but I can get some beer from Winnie's. It'll take five minutes.'

He grabbed one of her cheeks in his hand and held her eyes. She was so fucking beautiful. 'You wouldn't disappear on me, would you?' he asked.

'I'll be five minutes.'

'I'd kill you, you know that.'

'Yes, I know that.'

'Right.' He let her go, watched her slip the dress over herself and head for the door, careful not to look at the prone body under the window.

He supposed he ought to do something about that.

He put his trousers back on, grabbed the corpse by the feet and dragged it out into the courtyard. Anja had left the gate open, so he carried on into the darkened street, his ears straining for other sounds above the scrape of the man's head in the dust. After fifty yards he decided he had gone far enough, and simply left the body in the middle of the road. With any luck they would think he had been hit by a taxi in the dark.

Back in her room Anja was engaged in opening one of three bottles of beer on the edge of the table. He took it from her and sprang the cap off, remembering doing the same thing at other times in the past, in that same candlelit room.

'Do you mean you're in the army now?' she asked.

He shrugged. 'They want us to defend their revolution,' he said. 'They're going to give us guns in the morning. And then . . . I don't know. But I'm not going to get killed for a bunch of fucking politicians. I'll take their gun all right, but who I use it on is my business.' He smiled. 'And I've got a few ideas on that myself.'

'The Englishman who caught you,' she said, before stopping to think.

'How do you know about that?' he asked angrily.

'It was in the newspaper', she said. 'Someone showed it to me.'

'What was? What did it say?'

'That you were caught at the hospital by an Englishman, that's all,' she said. There had been more, but she reckoned he would not want to hear the details of his humiliation.

'It was bad luck,' he said. 'But yes, I owe him.' And the doctor too, he thought. He had had her naked once, and he would have her naked again, only next time she would not have the white bastard there to protect her. He would make her kneel for him.

He looked across at Anja, who was just as beautiful as the doctor, but had grown up as poor as he had. He felt the old desire mounting in his body. 'Take the dress off,' he said.

5

The column of five open lorries, each carrying twenty ex-prisoners, rumbled through Serekunda and south towards Yundum Airport. It had been light for only an hour or so, and the heat was not yet oppressive. Diba sat alongside Konko, the Kalashnikov leaning against his thigh, watching the countryside go by. He was not very happy with the situation. A town man, he felt much more confident of melting away into the scenery when it was composed of shanty compounds. Outside the town he felt too conspicuous.

Still, he had had no chance to get away again since returning to the temporary barracks an hour before dawn. Most of the other nocturnal absentees had also come back: like Diba they saw little hope of escaping the country under the present circumstances, and no hope of anything but longer prison terms from a returning Jawara. For the moment the new regime was their only friend – not to mention their only source of weaponry and ammunition.

The lorries with the Kalashnikovs had drawn up outside the barracks just as dawn was breaking, and the men had been told to claim their guns as they boarded. The new regime was obviously not composed entirely of fools.

Diba wondered if he really would find himself in a battle before the day was over. Not if he could help it, he told himself.

'Where do you think we're going?' Konko asked him.

'The airport,' Diba replied. It was a guess. There was nothing else of any importance in this direction, only three hundred miles of villages. Unless of course the new government had decided to invade the rest of Africa.

He was right the first time, for the lorries swung off the road to Brikama, taking the airport turn-off. The land was flat savannah, dotted with the occasional tree, but otherwise offering no more cover than that provided by the long wet-season grass. For the first time the possibility of being attacked from the air occurred to Diba. He remembered the opening shot of the film he had seen just before his arrest – a wall of palm trees exploding into flames. It had been about Vietnam, but he could not remember the title.

Also for the first time, he wondered whether leaving the prison had been such a good idea. His mind went back over the previous night, and told him it had been. And there had to be some way to make use of this situation for his and Anja's benefit. He just had to be patient, and recognize the opening when it came.

The lorries were drawing up in front of the airport terminal. The tailgates were lowered, the men ordered down and divided into groups of ten by two uniformed Field Force men. From the looks on their faces the latter hardly seemed enamoured of their new reinforcements. And Diba had to admit that his fellow prisoners hardly looked like soldiers. All were still wearing the clothes they had been wearing in jail, which ranged in condition from rags to almost reasonable, from utterly filthy to merely soiled.

The groups of ten were led off at intervals through the airport's main doors. When Diba and Konko's turn came they found that the building was only a temporary port of call: after each man had been issued with a hunk of bread and a couple of bananas they were led out through other doors at the back and onto a wide expanse of tarmac, where several large planes were parked. None looked like it was expecting to fly.

Diba's group, accompanied by a roughly equal number of Field Force men and other rebels, headed north up the main runway to its end, and then pressed on another two hundred yards until they reached a row of landing lights, protruding from the grass like fetish poles. Spades were produced and the ex-prisoners took turns excavating trenches while the others scanned the sky, talking nervously among themselves and occasionally throwing a contemptuous glance at the diggers.

Within an hour the group of twenty was arranged in a semicircle of trenches, the airport behind them, empty savannah and sky in front of them. The sweating Diba and Konko shared the latter's last cigarette and hoped that the rest of the day would be as peaceful.

McGrath was woken by a loudly honking formation of geese flying low over the hotel roof. He had been having one of those lovely English dreams, sitting in the conservatory his wife had spent so much effort on, watching the sparrows eating from the bird table on the lawn outside. It had all been so peaceful.

He looked at the sun, then at his watch. It was gone eight already, and his back ached from the hardness of the roof, but he felt reluctant to get up. Dreams like that – and he seemed to have more of them with each trip abroad – always

68

produced a vague aching in his heart, and made him wonder why, if he really missed her and the children so much, he spent so much of his time so far away from them.

I mean, he said to himself, what the fuck am I doing at my age sleeping out on an African hotel roof because it's not safe to sleep in my fucking room?

He reached for the transistor radio that he had recovered from his room the night before and tuned in to Radio Gambia. And like the night before, the programming consisted of replays of the new leader's message to the world, sandwiched between bouts of Bob Marley. The rebels were still in control.

McGrath manoeuvred himself into a sitting position, his back against an air vent, and thought about what he should do. For all he knew, the entire rebel army was out looking for him, although it seemed unlikely. He had heard no commotion in the hotel below him, and he tended to trust Jobo's judgement in the matter of the boy who had thrown himself into the creek. Of course it would be prudent to assume the new authorities were looking for him, and to stay where he was until he knew otherwise, but the thought of sitting on the Carlton roof for the rest of the day did not seem very appealing.

His first job, he decided, was to talk to the High Commission, and find out what the hell was going on. For that he would need a telephone, and the roof seemed lamentably short of them.

He walked down to his room, listened at the door for a few moments to make sure no one was waiting inside, and then let himself in. The water was on and hot, so he treated himself to a shower and changed clothes before going downstairs. The lobby was empty, the telephone dead as a doornail. He would have to revisit the Atlantic.

From the lobby window the road outside also seemed devoid of people, as if it was a Sunday morning. But two guards were standing guard at the gates to the Legislative Assembly, and several more men in uniform were talking to each other just outside the doors. McGrath was about to step out into the street when the Carlton's manager hurried out of the dining room to intercept him.

'Mr McGrath,' he said breathlessly. 'I wanted to talk to you. To give you warning.'

'What of?' McGrath asked, surprised at such concern.

'I remember your arrest at the hospital,' the man said, as if in explanation.

'Yes?'

'They have let all the prisoners out,' the manager explained.

'They've what!' McGrath exclaimed. 'Why, for Christ's sake?'

The manager shrugged. 'To fight for them, of course. They've given them guns and driven them off somewhere. But I thought you should know. The man you arrested . . .'

'Ah.' Now he understood. 'I understand. Thank you. I will be careful.'

'Maybe you can arrest him again,' the man said with a smile.

'Maybe.'

The manager smiled and retreated into the bowels of the hotel. Still absorbing this new information, McGrath walked out through the terrace and down the side of the building to where he had parked the Ministry of Development jeep. He wondered if Sibou had heard the news. He would have to make sure she had.

He eased the jeep out into Independence Drive. The guards outside the Legislative Assembly stared at him, but neither did nor said any more. McGrath drove the hundred yards or so to where the side road cut through to Marina Parade and turned onto it. Halfway down he had to swerve to avoid two bodies lying in the middle of the road. He stopped the jeep, got out, and went back to look at them. Both were oldish men, and both had had their throats cut. More than a few hours ago, for the pools of blood had long since dried into a brown crust.

He went back to the jeep and drove on, turning right again onto Marina Parade, oblivious to the beauty of the trees that hung across the road. The crust of civilization was so thin, he thought. Take away the repressive hand of the law, and hey presto, there would be a queue of sickos waiting to prove that morality grew out of the barrel of a gun. Or the blade of a knife. Or whatever came to hand.

The Atlantic Hotel was an oasis of order. Black waiters in red shirts were still serving breakfast to fat Europeans, and smiling at them as if their lives depended on it. Or at least their tips. He must have got out on the wrong side of the roof this morning, McGrath told himself. The world seemed cast in shades of sourness.

Or maybe moving from slashed throats to croissant-guzzling tourists in under five minutes was a little too swift a transition. He got himself a cup of coffee and carried it through to the lobby.

At least the telephones were still working. He called the High Commission and drank most of the coffee while whoever it was that had answered went looking for Bill Myers.

'Simon,' a voice said eventually, 'glad you're still alive.'

'Just about,' McGrath said. 'Banjul is getting a bit hairy. You know . . .'

'Help is on the way,' Myers interrupted him. 'Senegalese Army should be arriving sometime today.'

'Arriving where?'

'No idea. But wherever it is, I don't suppose it'll take them long to clear this shower out.'

'Maybe,' McGrath said noncommittally. He supposed it was good news to him personally – instead of being arrested for shooting a rebel he would probably be given a medal. 'Did you know they've emptied the prison?' he asked Myers.

'Oh shit, they haven't.'

'So I'm told. And armed the prisoners.'

'That's bad news. And the other thing is – we've got no idea what they've done with the old Government – it's only Jawara who was out of the country. And then there's the little matter of his family, too. It could still get very messy.'

'Sounds like it. Anything you want me to do at this end.'

'No,' Myers said after a brief pause, 'just stay in touch. According to London there's a rumour that Jawara has asked the PM for help. Who knows, she may even ask your old mob to lend a hand. So you may yet become indispensable.'

'Thanks a bunch, Bill,' McGrath said. 'Remind me to send you my invoice for services rendered to the Crown.'

Myers laughed and hung up. McGrath put the receiver down and thought about what he had heard. The SAS in The Gambia – that would be one for the Regiment's scrapbook. And if a hostage situation did develop . . .

It would be interesting, to say the least. For the moment, though, he had other things to worry about. Like Sibou Cham. He drove down Marina Parade to the hospital, and parked right outside the entrance. Soon, if not already, the rebels would be too busy worrying about the Senegalese to worry about him.

Once inside, he walked straight through towards her office, but an orderly barred his way at the threshold. Dr Cham was sleeping, and not to be disturbed. Dr Cham had not slept for two days, he added, in case the message had not got through.

'OK,' McGrath said. 'I just want to leave her a message. But it's important she gets it,' he added firmly.

'What's so important?' Sibou's voice asked from inside the next room.

'You wake her,' the orderly said indignantly.

'It's OK, Cissé,' Sibou said. 'McGrath, come and tell me your important message.'

She was lying fully dressed on the treatment table, staring up at the ceiling. 'They've opened up the prison,' he said, watching for her reaction.

Her eyes closed once, and opened again. 'He's out,' she said.

'Yeah. So I thought maybe I would hang around here for a while, and keep you company.'

'That . . .' She stopped herself. 'There's no need,' she said eventually. 'He can't get to me here . . .'

'He did before.'

'That was different. These days this place is swarming with armed men. I can't get rid of them.' She looked up at him. 'Thank you,' she said, 'but I'll be careful. And so should you be. I think he has more of a grudge against you than against me.'

He shrugged. 'OK. But I'll drop by every now and then . . .'

'Thanks,' she said again.

He went back to the jeep, drove it back to the Carlton, and climbed back up to the roof, taking his binoculars with him. It was about twenty minutes later, soon after 10.30, that the first Mirage flew low over Banjul, shattering the calm and more than a few hopes.

* * *

Cecil Matheson walked up the gracefully curving staircase to his first-floor sanctum in the Foreign Office. It had taken the chauffeur an hour to bring him the mile across London from his Pimlico home, and the *Times* crossword was proving unusually stubborn. All in all, he felt frustrated, and ready to take it out on the first available scapegoat.

Unfortunately, his first call of the morning, which arrived before he had even had time to re-order his desk, was from the Prime Minister.

'Cecil,' she began, without so much as a 'good morning', 'this business in The Gambia . . .'

'Yes, Prime Minister,' he said dutifully, wondering what the hell she was talking about. He had spent the previous day at home, watching the cricket and catching up between overs on the latest Argentinian claims to the Falklands. No one had thought to disturb him with news from The Gambia. Had the wretched little country left the Commonwealth, or banned the English cricket team, or stopped buying British? Maybe her son Mark had got himself lost again on some transcontinental rally devised exclusively for the idiot offspring of prominent world leaders.

'President Jawara called me late last night and asked if we could help,' she said.

Help with what? Matheson was thinking, when his eyes made contact with the relevant report. 'Exactly what does he have in mind?' he asked, scanning through the sheet in front of him.

'Just some military advice. The Senegalese are sending troops in this morning, but I think President Jawara would like some British help – The Gambia was a British colony, after all. And he was here in London for the Royal Wedding when it all happened.'

Matheson grunted to himself. According to the report he was reading, Jawara had been overthrown by an alliance of Marxist rebels and members of his own army. So he had had to ask for military help from his Senegalese neighbours. And now the crafty bastard wanted a counterbalance to his new allies. He did not want to clear out the criminals only to find that his house had been occupied by the police.

'So I thought a small advisory group,' the Prime Minister continued. 'The SAS would seem best qualified. And be a good advertisement for the country.'

'Yes, I'm sure they could undertake such a task,' Matheson agreed. The previous year's breaking of the Iranian Embassy siege had been efficient enough. Almost awesomely so. Yet it had not exactly quelled some doubts, particularly among the opposition, as to the Regiment's cut-throat methods. Over the five years of the SAS's deployment in Northern Ireland there had been rather a lot of fatal accidents involving terrorist suspects.

'Very well,' the Prime Minister was saying. 'I'll leave it with you to contact Hereford. Tell them we definitely want to offer the President some help, but it's up to them to suggest exactly what. You can arrange the necessary liaison with the Gambians.'

'Certainly . . .' Matheson started to say, but she had hung up. He made a face at the phone and read through the report properly. Reading between the lines, he doubted whether the Senegalese would have much trouble re-establishing Jawara's authority. But the large number of tourists did suggest an unpleasantly serious risk of hostages being taken. It could all become a bit of a mare's nest, he thought. Perhaps the SAS was not such a bad idea, after all.

First, though, he had better go through all the necessary international courtesies. The French first, he thought, and asked his secretary to connect him with his opposite number in the Quai d'Orsay. René Bonnard was one of God's more acceptable Frenchmen – on occasion Matheson even suspected he had a moral code. It was probably just a trick of the light.

'René' he said warmly, once the connection had been established. 'I'd just like a few words about the Gambian situation,' he went on, fighting the usual losing battle with his French.

'Let us speak English,' Bonnard said. Pride in one's language was one thing, but it was just too painful listening to Matheson's version of it. 'I hope you don't think we're treading on your feet . . .'

'No, no, not at all. The treaty between Senegal and The Gambia was there for just such an eventuality. We have no problem with Senegalese intervention, quite the contrary. I'm calling to let you know that we shall in all probability be sending a small team of our own – and at Jawara's request, of course . . .'

'Of course,' Bonnard agreed wryly. 'Hedging his bets – is that the English phrase?'

Matheson laughed. 'Indeed it is.'

'Well, we will be happy to offer any assistance we can. I assume Jawara will set up any necessary liaison facilities between the Senegalese military and your men, but if we can do anything . . .'

'Since the Senegalese were trained by your people, it might be useful for our men to get some idea of who they'll be dealing with – the quality of the ally, so to speak . . .'

'I'm sure that can be arranged,' Bonnard agreed. 'At the moment I don't imagine there's any chance of your boys flying direct to Banjul, so they'd have to come through Paris anyway, *en route* to Dakar. I could set up a meeting at Charles de Gaulle easily enough.'

'Thank you, René. I'll be in touch.' Matheson replaced the phone, asked his secretary to get him the State Department, and sipped at the coffee which had just appeared on his desk. Tadeusz Lubanski was a very different proposition from René Bonnard. A 'tad obnoxious' as some Foreign Office wit had dubbed him.

The buzzer announced the call had been put through. 'Good morning, Mr Lubanski,' Matheson announced brightly. The reply was a sound between a grunt and groan. Matheson smiled to himself. 'Sorry to wake you up', he went on, with the modicum of sincerity he could muster, 'but we're considering some military action, and I assume you would wish to be consulted before the fact, rather than after.'

'What are you going to do, Cecil? Invade China?'

'No, nor any other part of south-east Asia,' Matheson rejoined. 'We're just sending a few advisers to The Gambia – you know where that is?'

'Africa, by any chance?' Lubanski asked sarcastically.

'There's been a coup . . .'

'We do notice these things, Cecil.'

'Ah, of course. Well, the Senegalese Army is going in to put things back together and we're just sending in a few of our own men to lend them a helping hand.'

'Very commendable,' Lubanski said drily.

'So, the United States Government has no objections?'

'No, Cecil, I think I can say with some certainty that we don't. If you and the French want to play golden oldies down Africa way, then be our guests. Wear your pith helmets with pride.'

'Thank you,' Matheson said coldly.

'You're welcome. Now I'm going back to sleep.' There was a click as the line went dead.

'Bastard,' Matheson muttered. He took another gulp of coffee and asked for a number in Hereford.

Lieutenant-Colonel Bryan Weighell was sitting in his office at the Stirling Lines barracks of 22 SAS Regiment, thinking about his three children. Now that his ex-wife, Linda, had announced her imminent wedding to the idiot barrister he wondered what would happen to his relationship with Helen, Jenny and Stephen. As it was now, he only saw them for a few hours each Sunday, and presumably their moving to London would make things even more difficult. He supposed he could drive down from Hereford each weekend, but it would not be the same. He would always have to be *out* with them, at cinemas or zoos or McDonald's. And they would have new schools, new friends, new interests. And a new father.

He himself would become a more distant figure, and not just in miles. Maybe they had known him long enough for something to stick, something which could be brought back to life when they grew up, yet he was not at all sure of it. Helen, the eldest, was only twelve.

It was all profoundly depressing.

Like the state of the world, come to that. The Royal Wedding had been celebrated against a backdrop of cities torn by rioting, soaring unemployment, a new cold war. Something was up shit creek in the state of Denmark, Weighell told himself. Even his beloved SAS had been reduced to doing the dirty work in Northern Ireland. Shooting teenage joyriders in Armagh was not how he had seen the future of the Regiment.

Maybe he should take an early discharge and get a consultancy job – it would not be difficult. Maybe one in London to be near the kids. Or maybe one abroad, somewhere the kids could come and stay with him. A week of real contact would probably be worth a lot more than regular trips to McDonald's. And Linda would let them come, for she was determined to be civilized about it all.

Weighell glared savagely out of the window at the sunlit yard, half-wishing she had given him more real justification for anger.

The telephone rang.

'Lieutenant-Colonel Weighell?' a vaguely familiar voice asked him.

'Speaking.'

'I'm Cecil Matheson. Junior Minister at the Foreign Office . . .'

Now Weighell recognized the voice. A tall, smarmy-looking man who always seemed to be staring down his nose at TV interviewers. Not that most of the interviewers deserved any better . . .

'The Prime Minister has asked me to call you,' Matheson was saying. 'Are you aware of what's been happening in The Gambia over the last two days?' he asked.

'Can't say I am.'

'It's on the front page of this morning's *Times*', Matheson said curtly, neglecting to add that he had missed it himself in his eagerness to get to the crossword.

'I haven't seen the paper yet,' Weighell said, reaching across for the tabloid on his desk, and finding its front page devoted to the ins and outs, to coin a phrase, of the Royal Honeymoon.

Matheson briefly outlined the events of the previous forty-eight hours in The Gambia, and recounted the gist of his conversations with the Prime Minister and René Bonnard. 'She wants to know if you can – and I quote – make yourselves useful down there.'

'Doing what?'

'Advising the Senegalese, advising Jawara and his government.'

'Do the Senegalese *want* advice?'

'Probably not. But Jawara obviously wants some sort of counterbalance to them. You know what these situations are like.'

'Unfortunately. But why's the PM going along?'

'General goodwill. Fellow member of the Commonwealth, etc. Plus she has a fondness for . . . well . . .'

'Sticking her oar in?'

'You could put it that way. And she has a great admiration for your regiment,' Matheson added, wondering whether he had allowed himself to become a little too obviously disloyal. 'After the Princes Gate siege she thinks you can do miracles,' he added, reverting to his usual tone of disdainful detachment.

Weighell thought for a moment. 'Let me get this straight,' he said. 'You want us to send a small party to The Gambia to act as advisers to the President . . .'

'Two or three men, to offer help where help is needed.'

'Including military action?'

'We'll have to consider that if and when the need arises. The role will be essentially advisory. A hostage situation may develop, in which case your experience will no doubt be invaluable to whoever's in charge.'

'Advisory or not, I can't send my men into such a situation completely unprotected. They'll need clearance to carry handguns, at the very least.'

'I'm sure that can be arranged. Look, for all we know at the moment, the whole business may be over by this afternoon. I'll call you back, say around five, with the latest information. In the meantime, if you can come up with a game-plan . . .'

'Will do.'

'Thank you, Lieutenant-Colonel,' Matheson said before replacing the receiver.

Weighell stared idly out of the window for a few seconds, and then summoned his adjutant. 'Get hold of Major Caskey,' he said, 'and tell him I want to see him. As soon as he can manage. And get me a cup of tea. And a copy of the wretched *Times*.'

He took a quick look through the tabloid, on the off-chance there was any real news in it, and then resumed staring out of the window, this time thinking about his second in command – and the current duty officer – Alan Caskey.

The two of them really ought to get on better than they did, Weighell thought. They had two important things in common – the SAS and fucked-up marriages. It was not as if he disliked Caskey – he just did not feel drawn to him. The man seemed to have lots of close friends in the Regiment, but Weighell wondered how deep the friendships were. Caskey had always struck him as an archetypal loner, a law unto himself offering others little hope of real contact. Or was he just describing himself, Weighell wondered. It was an unwelcome thought.

The tea arrived, along with the *Times*. He read the front page report of the coup, and found it somewhat deficient in precise timings. Today was Friday, but the report could not even make up its mind whether the coup had taken place on Wednesday or Thursday. There were hints of dubious foreign involvement – the ubiquitous Libyans and Cubans, of course – but precious little in the way of proof. It was also suggested that majorities of the local armed forces both supported and opposed the new government.

He had never much liked the *Times* anyway, though Linda had sworn by its absorbent properties when it came to changing the cat litter.

He looked across to the photograph of her and the children which still held pride of place above the map cabinet. He supposed it was somewhat inappropriate now. He would have to get a new one of just the children. Or do what they had done in Stalin's Russia, and have her invisibly removed from the current photograph, and perhaps even replaced by someone new. First, though, he would have to find someone.

The two Mirages of the Senegalese Air Force had certainly made everyone jump when they first buzzed the airport, but no bombs had been dropped, no sticks of napalm unleashed, no missiles fired. For those in the trenches, like Moussa Diba, they represented a possible future threat, whose seriousness was completely unknown. Maybe all they were capable of was making a loud noise as they flew by.

On the other hand, the long lines of paratroops swinging down to earth from the giant transport planes a mile or so to the north looked like posing a depressingly immediate problem. It did not take a military genius to work out that their target had to be the airport. And once they had secured that, any number of troop-filled planes could land.

In the air control tower Junaidi Taal watched the descent of the airborne troops with a sinking feeling. There had to be at least five hundred, as many as he had available to face them, and the incoming Senegalese were trained soldiers, not a mixed bunch of policemen, Party activists and convicts who had been issued with rifles. At that moment, if Taal could have taken the coup back, he would have.

But he was not a man given to dwelling on what might have been. Their hopes might be fast receding, but they had not disappeared – not yet. He had an hour or so before the invaders got themselves organized enough to begin advancing on the airport. How could he use the time?

He picked up the phone which connected him with the officer he had left in charge of the airport terminal. 'Have the explosives arrived yet?' he asked, knowing full well the answer would be no. The man would have phoned him if they had.

'No, sir, not yet.'

'Call me the moment they do,' Taal said.

'Of course, sir.'

It was truly ironic, Taal thought. Because The Gambia had never had an army, it had never had a central ordnance depot, and no stockpile of military explosives. And since the coup had seriously disrupted communications and shut down work on most official projects, it had proved extremely difficult to track down any civilian sources. The nearest one that Taal's subordinates had been able to find was in Soma, a hundred miles away, where explosives were being used to blast irrigation channels for rice cultivation. Plans to fetch a supply by helicopter had fallen through due to the lack of anyone capable of flying one of the several machines parked on the tarmac. Instead, a taxi had been dispatched along the pothole- and rut-strewn highway to the east. If the explosive was at all volatile then Taal would not have fancied being the driver making the return trip.

All in all, their chances of rendering the runway unusable before the Senegalese captured it seemed less than good. Like their chances overall. If Taal had been a betting man he would have put money on the Senegalese taking the airport by mid-afternoon, and Banjul by the following noon.

A mile to the north Diba's thoughts were more personally oriented. The flow of transport planes and parachutists had seemed depressingly relentless for a while, but the staunching of the flow, and the promise of imminent contact with armed troops made him wish for more planes.

He doubted whether those in charge on his own side had any idea of what they were doing. The big chief back at the airport was just a converted policeman, and the man in charge of this small company dug in behind the runway guide lights – a Wollof zealot named Jahumpa – seemed endowed with more enthusiasm than brains. In fact Jahumpa had the idiot eyes of someone who was willing to die for a cause, and Diba was fucked if he was going to join him for the ride.

'That cell of ours would look pretty good now,' Konko muttered beside him.

Diba was opening his mouth to reply when the silence was shattered by a swelling, high-pitched whooshing sound. A blinding flash and an exploding fountain of earth some forty yards behind them preceded, by a split second, the deafening crash of the explosion. Diba instinctively clasped his hands to his ears, which were already humming with the impact.

'Fuck,' he grunted, pulling himself as low as he could in the trench, just as another mortar landed in almost the same spot, providing a second white splash on his retinae and more whirring in his ears. He could just about hear Jahumpa, two trenches away, talking excitedly into the walkie-talkie.

Up in the air control tower Taal thought he could make out the Senegalese mortar positions a mile or so to the north. The enemy had no high ground and no air reconnaissance – not yet, at least – so it would be difficult for them to zero in on the defending positions, but that would slow them up rather than stop them. Already he could see groups of distant infantry on the move in wide flanking directions to either side of the airport. Even if the explosives arrived now he could see no hope of their being laid and detonated in time to cause any significant damage to the runway. The airport was a lost cause. And if he did not move fast the Senegalese would reach the Banjul road, and cut him and his men off from the capital.

'Pull them back,' he told his immediate subordinate. 'As quickly and as invisibly as you can. Then start moving them into the fall-back positions. I'm going to Banjul, but I'll be back in a couple of hours.' He turned to descend the spiral staircase, hesitated on the top step, then continued down. He had been about to order the destruction of all the aircraft on the tarmac, but had thought better of it. In the circumstances such an action would be little more than vandalism.

It was five past eleven, and the Australians had successfully survived the first over of the second day. The weather at Edgbaston looked much as it did outside Caskey's window – depressingly sunny. The English bowlers needed a few clouds, or the team as a whole would pay dearly for batting so ineptly on such a good wicket the day before.

Always assuming Botham did not provide another miracle.

It could hardly happen twice, Caskey thought. And anyway, once was enough. He would carry that innings at Headingley to his grave, smiling at the memory every time it surfaced.

He reached for the bottle of claret he had been allowing to breathe, and poured himself a small glass. It might be a dull time for the Regiment, and to describe his personal life as a disaster area might legitimately be considered an understatement, but there were still test matches which he could sink himself into, body and soul. There were still twenty-five days a year, rain permitting, when he could forget about the real world.

Cricket was like marijuana, as he had once explained to a shocked New Zealander. It slowed everything down. Once you accepted cricket time and forgot real time, accustomed yourself to the new pace, it became as beautiful to the spectator as a Grateful Dead concert did to a dopehead. Needless to say, every West Indian he had ever met understood this instinctively.

He sipped appreciatively at the wine and willed the nightwatchman Bright to lose his concentration. Without success. He had a bad feeling about the coming day – he could see the Australians making four hundred on a wicket like this, and then skittling England out for half as much. Botham's innings at Headingley deserved better.

He had just put his feet up on the coffee table when the phone rang.

6

The knock on Lieutenant-Colonel Weighell's door was swiftly succeeded by the appearance of Caskey's willowy figure.

'Good morning, boss,' Caskey said, taking the proffered chair on the other side of his CO's desk.

'Good morning, Alan,' Weighell said. Somehow, Caskey's use of the SAS's customary 'boss' when addressing a superior officer always grated on him. Perhaps it just sounded too working-class for Caskey, whose background, unlike that of most men in the Regiment, was colonial and public school. 'I take it you've got nothing important on right now?' he asked.

'Nothing. What's up?' Caskey asked.

'Read this,' Weighell said, handing him the *Times* and pointing out the story.

Caskey read it through, and looked up quizzically.

Weighell explained the Prime Minister's request. 'And I thought with your African experience . . .' he concluded.

'I'd be delighted,' Caskey said. Even five days of cricket could hardly compete with a mission abroad, always supposing England's batsmen held out that long. It would put a distance between him and his wife, and between him and Liz. He could forget the whole damn business for a few

87

precious days or weeks, and enjoy some real excitement while he was at it.

'The Foreign Office are ringing me back this afternoon. Can you dig up a third man for the party . . .'

'Third?'

'I've already picked a second. Trooper Franklin of G Squadron.'

'Because he's black?'

'Yes. I think putting three white faces into a situation like this might be less than diplomatic, don't you?'

'Did the Gambian Government request it?'

'No. I doubt if it occurred to them that the SAS might have black soldiers.'

'There are only two. West Indians, that is.'

'I know. And you know as well as I do that we've made no effort to increase the number, mostly because it would be hard to use West Indians in the sort of operations we've been involved in lately. They tend to be rather conspicuous in rural Fermanagh. But in Africa . . .'

'In Africa they give us credibility?'

Weighell grunted. 'Something like that. But Franklin's a damn fine soldier. If he wasn't, I wouldn't send him. The fact that he's black is just a bonus as far as this operation's concerned.'

'OK. I get the picture. And if he's as good as you say, I'll have no trouble with him.' He got to his feet. 'For the third man I'll see if I can find someone who's actually been to The Gambia.'

Joss Wynwood stretched his legs as silently as he could manage within the confines of the hedge. It was more than six hours now since dawn had rendered movement inadvisable. After all, who knew what Irish eyes might be smiling at him down the end of a sniper's 'scope?

Admittedly it was unlikely. From where he lay, half in the hedgerow, half in the long grass behind it, Wynwood could see empty country stretch away to the north, down to the distant glimmer of Lough Neagh some fifteen miles away. In the foreground, and not much more than twenty-five yards away, the road from Armagh to Newry ran from left to right. Parked off the road on his near side, and apparently changing a tyre on his Leyland van, a man in a blue woolly hat was happily whistling 'Danny Boy'.

It was a lovely day for an ambush. The sun shone intermittently, as fluffy white clouds sailed majestically across the blue sky, trailing their vast shadows across the green hills like a fleet of Zeppelins.

It all looked a lot more peaceful than Wynwood felt. He had been a badged member of the SAS for only a few months, and this was his first major action with the Regiment. His nerves were all on edge, from what felt like a tick in his eyelids to the prickling sensation on his skin. Every now and then he had to wipe the sweat from the stock of the Heckler & Koch MP5 sub-machine-gun he was holding.

He stole a glance to his right, where Trooper Davey Matthews – Stanley to his friends – seemed immune to such anxiety. He was probably fantasizing about the barmaid in Newry, Wynwood thought, for apart from football, Stanley's only interest in life seemed to be sex. Getting it, having it, talking about it, imagining it.

'What do you think the Pope does with an erection?' Stanley had asked him in the middle of the previous night. Wynwood had been too dumbstruck by the incongruity of the question to think up an answer. 'Takes it to confession,' Stanley had told him.

Wynwood smiled at the memory. Everyone in the SAS was fucking crazy, he thought. And he must be fucking crazy too.

When in Rome . . ., he thought. Making love with Susan had been wonderful from the very first time, half-pissed out of their skulls in her room at the training college. It had been wonderful in the back of his car, wonderful on that Gower beach with the moon coming up, wonderful in their Gambian honeymoon hotel, the fan whirring lazily above them.

Jesus, why does Stanley do this, he asked himself. What did he do with his own hard-ons?

Wynwood turned his attention back to the scene in front of him. The man in the woolly hat had now been changing his tyre for almost an hour, performing each task in the process with a speed that would have embarrassed a snail. Soon he would have no choice but to start changing the two tyres back again. His name was Martin Langan, and he was a corporal in the Regiment's B Squadron.

Watching him reminded Wynwood of how nice it felt to be cramped up in a hedge. It was always better to be the trap than the bait. Though this particular trap seemed unlikely to spring. If the Provos were coming, they should have come by now. Like all the old hands said: for every successful ambush you got ten that just end in premature arthritis.

The preparations for this one had taken a lot of time and effort. About a fortnight before, 14th Intelligence Company had got word from one of its informers that the IRA had plans to murder an ex-UDR officer. This man, William O'Connor, was now in the building trade, and currently engaged in a restoration job in Markethill, a small town halfway between Armagh and Newry. Each day he would drive there from his home in Armagh, in the Leyland van now sitting in front of Wynwood, wearing the blue woolly hat now clamped over Corporal Langan's head.

O'Connor had been persuaded by 14th Intelligence to keep to his usual pattern while they kept tabs on the local IRA brigade and mounted a round-the-clock observation at the already discovered site of their arms cache. Yesterday, one man had come to collect the guns in a Renault 4. Overnight, Wynwood, Stanley and a third man – Trooper Sansom, who was concealed in the derelict barn to Wynwood's left – had walked to the site of the intended ambush and concealed themselves. That morning O'Connor had happily surrendered his van and cap to Corporal Langan. It was now an hour and a quarter since the latter had faked his punctured tyre, and if the Nationalist grapevine worked half as well as everyone thought it did, the IRA men – lying in wait further up the road – should have known about it by now.

Out of the corner of his eye Wynwood saw Stanley pick up the walkie-talkie which connected them with Sansom. Maybe this was it. He waited while Stanley listened, watched the other man's face tighten with anger, heard the repressed frustration in his voice as he signed off.

'The useless bastards have lost them,' he hissed to Wynwood. 'So they may be on their way. They *were* in a blue Sierra, but Christ knows what they're in now.'

Langan went on tightening the bolts on the wheel, having presumably heard the same message from the walkie-talkie in the van's front seat. A car could be heard approaching from the right, which was the way they would come. Wynwood's grip on the MP5 perceptibly tightened. It was a Sierra, but red. And it went right past, the driver flashing a single sympathetic look in Langan's direction.

Wynwood did not envy Langan – that look could just as easily have been a gunshot.

Another car was approaching – it must be rush hour. This time it was a white Fiat, and as it slowed down Wynwood thought he saw the metallic gleam of a gun. Perhaps they had hoped to get a clear shot from the car, but Langan had arranged matters so that he was protected by the van from any but the most oblique angle.

The thought that it still might not be enough flashed through Wynwood's mind as the doors of the still-moving car swung open to eject two men in boiler suits, their heads covered by slitted balaclavas, gloved hands holding AK47 assault rifles. A third man was close behind them, dressed the same, but brandishing only a Webley revolver.

He was the first to fire, as Langan took a flying dive across the nearest wall. He might have been the first to die too, but it was hard to tell. All three Provos were shredded by fire from Stanley, Wynwood and Sansom before they had gone three paces. The driver of the car was still wrestling frantically with the gear lever when the windows of his vehicle were blown away by the redirected fire, and there was a momentary glimpse of something red collapsing out of sight.

A dreadful stillness settled on the scene.

Langan was already in the front seat of the van, talking on the radio, telling someone or other to seal off the road. 'They're all yours,' he was saying. 'We'll be out of here . . . yeah, well, we're all a bit shy, you know how it is . . .'

Sansom walked across, having examined the body in the car. 'His head would make a great pincushion,' he reported laconically. He looked down at the other three, spread-eagled across the grass verge. 'Looks like the Armagh Brigade will be needing some new recruits,' he added.

Wynwood forced himself to look at the men he had just helped to kill. He did not know their names, had never even seen their faces. He had an urge to tear off the balaclavas, and at least get some sense of who they were – who they had been – but he restrained himself. It was partly, he admitted to himself, that he did not want to appear concerned in front of the others, but it was also partly because he knew it was unnecessary. He had no need to see their faces to know they had been human beings. He had just helped to kill four men – four terrorists who would have killed them with an equal lack of compunction. No matter what the fucking government in London said, this was a war. The IRA said it was, and the SAS believed them.

But Wynwood had never killed anyone before, and he was not quite sure what he was supposed to feel. It had been so quick. Ten hours of waiting and about ten seconds of death. He did not feel like throwing up – nor guilty, angry, excited or happy. If anything, he just felt sad. And maybe a little numb.

Stanley put a friendly hand on his shoulder. 'All part of death's rich pageant,' he said. Wynwood became aware of the sound of an approaching helicopter, and almost immediately a Lynx hove into sight above the hill behind them. The pilot put it down in the field behind the barn, and at Langan's signal the four SAS men trotted across to climb aboard.

Wynwood had one last glimpse of the shattered car and scattered corpses, before the pilot swung the Lynx away to the east.

Taal arrived at the Legislative Assembly in Banjul shortly before noon. The rest of the twelve-man Revolutionary Council was in session around the long table in the conference room, discussing the changes in educational policy they wanted to introduce. Taal felt a pang of sadness. It was with such intentions in mind that he had joined Jabang and the Socialist and Revolutionary Labour Party, and yet it was hard to imagine a less appropriate subject for discussion on this particular morning. Mamadou Jabang, he noticed, even had a smile on his face. Taal felt like a – what did the Americans call it? – a party pooper. In more ways than one.

'Comrade,' Jabang cut short the young man who was speaking, 'we must interrupt this discussion for a report from the Defence Minister. Junaidi?'

Taal thought about standing and decided not to waste his energy. 'I have not brought any good news,' he said shortly, and watched eleven faces react to the statement. 'As you no doubt know, the Senegalese have landed several hundred paratroops in the area to the north of the airport, around Kerewan. They are advancing on the airport, and will take it sometime within the next few hours . . .'

'What happened to our troops?' one voice asked, more in confusion than anger.

'They are fighting bravely,' Taal said, though since his departure they could, for all he knew, have scattered like rabbits. 'But they are outgunned and outnumbered. The enemy has mortars and air power, and the most we can hope for is to slow them down. They will take the airport, probably wait while they fly in more troops, and then they will start advancing along the road to Serekunda and . . .'

'How long do we have, Junaidi?' Jabang asked quietly.

'I would guess that they will be in Banjul by tomorrow morning,' Taal said. 'At the latest.'

Everyone seemed to start talking at once, and for almost a minute it seemed to Taal as if a collective panic was seizing hold of all those present.

But not Jabang. He got to his feet and stood there, not saying anything, reducing the rest to silence merely by the force of his personality. 'Comrades,' he said finally, 'we never believed this would be easy. And now we know for certain it will be hard. Jawara and his Senegalese friends have the

94

military power – that is plain. There is no way that we can win on that battlefield. So . . .' He looked round at them all. 'What power do we have? What can we use? How do we stop their soldiers if not with soldiers of our own?'

There was a silence.

'What do we have?' Jabang said softly, as if he was asking himself. 'We have the support of the mass of the people, but that will mean nothing if we cannot hold onto power. We have our dedication, and our willingness to work for the regeneration of our country, but all this will mean nothing if we cannot retain power. You see, Jawara and the Senegalese put no value on what the people want, or on our dreams for the country. So what do we have that they do put a value on?'

'His wife and children,' Sharif Sallah said.

'The Senegalese envoy,' said another voice.

'And all the white tourists,' a third man added.

There was another silence, as the meeting contemplated such a step.

'They will call us terrorists,' someone said.

'They already call us that,' another replied.

'That is not the point,' Junaidi Taal said quietly. He now knew he had been expecting this moment, without realizing he was expecting it, ever since they had known that the Senegalese were on their way. 'Whether or not they call us terrorists or criminals is of no importance,' he went on. In any case, they had already crossed that line when they emptied Banjul Prison. 'What matters is whether it will *work*.'

'How will we know that unless we try?' someone asked.

Taal grimaced. 'What are we going to do – threaten to kill Lady Chilel and the Senegalese envoy? In what circumstances? Does anyone really think the Senegalese will stop their army because of one man and his family? Or that Jawara will agree to give up the country in exchange for the life of one of his wives? And the fattest and ugliest one at that?' He allowed himself a smile, but there was no humour in it.

'Perhaps the white tourists would make better hostages,' Sallah suggested. 'Jawara and the Senegalese would not dare to go against the wishes of the English and French.'

'There are no French tourists,' Taal said. 'And it is the Senegalese we have to stop.'

'This is true,' Jabang agreed. 'And I think Junaidi may be right in this matter. But . . .' He paused, looking sadly at Taal. 'I'm afraid I can see no other course of action open to us. If threats do not work, we have not lost anything . . .' He smiled bleakly. 'Except for the good reputation we already lack. I recommend we put Mustapha Diop and Lady Jawara on the radio, and try to bluff them. At the very least it may win us some time. And who knows what can happen then? Perhaps the Senegalese opposition will come out for us, and make it more difficult for Diop to help Jawara.' He looked pointedly at Taal, as if asking for a response.

Taal was trying to remember another of those English phrases – his head seemed full of them today. Whistling in the dark – that was it. Highly appropriate in Banjul. 'No one will be happier than I will if we can stop the Senegalese with a bluff,' he said, getting to his feet. 'But in the meantime I must be getting back to Yundum.' And to the real world, he said to himself.

Alan Caskey made his way to Records, where he found the formidable figure of Sergeant Rainey with his feet up, a half-eaten ham roll in one huge paw, listening to the cricket on a small transistor radio. If Caskey had not already known it was a quiet time for the Regiment, the sight of Rainey taking it easy, even in his lunch hour, would have convinced him. Since his disablement in Oman, Rainey had set about duplicating the raw data of Regimental Records in his own mind, and of pursuing avenues of cross-checking of which no one had previously dreamed. It was rumoured that he occasionally went home to his wife, but no one could actually swear to seeing him leave the barracks.

'Any wickets yet?' Caskey asked, making himself a seat by moving a stack of files to the floor. He idly wondered how Rainey would adapt to the imminent computerization. Like a fish to water, probably.

'No, boss. Is this a business call?'

'Yep. But keep eating. I need someone who has been to The Gambia, preferably in the not too distant past.'

Rainey was silent for a while. 'I may be able to help you there,' he then said, carefully balancing the remains of his roll on the corner of a typewriter and getting up. He limped down the line of filing cabinets, opened the one at the end, and extracted a file. A quick glance inside it made him smile.

'Success?' Caskey asked rhetorically.

Rainey limped back and handed him the file. It belonged to one Trooper Joss Wynwood.

'Honeymoon,' Rainey said. 'Last year. And I think he's the only one, but I'll check.' He reached for one of several card-index boxes, and flicked through its contents. 'He's the only current member of the Regiment listed under The Gambia,' Rainey confirmed. 'But Simon McGrath – remember him?' he asked.

'I know of him, but we've never really met. I think our terms tended to alternate rather than overlap.'

'Well, he's out there now as head of a technical assistance team supplied by the Royal Engineers. In a civilian capacity,

97

that is. Help with bridge-building, I think. Someone at REME HQ will know the details.'

'Do you have a file on him?'

'Of course.'

'OK, well I need to borrow his, Wynwood's here and Trooper Worrell Franklin's. And I promise to bring them all back.'

'You'd better,' Rainey said over his shoulder. 'Boss,' he added as an afterthought.

Sibou Cham was halfway through extracting a bullet from a child's forearm when the new Minister of Health arrived. The bullet's force must have been almost spent, because it had simply gouged itself an inch or so into the softer flesh, far enough to cause the girl excruciating pain but not far enough to do her any lasting damage. As it was, she was being a lot braver than Sibou could imagine herself being at such an age.

The new Health Minister did not seem impressed by this delay to his progress, and Lamin Mansebe, the Royal Victoria's chief administrator, was obviously keen to impress. 'Dr Cham, surely that can wait for a few minutes,' he said. 'Mr Sabally does not have much time to spare.'

She looked up at the two of them: Mansebe with his tinted glasses and Sabally, a tall, wide-browed man who was probably younger than she was. 'This will only take a few minutes more,' she said, and went back to her work.

'It is good to see there is still one place where ordinary people have equal access to health care,' Sabally said. 'We shall of course be expanding the state sector,' he added quietly, as if he might be guilty of betraying a confidence.

What with? Sibou wondered, as she placed the gauze across the girl's wound.

'Of course, the Royal Victoria has a long tradition of serving the whole community,' Mansebe said self-importantly.

And serving it badly, Sibou thought to herself.

'It will be the model for the new service,' Sabally said.

Sibou fastened the bandage and stood up. 'How can I help you?' she asked.

'In your office, Sibou,' Mansebe suggested.

She acquiesced, leading the way through the door and turning to find only Sabally had followed her. 'I have an infection,' he said, and started unzipping his trousers.

She considered pointing out that equal access to health care meant joining the queue of those still waiting for her attention outside. But she thought better of it. Mr Sabally might have the power to confiscate those stocks of blood and medicine which the black marketeers were hoarding. There was no point in offending him unnecessarily.

She was, perhaps, not quite as gentle as she usually was in her treatment of infections like his.

By the time Caskey got back to his quarters the teams had gone in for lunch, and after listening for the latest from The Gambia on the *One O'Clock News* – Senegalese troops had been airlifted in, though it was not clear exactly where to – he started looking through the three files he had borrowed from Records.

Joss Wynwood was twenty-four and, if appearances were anything to go by, seemed to be enjoying life. The smile that beamed out of his photograph seemed to say, this is fun. The eyes were slightly more watchful, the dark, tangled hair an anarchist's dream. So much for photographs, Caskey thought.

Wynwood was a Taff, born and raised in Pontardulais, where his father had been a miner. He had gone to the local grammar school while it still existed, which suggested a certain amount of intelligence, though not necessarily of the type that was useful in the SAS. After taking and failing two A levels he had joined the Welsh Guards, probably as the single sure way of avoiding life down the pit, and five years of service later had applied to the SAS. In both Selection and Continuation Training he had shown outstanding aptitude in those skills considered necessary in an SAS trooper. He had celebrated selection by getting married, and taking his wife on honeymoon to The Gambia.

Caskey thanked fate for dealing him such a good card. The lad sounded ideal material. With rather less optimism, he turned to the file on Worrell Franklin.

He too was twenty-four, and had arrived in the UK in 1957, as a baby. His father had worked as a guard on the London Underground until his death in an unspecified accident twenty years later. His mother still worked as a sister at the South Western Hospital in Clapham. Worrell was the oldest of three children, all of whom had attended the local comprehensive. He had gained two A levels – in History and Economics – before enlisting in the Royal Engineers. He had seen service in Northern Ireland, West Germany, and already, after only a year in the SAS, had proficiency marks in demolition and medicine. Like Wynwood he had almost sailed through Selection Training. Franklin had also, Caskey noticed in passing, been second in the British Army of the Rhine Championships 400 metres for two successive years.

The photograph showed a handsome West Indian face, wide-set eyes over high cheekbones and a straight nose. The effect would have been almost ingenuous but for the mouth, which seemed set in defiance, as if daring the photographer to do his worst.

Another good card, Caskey thought. What had he done to deserve such luck?

Don't count your chickens, he told himself. First he had to find the two of them, preferably in Hereford and good health. He picked up the internal phone and dialled the operational roster desk number.

'Franklin's on a week's leave,' he was told. 'Due back Sunday night.'

'Where is he?' Caskey asked, half-afraid that the man would be up a mountain or down a pothole. He would be hard to spot down a pothole, Caskey thought. He hoped Franklin was not going to be unduly sensitive about such remarks.

'The contact number's a London one,' the adjutant told him. 'But Wynwood's more of a problem. He's on operational assignment in Armagh.'

'Bugger.' Caskey thought for a moment, and decided he could clear it with Weighell later. 'Get him back here, will you,' he said. 'ASAP. As in tonight at the latest.'

He hung up the phone just as the English team took to the field on his silent TV. Resisting the temptation to turn up the sound, he opened the file on Major Simon McGrath.

Beyond confirming what he suspected – that McGrath had served his two terms as an SAS officer in the gaps between Caskey's own three terms – the file told him next to nothing. The photograph showed a man with short, dark, curly hair and prominent eyebrows over dark eyes. He had a slightly upturned nose, a smallish mouth and the look of someone who had to shave twice a day. Despite this, he had a notably cheery expression on his face.

Caskey scratched his chin, realized he himself had not yet shaved that day, and wondered who could tell him more. The CO seemed a good place to start.

'Oh yes, I know McGrath,' Weighell told him, and suggested Caskey should come over for a cup of tea.

Both the tea and a suspicious-looking rock cake were waiting for him when he arrived at the CO's office for the second time that day. Ever since the day several years before when a shortfall in grenades had led to their substitution in a training exercise by the canteen's rock cakes, a vengeful kitchen staff had been devoting their not inconsiderable ingenuity to producing the hardest cakes in Britain, and perhaps the world. It had even been rumoured that they used cement.

Weighell, however, was a known devotee, claiming that the cakes reminded him of the boiled sweets of his childhood.

Caskey pushed his to one side and tried to ignore it.

'McGrath's a difficult man to describe,' Weighell said. 'But then a lot of our chaps are. He's . . . well, I suppose he's a bit of a Jekyll and Hyde . . . I don't mean he's two people, one good and one evil. More like . . . No, let me put it this way: he's a very gregarious man, gets on well with most people. He always says exactly what's on his mind and he seems to operate on a short fuse, but no one holds it against him because the outbursts never last more than a few minutes. He's unconventional to a fault. And he's had more women than I've had rock cakes.

'All of which might lead you to expect someone who always acts on the spur of the moment, and never stops to think before he acts. In short, a loose cannon. Which he is, at least to some extent. But he's also a devoted family man with three children – they live in Leominster – and a fanatical mountaineer. Note the mountaineering. That's a hobby for people who like taking risks, but it's also a hobby which demands real planning and precision. Then add the final piece of the puzzle – the man's an engineer, and a specialist in bomb disposal at that. You see what I mean?'

'Not exactly,' Caskey said.

'Well, what we have here is almost a definition of a good soldier: someone who's emotionally capable of taking risks, but has the sense to calculate them as well as he can.'

'Sounds like a good man to have around,' Caskey commented.

'Yes . . . I don't know whether I should say this or not,' Weighell went on, 'but I've never felt comfortable with the man, either on the job or off it.' He smiled. 'Which may just be a matter of two people who rub each other up the wrong way.'

'I see,' Caskey said, in a tone which suggested the opposite.

'Anyway, you'll probably get the chance to make up your own mind about him. If there's stuff going on all round him, I don't expect Simon McGrath has been sitting in his bungalow waiting for things to get back to normal. He'll be out there in the thick of it.'

Mustapha Diop had now been confined to the house on Marina Parade for almost thirty-six hours. He was sharing this confinement with his wife, their three children, and five of their children's friends from the embassy, who had been staying the night with them, and who had not been allowed to return home. All the Gambian staff had vanished, leaving his wife with all the cooking to do and the children in a state of near-permanent riot.

At first Diop had clung to the hope that things would blow over, that the new government would prove acceptable to everyone and that things would return to normal. After being taken on the strange taxi ride through Banjul, he had reluctantly reached the conclusion that these were not the sort of people the international community was likely to welcome to its bosom. They were either idealists or madmen, two groups which Diop had always found hard to disentangle. The history of the twentieth century – not to mention the last quarter of a century in Africa – seemed to bear out his thesis: the only thing that ever really worked was doing things one step at a time. Grand ideas always seemed to end in someone's tears.

He hoped this particular grand idea was not going to end in his. There seemed little doubt that the planes he had been hearing all morning belonged to the Senegalese Air Force, for his government was holding to the Treaty and intervening on the overthrown Jawara's behalf. Diop hardly dared think about what the rebels were doing at this moment, or what their intentions might be towards him and his family. If they were looking for someone to take their frustrations out on, they could hardly find anyone more suitable.

The thought had no sooner escaped him than it took flesh, materializing in the form of three men walking towards his front door. One of them was the man called Sallah, who had been on the taxi ride with him and the coup leader, Jabang. The latter, Diop had to admit, had been reasonably personable for someone so intense, but Sallah had seemed neither likeable nor trustworthy. His heart sank.

They knocked on the door, which Diop thought had to be a good sign. He was not so sure when he opened it, and found two rifle barrels pointed at his stomach.

'You will come with us, please,' Sallah said.

'Where to?' Diop asked, not moving.

'The radio station. You are going to tell the world what is happening here,' Sallah told him. 'And what might happen,' he added.

Diop did not like the sound of those last four words. 'May I tell my wife where I am going?' he asked with as much dignity as he could muster.

'There's no time,' he was told, and the rifle barrels twitched as if to emphasize the point. Diop followed Sallah out to the road, where the inevitable taxi was waiting. They got in the back with one of the armed men, who had to lay his rifle across all their legs. The other got in front with the driver.

No one spoke during the five-minute drive to the radio station. Once there, Sallah accompanied Diop up the stairs to the studio, where Jabang was already waiting with Jawara's senior wife, the Lady Chilel. To suggest that the atmosphere was cool would have been to vastly understate the situation: it was positively frigid.

'Lady Jawara,' Diop said, extending his hand in greeting before Sallah could say anything.

'Monsieur Diop,' she said graciously. 'I apologize for the behaviour of my countrymen.'

'Sit down and read this,' Sallah told Diop coldly, handing him a typewritten sheet of paper. 'You will be reading it over the air in a few minutes.'

Diop glanced through it. According to the text he demanded to be taken to meet the Senegalese commander, and wished to appeal to the Senegalese Red Cross, on behalf of the Gambian Red Cross, for medicine, food and vehicles. The text claimed he had seen people on the streets of Banjul making clenched-fist salutes in support of the revolution – well, he supposed he had seen one or two – and contained a personal plea from him to his own Government to negotiate a ceasefire with the newly formed Gambian Supreme Revolutionary Council.

Diop was pleasantly surprised. There were no threats in the message, either to his own safety or anyone else's.

His relief was short-lived. Lady Jawara was the first to take the microphone, and she had a list of hostages to read out. It included herself, eight of her husband's children, seven members of his cabinet, and Diop himself, together with his wife and children. All would be killed if the Senegalese troops were not withdrawn by five o'clock that afternoon.

Since no one intervened to correct her, Lady Jawara had presumably read the text she had been given, but the tone in her voice – a mixture of contempt and disbelief – was one which Diop wished he could have emulated. Unfortunately the shock of having his life threatened – and with a deadline less than four hours away – had somewhat unnerved him, and his declaration sounded, to him at least, both nervous and hesitant. It was only when he had finished, and saw Sallah and Jabang exchanging smiles, that he realized that this was exactly what they had wanted.

The leader now took the microphone himself. There had already been a grievous loss of life, Jabang said, and no one could desire more. But, reluctantly, he felt compelled to announce himself ready to kill Jawara's family and cabinet if that was the price of preserving the revolution. 'The country is with us,' he claimed, and he had the power to execute the prisoners. Ultimately their fate lay not in his hands but in those of the Senegalese invaders. The latter had but to announce a withdrawal and the prisoners would all be freed.

Jabang stared at the microphone, as if willing it to believe him, and abruptly got up from the chair and walked to the window. Diop studied his face: the mouth pursed with anxiety, the skin drawn tight by tension across the forehead and cheeks, the eyes burning with their apparently inexhaustible intensity. Did the rebel leader mean it about killing all the prisoners? Diop asked himself. Did he have only a few hours of life left?

There was no way of knowing. Indeed, Diop suspected that Jabang himself had no clear idea of how far he was prepared to go.

7

It was four-thirty, and only thirty minutes remained until the expiry of the deadline. Nothing had been heard from the Senegalese forces or government – no radio broadcast, no telephone call, no visit from an intermediary, no white flag. And none of them was really expecting any, Taal thought. He had just returned once more from the front line, which was now located in the middle of the village of Lamin. The good news was that only one group of twenty fighters had been unable to escape from the Senegalese encirclement of the airport; the bad news was that several hundred more of the enemy had since been landed on the captured runway. If one thing was certain it was that the Senegalese were under no military pressure to negotiate.

The other eleven members of the Revolutionary Council had received Taal's report in the manner of condemned men hearing that their latest appeal had been denied. His suggestion that they relocate the government to Bakau, where the Field Force depot offered at least a defensible perimeter, had been voted on, and unanimously agreed, with a similar level of enthusiasm. Taal felt, but restrained himself from suggesting, that his fellow Council members would be better served getting out of this chamber and back among their Party comrades.

First, however, there was the business of the hostages to conclude. Or not to conclude. Taal fought back the temptation to say, 'I told you so.'

'We have here the classic dilemma,' Jabang said, as if he was discussing an interesting academic problem. 'If we do as we threatened, and kill them, then we will have no cards left in our hands at all . . .'

'And will not be able to expect any mercy from the victors,' Sallah interjected.

This amused Jabang. 'I am not expecting any now,' he said. 'As I was saying – if we kill them we have nothing left to bargain with. If we do not then we lose at least some of our credibility. Either way we lose. Of course, some' – he looked at Taal with a smile – 'might say we should never have made the threat in the first place, but we had to do something, or we would have lost the initiative entirely . . .'

'Why not kill one hostage?' one of the younger men asked. 'That would show we were serious, yet still leave something to bargain with.'

'That is true,' Jabang admitted.

But reluctantly, Taal thought, and that made him feel better. He did not like to think of his friend acceding to such a cold-blooded course of action. 'If we kill any of the prisoners,' he added in support, 'we will sacrifice any hope of receiving help from abroad.'

'Is there any such hope?' the younger man wanted to know.

'Our friends in Libya are trying to intercede with the Senegalese,' Jabang said, 'and through the Islamic Conference.'

'There is also another point,' Taal said. 'I don't want to sound too pessimistic,' he went on, thinking that would be difficult, 'but if this time we are defeated, we shall want the chance to fight again, and that means being accepted into exile in other countries. If we kill any of the prisoners – particularly Jawara's family or Diop's – no one in Africa or Europe will offer us safe haven.'

'I agree,' Jabang said, 'but I think we must continue to give out the message that, in the last resort, we will have nothing to lose by killing them. Otherwise what is to stop the Senegalese from just rolling straight over us?'

'We can claim that the deadlines have been extended for humanitarian reasons,' Sallah suggested, which made Taal smile.

'That is agreed, then,' Jabang announced, looking round the table. 'Sharif, make the announcement on the radio. Jallow, see that all the prisoners are moved into the Field Force depot tonight. And if we're moving our men out of Banjul, we can put larger numbers outside the tourist hotels. The embassies in Bakau will get the message, and they'll see it gets passed on to the Senegalese. Which should give them something to worry about. And at least slow them down. And by the way, Junaidi,' he said, turning to Taal, 'we have information that an Englishman shot one of our people on the Denton Bridge. It was decided he should be arrested – as a sign that we are serious.'

It was on the stroke of five that the phone in Lieutenant-Colonel Weighell's office rang.

'Matheson,' the now familiar voice said curtly. 'Have you made any progress?'

'We're assembling a three-man team at the moment. They can be in London by eleven tomorrow morning. I assume you'll want to brief them before they go.'

'Someone will. We've just had news that hostages have been taken. We don't know how many, or who they are, except that one of the President's wives seems to be among them . . .'

'*One* of his wives?'

'He's a Muslim,' Matheson said drily. 'At least I assume he is. It seems unlikely that he'd be a Mormon.'

'I suppose not.'

'Very well,' Matheson said, his tone more businesslike. If you can get your team to the MOD by eleven a.m. I'll have someone there to brief them on the situation.'

'And the context, Minister,' Weighell insisted. 'The more they know about the country they're going into the less chance there is of their making any major gaffes.'

'Understood,' Matheson said.

'One other thing I wanted to check with you,' Weighell said. 'Are my lads wearing uniform on this outing?'

'No. At least, assume not unless you hear to the contrary.'

After putting down the phone Weighell sat at his desk for a minute or so, letting his mind wander through tropical sunshine and palm trees. Maybe he should have gone himself, he thought.

He smiled to himself and called Caskey. 'You're on,' he told him. 'MOD, 1100 hours. Have you got hold of Wynwood yet?'

'He was still in debriefing when I called. I'll try again now, and give Franklin a call in London.'

'The FO says no uniforms, Alan,' Weighell told him, 'but they may change their minds.'

On the Yundum-Serekunda road there were some signs that the invaders were at least pausing for breath. Even so, crouched behind an overturned market stall, the Kalashnikov in his hands hot from firing, Moussa Diba was in no doubt that any such pause would only be temporary, and he was still looking for the perfect opportunity to wave his short military career goodbye. In the sky to the south-east he could see even more Senegalese planes coming in to land at the airport, carrying God knew what in the way of more men and weaponry. If this was not a lost war then he was Nelson Mandela.

A single bullet whistled above his head and embedded itself in the concrete colonnade of the abandoned Field Force station behind him. Fifty yards or so down the street a couple of Senegalese were inching their way forward from cover to cover. Diba fired a burst in their direction, and had the satisfaction of seeing them dive into the shelter of a building.

He wondered how they intended shifting the barricade which filled the street in front of him. Two taxis had been lined up nose to nose, several wooden carts and stalls from the marketplace piled up in front of them, and sundry other rubbish piled on top.

Maybe they would bypass it, he thought – just circle through the fields and meet up again on the other side. Or maybe not. In the distance a rumbling sound was growing louder, causing Diba to think the worst – a tank.

The source of the noise came into view. It turned out to be an armoured car, but that would be enough. It stopped about a hundred yards from the barricade, like a runner pausing to inspect a fence he intended to jump, then slowly gathered speed once more, crashing through the two taxi bonnets and coming to a triumphant halt on the rebels' side of the broken wall. Its machine-gun suddenly opened up, spitting fire in Diba's direction, sending splinters of wood flying from the upturned stall in front of him. One impaled itself in his cheek, causing blood to run.

He swore and looked round for Jahumpa, expecting the signal to retreat, but the idiot was firing impotently at the armoured car. Diba raised his Kalashnikov and took a sighting on Jahumpa's chest, but before he could pull the trigger his target picked up the walkie-talkie, said one word into it, and looked round, waving everyone back.

Diba forgot about him, and keeping the stall between himself and the armoured car, crawled his way backwards into a gap between two houses. He then regained his feet and started running towards the open countryside.

He had just decided that this was the ideal moment to abandon his unit when he rounded the last house and practically ran into the rest of them. Their lorry was bumping its way across the savannah to pick them up.

Simon McGrath spent the afternoon on the roof of the Carlton, watching the increased traffic over the distant airport, and mentally following what he imagined would be the pace of the Senegalese advance. Most men would have gone mad with boredom after the first couple of hours, but a life in the military – and particularly his years in the SAS – had taught McGrath how to survive enforced inactivity with almost complete equanimity. At around five in the afternoon, with the sun sliding swiftly down towards the western horizon, it was hunger and thirst which drove him off the roof, not a restless mind.

His timing turned out to be extremely fortunate. A minute later and he would have walked straight into trouble; a minute earlier and it would probably have walked straight in on him. As it was, he was still descending the two flights of stairs to his room when he heard the clump of several booted feet on their way up from the lobby below.

He crouched down in the stairwell, just around the corner from the last flight down to his floor. The visitors seemed involved in a less than friendly conversation, and McGrath thought he recognized the hotel manager's voice among them. The language sounded like Wollof.

The bootsteps headed, as he had feared, for his room. There had to be at least four men, probably five. The bootsteps ceased, presumably outside his door, and further argument followed, this time in loud whispers. What the fuck are they doing? McGrath wondered.

A loud splintering noise provided his answer. They were breaking down the door, rushing into his room, and finding it empty. And now the manager was shouting at whoever had given the order to destroy his door.

McGrath smiled to himself, silently descended the flight of steps, and looked around. The third room along, in the opposite direction from his own, had its door open. He slid inside, careful to leave the door the same distance ajar, and waited, the Browning in his hand.

The party emerged from his room, still arguing, this time in English. The manager was demanding to know where he should send the bill for his door, while his adversary was accusing him of harbouring a terrorist.

That's me, McGrath thought with a grin.

The existence of the roof seemed to have escaped them, or perhaps the manager had convinced the visitors that McGrath must have gone out, because the whole party simply started back down the stairs. McGrath listened to their diminishing footfalls, and then headed down the corridor in search of a window overlooking the entrance. He found one just in time to see two men in Field Force uniform head back across the street towards the Legislative Assembly. Which presumably meant another pair were staked out in the lobby downstairs.

He went back to his room, stepping over the unhinged door and onto a floor covered with his personal possessions.

He left them where they were, and stood at the window for a moment, staring out at the row of huge palms growing out of the corrugated sea, and the twin minarets of Banjul's Great Mosque rising behind them against the yellowing sky.

If they were after him, he thought, then they would also be after Jobo Camara. Always assuming that this was about the dead man on the Denton Bridge, and not the beginning of some pogrom against all the whites in Banjul.

The latter was not very likely. He would have to warn Jobo, and that meant getting out of the hotel.

He edged his way carefully down the three flights of stairs which led to the last bend above the lobby. The hotel seemed even emptier than the day before, which he supposed was hardly surprising. It was a favourite of Gambian businessmen, and Gambian business was presumably at a complete standstill. The businessmen would all be at home, waiting for the smoke to clear.

For a fleeting second McGrath felt the attraction of being at home himself, feet up in the music room, eyes closed, Bach filling the air. The moment passed. Even at the age of thirty-nine, he enjoyed this sort of thing too much.

He inched an eye round the corner of the wall. Two Field Force men, both carrying Kalashnikovs in their laps, were sitting on either side of the door which led out to the terrace and street.

McGrath went back up to the first floor, along to the back of the building, and down the fire-escape stairs. He carefully opened the door to the yard outside, but more out of habit than from any expectation of meeting anyone. The Field Force men were waiting for him to come back to the hotel, not trying to stop him leaving it.

The Ministry of Development jeep was still sitting where he had left it, temptingly available, but McGrath swiftly but reluctantly came to the realization that he would be a trifle conspicuous driving it round the streets of Banjul. It would take only ten minutes to walk to Jobo's compound, and there was still enough light left to see where he was going.

He vaulted the wall separating the yard from Otto Road and started down it, keeping to the centre of the road, his eyes constantly searching the shadows on either side. After a moment's thought he took the Browning out from its holster and carried it openly in his hand – this was neither the time nor the place for false modesty. 'How can you tell me you are lonely?' he started to sing. 'Let me take you through the streets of Banjul . . . I will show you something that will make you change your mind . . .'

Ralph McTell, eat your heart out, he thought.

He got several strange looks, and one local even burst out laughing at the sight, shouting 'mad dogs and Englishmen' at him several times, despite the obvious lack of a midday sun. But no one tried to arrest him, mug him, or in any way interfere with his passage through the darkening city.

Jobo's compound in Anglesea Street seemed unusually full of light, though his knock on the gate seemed to diminish the illuminations somewhat. 'It's McGrath,' he shouted, hearing whispering and footsteps.

The gate opened, and the face of Jobo's uncle appeared. 'What you want?' he asked.

McGrath noticed that the man was wearing his Field Force uniform again, and hoped he had not walked out of one trap and into another. 'I've come to warn Jobo that the rebels may be coming for him,' he said, keeping the Browning behind his back.

'They have already come,' Mansa Camara said. 'Come inside.'

McGrath followed him across the compound yard, and into a large room on the ground floor of the colonial-period house which comprised the principal living quarters. Inside he found Jobo, smiling cheerfully despite the fact that he was still partly immobilized by his wound, and eight men in Field Force uniform. On closer inspection it became apparent that two of them were less than happy at being there.

'They came to arrest me,' Jobo explained, 'so we arrested them.'

'We have decided it is time to begin fighting back,' his uncle added. 'We are not sure what we can do, but we feel we want to do something.'

'Mr McGrath will know what is happening,' Jobo suggested.

Mansa raised a quizzical eye.

'The Senegalese will be in Banjul tomorrow,' McGrath told him.

'Then perhaps we can offer them some assistance,' Mansa said.

'They reckon another one's going to die tonight,' Wynwood said quietly. He and Stanley were halfway through their second pints in the base canteen they shared with the Armagh section of 14th Intelligence Company.

'Oh yeah. So how many's that?' Stanley asked, his thick Brummie accent offering an interesting counterpoint to Wynwood's soft Welsh lilt.

'He'll be number seven. Langan reckons it'll be a hot night in Belfast, what with that and our business this morning.'

'Probably. I suppose they're saying we gunned down four young innocents . . .'

'Something like that.'

'I suppose they were all on their way to a Mr Balaclava contest.'

Wynwood grunted. 'Probably. But . . . I don't know, Stanley . . . don't it make you wonder a bit, all these men willing to starve themselves to death. I mean, the TV's always calling the IRA a bunch of cowards, but from what I can see . . . well, they may be a bunch of psychos but they're not cowards.'

Stanley shrugged. 'My mother's got a martyr complex,' he said. 'Hard to imagine her on a hunger strike, though,' he added thoughtfully. 'They'd have to surgically separate her and the fridge.'

'Seriously.'

'What do you want me to say? That I admire the bastards? I think they're idiots. What are they dying for – so that Northern Ireland can be run by Catholic shitheads rather than Protestant shitheads? A, it won't happen. B, it wouldn't make any difference if it did. And C, they should realize what's important in life, like beer and women.'

'And football,' Wynwood volunteered.

'Exactly,' Stanley beamed. 'Now you're getting the hang of it. I'm sure going on hunger strike is a turn-on for all the Provo groupies, but actually dying seems a bit over the top.' He drained his glass and reached out a hand for Wynwood's. 'Same again?' he asked, somewhat unnecessarily.

Wynwood watched the ginger-haired Brummie walk up to the bar, and wondered if Stanley could be as straightforward as he seemed. There was certainly no indication to the contrary. Wynwood sighed. He liked the man, but he would not have wanted to be like him, even if he could. Beer, women and football – rugby football, that is – were necessities of life all right, but then so were eating and crapping. And when it came to what he did with his life, Wynwood liked reasons. Maybe some people could just follow their instincts, do whatever came naturally in any given circumstance and never look back, but he had inherited his father's tendency to reflect on things past and present, not to mention those in the future. His dad had always displayed a tendency to grow maudlin, usually about two-thirds of the way through his fifth pint, and it was a tendency which, according to his wife, Wynwood shared. But then she was English, and the bloody English thought emotion was something you reserved for gardening.

Where was I? Wynwood wondered, as Stanley accepted change from the barmaid, and said something which made her laugh. Reasons, that was where. Reasons for four men dead on a nice afternoon, reasons for men starving themselves to death. And not *political* reasons – he knew all that fucking crap . . . So what kind of reasons did he want? He was buggered if he knew. And probably buggered if he didn't.

He had a sudden desire to see Susan, to hold her and be held by her, to feel her gentleness . . .

'Great pair of tits on that one,' Stanley said, gesturing with his head back towards the bar.

Wynwood burst out laughing.

The credits for *It Ain't Half Hot Mum* were rolling up the screen when his mum asked, 'Are you happy, Franklin?'

'What do you mean?' he asked, startled.

'It's a simple enough question, boy.'

'Yes, I s'pose. Why do you ask?'

'Cos you wearing the longest face I ever seen for about three days now.'

'You want me to be laughing and singing when Everton's in jail?'

'No, of course not. But I don't think Everton's problems is all that's worrying you. Is your soldiering going OK?'

'Yeah. It's great.'

'And they don't treat you different cos you're a coloured?'

'No. Leastways, the system don't. There's always a few, but I can deal with that. And they know I'm there cos I can do the job. That's what the SAS is about, mum. Just doing things well.'

'So you tell me. I sometimes wonder what these things are you do so well, but I don't really want to know. I knows you're not a mean boy . . .'

'I'm not a boy, mum.'

'I knows that too. Have you got a girlfriend?'

Franklin hesitated. 'Not really.'

'I takes it from that she's white.'

Franklin burst out laughing. 'They'd have burned you as a witch,' he said.

'Ain't there no black girls in Hereford?'

He shook his head. 'Not really. It's a white town, through and through.'

'So what she like? What's her name?' his mother wanted to know.

'Miriam. She's a student teacher. She . . . What else do you want to know?'

'I want to know why she's after a black man.'

Franklin told himself to take a deep breath and count to ten. 'Maybe she's after me,' he said eventually. 'Maybe she's not as hung up on colour as some people.'

'Maybe,' his mum conceded. 'But it ain't common. And the ones like to think they colour-blind is often the ones using it to make themselves feel special.'

'I don't think she's like that.'

'You don't *think?*'

'I've only been out with her once.'

'OK, I say no more. You do what you want. You always did . . . no, I don't mean you selfish – you not – I just mean you always like to find things out for yourself.' She smiled at him. 'So I still don't know why you so miserable.'

'I'm not. Not really.'

'There's an awful lot of "not reallys" coming out your mouth this evening.'

'Brixton's depressing.'

'Especially for us who have to live here.'

'I know. I lived here, remember. The whole country feels depressing, mum . . . I . . . I don't know. And anyway,' he said, looking at his watch, 'I got to get to this meeting Barrett arranged.' As he got to his feet there was a knock on the front door. 'Expecting anyone?' he asked her. She shook her head.

It was Everton.

'They released me,' he said eventually, after managing to free himself from his mother's embrace. 'They're dropping the charges.' He looked at Franklin, and it was not a look of gratitude. 'You pulled some strings, didn't you, bro?' he said.

'No.' Unless simply showing up in uniform had been enough. 'Didn't they tell you why you were being released?'

'They said it was insufficient evidence, but they didn't think that the day before. The magistrates didn't think that. And I was the only one released. You know how that gonna look, bro?'

'You's out and that's the main thing, Everton,' his mother said.

He ignored her. 'You know?' he asked Franklin again.

'Yeah, I know. But if I pulled any strings I didn't know I was doing it. I was just trying to get you out.'

'Like I asked him to,' his mother added.

Everton let his anger give way to sorrow. 'I know you means well,' he told Franklin, 'but it just don't work any more, you looking out for me. Not wearing that uniform.'

'We're still brothers, Everton.'

'Yeah, I know.' He turned away. 'I need a bath, mum.'

'You knows where it is.'

Franklin and his mum were left standing at the bottom of the stairs.

'I think I'll go out for a drink,' he said, taking his jacket down from the hook.

'You don't want to take what Everton says to heart,' she said, but without any great conviction.

'I know,' he said, colluding in the self-deceit. 'But I could do with a drink.'

'Well you go and have one, then,' she said with forced cheerfulness. 'I'll make Everton some supper.'

Franklin let himself out and started walking. Maybe he would have a drink later, but his main aim had been just to get out of the house.

It was still light, and being Friday night the streets were full of people going out, people carrying booze home, music and ganja smoke floating out through the windows, as both smokers and loudspeakers limbered up for the night's parties. Down on Brixton Road the usual groups were gathered, wondering what would happen, wondering whether this would be one of the nights which exploded. There was no sense of inevitable violence, only of a general willingness to contemplate it if the moment seemed propitious.

Was this the Britain he had agreed to serve? Franklin walked away from it, up the hill towards Streatham, his long legs eating up the pavement. His mother's question would not leave him alone. Why was he unhappy?

It was simple really, but it was not something he could explain to her. He loved being in the SAS, loved nearly every minute of it. He had even loved the selection procedure, and especially enjoyed scoring higher than the other entrants, all of whom had been white, in just about every test.

He loved mastering all the different skills involved, and facing so many different challenges. Even Northern Ireland had been a real eye-opener when it came to learning things about himself and what he could do. And there had been the jungle training in Borneo, and a month in Hong Kong as part of a training mission.

He had made friends too. White friends. A lot of the banter might be unconsciously racist, and occasionally it made him want to scream, but on most occasions there was no evil intent in it, and it had always seemed to Franklin – right through school and beyond – that picking fights over dumb or insensitive remarks proved nothing. If blacks took on the challenge and showed the whites that, on an even playing field, they could match them at anything, then the stupid remarks would start to die of their own accord.

That was why he had joined the white man's army and the white man's world. If enough other blacks did the same then maybe people could start forgetting about colour and getting down to the real problems – like poverty, unemployment and homelessness.

At least, that was how he had explained it to himself. The problem was, he was not sure he believed it any more. He loved his life in the SAS, but it only seemed to work within the cocoon of the Regiment. It did not work in Brixton, or within his family. It was like one of those relationships which could not be brought into the outside world, because the two people had nothing in common outside the love they shared.

Like him and Miriam probably. He hoped not, but he would hardly be heartbroken if he never saw her again. And every time he went out with a white women there was this voice in his head reminding him how much easier it would be to find a black woman and have black kids and not have to deal with race all his life.

That was it in a nutshell. He did not want to deal with race. Nor be oppressed by it. It just got in the way of who he was. It was so stupid anyway, just a skin pigment, for fuck's sake. It should not matter. But it did. In Brixton Police Station he had been a black first, a human being second. Even to Everton, it sometimes seemed like he was a black first, a brother second. Only in the SAS had he felt respected for what he could *do*. Not for who he was, not yet. But for what *he* could *do*.

He stopped walking, and looked round to see where he had got to. He was at the crown of Brixton Hill, and it was finally getting dark. He no longer wanted a drink.

When he got home his mum had already gone to bed, and Everton had gone out. But there was a message from his brother on the kitchen table: 'Man named Major Caskey' – a phone number followed – 'wants you to call him back tonight. If you're gone before I get back – thanks.'

Franklin reached for the phone.

Caskey let himself into his top-floor flat in Cathedral Street shortly before eleven. Everything had been arranged for the next day, and he had even had time for a couple of pints in the Slug and Pellet on his way home. Solitary pints: usually you could count on at least half a dozen troopers propping up the Slug's bar, but tonight there had been nobody. Maybe there had been a party somewhere which no one had invited him to.

124

The flat looked no different from usual, yet somehow it seemed a little sadder tonight. In the photograph on the mantelpiece his wife looked a little more accusing, the kids a little more indifferent. He had thought of ringing Liz from the pub, but lately her husband had taken to answering the phone, and even he had to be getting a little suspicious at how many wrong numbers they were getting.

What a fucking mess. He was glad to be getting away, at least for a few days.

The *Radio Times* told him he had fifteen minutes before the test highlights, so he walked into the bedroom and started packing the small blue holdall he always used in such circumstances. It looked a little worn now, but he almost thought of it as a lucky charm.

Six pairs of underpants, six pairs of socks, six shirts, a spare pair of trousers. Compass, star chart, torch. Etc., etc., etc. Christ, after twenty years he knew the list off by heart.

The bag packed, he went back to the living room and poured himself a glass of the claret he had been forced to abandon earlier that day. The cricket was late as usual, but wonderfully restful, even in the ludicrous highlights formula. Cricket highlights – what a contradiction in terms! In cricket the moments only made sense in terms of the hours.

And it had been a bad few hours for England, with the Australians building a sixty-nine-run lead without ever looking more than merely competent. England had cut it to twenty by the close for the loss of only Brearley, which Caskey supposed was something. Throughout the day both sides had seemed in a thoroughly bad mood, and Richie Benaud was suitably disapproving.

For a few moments he sat there with the last quarter of an inch of claret, watching the BBC2 logo, knowing he was not ready for sleep. It was good to be going somewhere, he thought once more. It would change nothing, and the same mess would be waiting for him when he got back, but it was good to be going somewhere. Anywhere.

8

After several days of unseasonable dryness, the heavens opened in the early hours of Saturday 1 August. Moussa Diba's trench soon turned into a warm bath, and he was forced to sleep out on the open ground. An abandoned piece of corrugated-iron fence provided him with a hard, uncomfortable blanket. Still, at least it kept most of the water off him.

The rain stopped before dawn, and he had an hour or so of real sleep before Jahumpa did the rounds with his toecap, waking everyone up. The sun was already above the horizon, a large white disc behind a line of silhouetted palms, and the pools of rain on the road were beginning to evaporate, each forming its own private cloud of mist in the clear morning air.

There was no breakfast.

Diba washed his mouth out with some rainwater that had gathered in a fold of his iron blanket, and began baling out his trench, wondering what he should do. Or at least plan to do.

He supposed the Senegalese would be along in the not too distant future, though there was always the chance that they would head straight for Banjul. His company had been taken out of that line of march, and pulled back to form part of a defensive arc around the beach resort areas of Bakau and

127

Fajara. Their current location lay astride the Serekunda-Fajara road, close to the village of Kololi, a mile or so from the coast. In front of them the road stretched arrow-straight for about a mile towards the outskirts of Serekunda. They would have no trouble seeing the bastards coming.

Diba wondered what was going on in the heads of the revolutionary leaders. Had they abandoned Banjul, or were they going to make a last stand somewhere? The Denton Bridge was the obvious place. If they could stop the Senegalese there, or blow it up, then Banjul could be held for a bit longer.

But what for? The rebels must know that they had lost. So what were they still fighting for? Because they could think of no alternative? Because they needed time to make a getaway? Who fucking cared anyway? He should be thinking about his own getaway.

Which was getting more and more complicated. If the Senegalese took Banjul – or even if they just got as far as the bridge – then they were between him and Anja, him and the Englishman, him and the doctor. That had occurred to him the previous night, but for one thing there had been no chance to slink away, and for another he was not at all sure Banjul would be a healthy place to be over the next couple of days. With the Senegalese in control, Jawara and his cronies would all be coming back, and they would be turning the town upside down, looking for the rebels, who they probably had no photographs of, and the released prisoners, whose mugshots they most certainly did have.

No, he would have to revisit Banjul before he headed for the border, but not just yet. For the moment Bakau seemed a safer bet. When the time came – and recognizing the right moment would be the difficult part – then he would do what he had to do. Steal enough money to buy a new life, kill the fucking Englishman, have a time to remember with the doctor, collect Anja and go. Guinea, the Ivory Coast, anywhere.

Four miles to the east, Colonel Taal's thoughts were running in similar channels whenever the exigencies of the situation allowed him the luxury of such reflection. It could all be summed up in one phrase, he thought: when do we cut our losses and run? And he suspected they would all have different answers. The Sallahs of this world would leave too early, the Jabangs would probably leave it too late. So they were both lucky to have him around, he thought with a sour smile.

He looked back along the bridge towards the Banjul end, but there was no sign of any vehicle approaching from that direction. It was hard to believe that there were no explosives in the entire western half of the country, but he was reluctantly coming to that conclusion. He supposed that when it came down to it, explosives were mostly used by armies and miners, and The Gambia had neither. But still . . .

It hardly seemed worth blowing up the bridge anyway. It might slow down the Senegalese, keep them out of Banjul for another day perhaps, but the Revolutionary Council had essentially abandoned the capital in any case, and there was always the argument that if they could not march into Banjul the Senegalese might just march all their forces straight into Bakau.

Taal could not help feeling he was wasting his time. There were nearly a hundred men dug in on either side of the bridge, and it would take the Senegalese a while to shift them, but he knew his side had lost both the battle and the war, and that now it was just a matter of how much they could salvage through the hostage negotiations. In which case, these hundred-odd men would be better served defending the Field Force depot in Bakau.

Jabang, however, had insisted on at least a token resistance to the enemy occupation of the capital. The longer they held Banjul, he said, the longer the radio station could continue broadcasting. How his leader had reached the conclusion that another two hours of broadcasting threats and demands were worth a hundred men, Taal could not say. But he did know he had come too far with Mamadou Jabang to start arguing with him at such a moment. It was, as the American military liked to say, a 'no-win situation'.

At the radio station Mustapha Diop was trying, without much success, to quell a slowly growing sense of panic. After his broadcast the previous afternoon, and the threats to kill him and his family at five p.m. if the rebels' demands were not met, he had been taken back to the house in Marina Parade. There he had agonized about whether or not to tell his wife, torn between a need to share his fear and an unwillingness to see her suffer. Instead, he had paced up and down for three hours, one eye on the window for the arrival of nemesis at his gates.

But five o'clock had passed without any visitors, and after another hour had passed Diop was beginning to let himself believe that the worst was over. When Sallah, accompanied by the same two 'comrades', did appear a few minutes later, Diop felt as if his stomach had dropped through the floor. The next thirty seconds were the worst of his life, and when Sallah coldly told him they only wished him to make another broadcast, he could have kissed the ugly bastard.

He had accompanied them to the radio station in the same taxi, by the same route. It would all have smacked of *déjà vu*, but this time there was to be no talk of prisoners or deadlines; they simply wanted him to politely ask his compatriots for two things: a ceasefire between the warring armies and nego-tiations between the rebels and the Senegalese Government.

Once he had done so Diop had expected to be driven back to Marina Parade, but no such journey was forthcoming. They might need him again, Sallah had told him, and there seemed no point in making continual trips to and fro. And in any case his family were at this moment being moved to the Field Force depot in Bakau – for their own safety, of course. He would be joining them as soon as circumstances allowed.

A long evening had followed, during which Diop reached the unhappy conclusion that even a terrified man can experi-ence numbing boredom. Sallah had left soon after dusk, and his other minders seemed disinclined to talk. The radio played either mindless Afro pop or repeats of his own broadcast, which sounded stranger and stranger as the evening wore on. Sleep, even the fitful kind in an upright chair, had proved a merciful release.

He woke with all the old fears and a few new ones, but soon found reasons for hope. To judge by the faces of his companions, he was no longer alone in feeling afraid. It seemed that at some point in the night they had belatedly come to the realization that theirs was likely to be the losing side. And one of the consequences of this realization was a desire to ingratiate themselves with him. He was allowed some privacy in the toilet, and even asked what he would like for breakfast.

It never arrived, of course, but it was nice to be asked. The rebel in charge, a Mandinka named Jimmy Gorang, spent most of his time on the telephone, presumably talking to his superiors. The look on his face just before eleven, when the connection was suddenly severed, would have been comic in any other situation. His mouth gaped open, he shook the receiver, then pressed a few times on the cut-off button. He then tried redialling, once, twice. Eventually it seemed to sink in that the line was dead.

His countrymen had taken the Denton Bridge, Diop guessed, and put a temporary block on all communications between Banjul and Bakau. The question was: how would his captors cope with their new isolation?

Caskey had told him to pack for the tropics, so Franklin just gathered together the most lightweight clothing he could and stuffed it into the somewhat battered suitcase his father had originally brought from Jamaica. His mum was already at work, his sister at school and his brother still in bed, so he ate breakfast alone and walked down to the tube. He changed onto the Piccadilly at Green Park and got off at Holborn, with almost an hour in hand for the ten-minute walk to the MOD building in Theobald's Road.

It being Saturday, the area seemed almost empty, and most of the cafés were closed. He eventually found an Italian sandwich bar open, bought coffee and a doughnut, and sat in the window watching the buses go by. Major Caskey had not told him much on the phone the night before – in fact all he knew was that three of them were going to Africa. Which was a big place. His first reaction had been to be thrilled by the news, and the fact that he had been selected. His second had been to wonder whether even his soldiering was now a hostage to his race. Had he been chosen for this mission simply because he was black? Franklin intended to ask Caskey precisely that question the first chance he got.

At least the third member of the party was not the Regiment's other West Indian.

'Joss Wynwood, B Squadron,' the man in the MOD hospitality room introduced himself, the chirpiness of the Welsh accent somehow made more apparent by the unruly shock of dark hair and wide grin which accompanied it. Franklin found himself taking an instant liking to the man.

'Worrell Franklin,' he replied, smiling back. 'G Squadron.'

'Any idea where we're going?' Wynwood asked.

'Africa was all the boss told me. What did he tell you?'

'Nothing. Which boss? All I know is that I was given a flight ticket to London and ordered to report here at eleven.'

'Where were you?'

'Armagh. But if it's Africa I can see a connection,' he added. 'I had my honeymoon in The Gambia last year, and I was just reading in the paper that there's been a coup there.'

'Dead right,' a voice said behind them. Caskey dropped the blue holdall, introduced himself and shook each man by the hand. They looked young, he thought. Both of them. Which was hardly surprising – when he was their age they would have just been starting primary school. 'We're on the second floor,' he said, picking up the holdall again.

They took the lift up, and the two troopers followed Caskey down a long corridor and into a large room. It made them think of school – rows of tables and chairs facing a blackboard and map easel. A thin man in a dark-blue suit was busy draping several maps over the latter. He looked about thirty, had black, sleeked-back hair, a cheery smile and a public-school accent.

'Be with you in a mo',' he said.

'From the Foreign Office,' Caskey explained. 'This is just the background briefing. We'll get a more detailed briefing on the current military situation from the French in Paris.'

Wynwood and Franklin exchanged impressed glances.

'Any chance of a night at the Folies Bergère?' Wynwood asked.

'A night in the Charles de Gaulle departure lounge if you're lucky,' Caskey said. 'Two if you're not.'

'And they said the SAS was the glamorous Regiment,' Wynwood lamented.

The FO man was clearing his throat. 'I'm not sure how much you need to know,' he began, 'so if it's too much or too little, just tell me.' He turned to the map. 'This is West Africa,' he said, 'and this uneven sausage shape is The Gambia. It's about two hundred miles long and between twenty and forty miles wide. The River Gambia runs down the middle of it and is the reason why it looks that way – the British just wanted control of the river for strategic reasons, and enough land on either side of it to make the territory viable. As you can also see, it is completely surrounded by Senegal, which was a French colony.

'In fact the two countries would make a lot more sense together than they do separately – the River Gambia would provide exactly the transport artery for a united country which Senegal lacks, and Senegal would provide the hinterland which the river lacks. And that's the main reason why the two countries have been moving towards a confederation – or at least they had been until the current crisis.

'But I'm getting ahead of the story. The population of The Gambia is about 600,000, of which about a quarter live in the towns at its western end. Here' – he pointed at the map with a ringed finger – 'is the capital, Banjul, which used to be called Bathurst. Business and government are still centred there, but it tends to be like the City of London: most of the people who work there don't actually live there. So by day you have business as usual in peeling colonial mansions, and by night it reverts to being a large shanty town.

'Here is where most of the middle class tends to live' – the finger pointed again – 'about eight miles away along the Atlantic coast. Bakau and Fajara are basically outer suburbs, much plusher, much less fraught. Most of the embassies are there, and that's where the big hotels are being put in for the European package tour trade.'

'Finally, here, forming the third corner of a triangle with them and Banjul, almost like a gateway to the rest of the country, is Serekunda, which is probably more populous than Banjul by now, but is basically just an African township. It's the place which looks most authentic to the tourists when they drive from the airport to their hotels. They can say they noticed Africa somewhere between the duty free and the beach.'

Wynwood smiled to himself at this. He remembered driving through Serekunda in the coach quite well, but had only a dim recollection of the beach – somehow the chalet had seemed a more appropriate setting for what Susan and he had in mind. It occurred to him that if he had been picked for this mission on account of his knowing The Gambia, then he was travelling on mostly false pretenses.

'The people,' the FO man was saying, 'are mostly Muslim – about ninety per cent. The largest tribal grouping are the Mandinka, who make up just under half the total, followed by the Wollof – about sixteen per cent – and then several other small minority groups. The tribal boundaries don't follow the national boundaries. For example, there's a lot more Wollofs over the border in Senegal. Generally though, tribalism has never been a serious problem in The Gambia. All the chiefs got their own patch to lord it over, and none of the minorities seems to feel any real grievance. All of them are represented – were represented, I should say – in the Government.'

'Is it a democracy?' Caskey asked.

The FO man smiled. 'Formally, yes. But Jawara has been in charge now for almost twenty years, since before independence, and – how should I put it? – well, he's always the one in the best position to win the elections. He's not a bad ruler, and not a very good one either. The Gambia is poor, make no mistake about that – the annual per capita income is about £100. It doesn't have anything much in the way of natural resources – peanuts and sunny beaches are the only things they have which anyone else wants, and Jawara's made a fair fist of encouraging tourism. But there are other things he could have done, which other small countries have done to earn revenue, like printing lots of stamps, or running lotteries, or setting up a free port . . . There hasn't been much imagination devoted to the country's problems, and the few major schemes which have been launched since independence have nearly all been ill conceived and incompetently handled. And in the last few years the economic chickens have started coming home to roost: there was widespread famine in 1978, and more shortages last year. Like I said, Jawara's not a bad ruler, and he's certainly not a half-baked psycho like Amin or Bokassa. He's more like an African Mr Average.'

'And what about the guys who mounted the coup?' Caskey asked.

'We don't know much about them. The Socialist and Revolutionary Labour Party seems in charge, and that goes back a few years. It was banned last year after a policeman was shot, although it was never clear whether that was the reason or the excuse. Ideologically, they spout the usual Marxist rubbish, which sounds even more comic coming out of a continent without any industry or workers than it does anywhere else. But that may just be window-dressing. A lot of their inspiration – and probably their weapons – comes from Gaddafi, who also likes the phraseology, but takes its meaning about as seriously as I do. And since it seems that over half the military – the Field Force as it's called – has supported the coup, it's obviously not just a matter of a small bunch of loonies seizing power. I'd guess that Jawara must be pretty unpopular outside the tourist areas.'

'Has it been a bloody coup?' Franklin asked.

'Hard to say. The reports we've had have only put deaths in the low hundreds, but the coup leaders have appealed for blood donors, so it may be more.'

'What's the latest news you have?' Caskey asked.

The FO man went back to his map. 'The Senegalese took the airport yesterday, and since then they've been advancing on Banjul up this road. I'd guess they'll take it sometime this morning.'

'That won't leave us much to do,' Wynwood complained.

'The rebels still seem to be in control of this area,' the FO man said, indicating the Bakau-Fajara coastal strip. 'That's where their main depot is, and that, I should imagine, is where they've taken their hostages.' He smiled. 'I'm sure they'll find something for you to do. Any questions?' There were none. 'Then good luck,' he said, removing the portfolio of maps from the easel and heading for the door.

Caskey turned to the other two. 'Here's the drill,' he said. 'Next stop is the Hospital of Tropical Medicines for our shots, then the Regent's Park barracks for kitting out and lunch. We've got a four o'clock flight from Heathrow to Paris, and then a five-hour wait for the Dakar flight . . .'

'Why Dakar?' Wynwood wanted to know.

'That's where Jawara is at the moment. He wants to see us, or at least me. And the only people flying into The Gambia at the moment are the Senegalese Air Force.'

* * *

The Denton Bridge was still in rebel hands, at least for the moment. The first Senegalese attempt to take it, using two armoured cars and a hundred or so infantry, had been an ignominious failure. The rebels' bullets had simply bounced off the cars, but without infantry support they could hold no ground, and the vulnerable foot soldiers had been forced back by well-directed fire. For the first time since the airborne landing, Taal had reason to feel proud of his men.

It could not last. The Senegalese were now simply waiting, and Taal could guess what for, long before he actually heard the sound of the approaching Mirages. There were two of them, and they streaked in across the waters of Oyster Creek, cannons firing. The rebels hunkered down into the shallow trenches they had dug in the soft earth of the flood plain, but to little avail. Both Mirages unleashed a cloud of small objects: anti-personnel bombs, designed to explode above the ground into a thousand deadly shards.

Suddenly the air was full of crying, screaming men, and those who had escaped were not about to give the planes a second chance. They were already running in all directions, most of them towards Banjul, but some into the mangrove swamps, and others straight into the dubious safety of the water.

Taal took a deep breath, and waited to see if the Mirages would return for a second strike. He could not see them, but at the swelling sound of their engines, he scrambled underneath the bridge.

The planes swooped in again, but either the pilots had shot their only bolt or their humanity prevailed, because no more splinters of death were cast across the fleeing soldiers. At the other end of the bridge Taal heard one of the armoured car engines pushed into gear.

It seemed like a good time to make his departure. He walked swiftly down to the water's edge and stepped aboard the President's speedboat, which had been liberated from the Palace moorings and brought around the coast with exactly this eventuality in mind. 'Go,' he told the driver, who needed no further encouragement to open the throttle and send them shooting out from under the cover of the bridge, with such force that Taal was almost thrown backwards over the stern. If anyone shot at them the sound was masked by the noise of the outboard, and within a minute they were out of range, the bridge receding behind them, the ocean filling the horizon in front.

Most of Banjul either saw or heard the two Mirages as they swooped low across the town after their attack on the rebel positions at the bridge. One of Diop's guards put his head out of the second-floor window at the radio station, and was spotted by most of the small group of men concealed in the building on the other side of Buckle Street, a deserted school.

'There's five of them out front,' Mansa Camara said. 'Maybe two inside, maybe more. But nothing we can't deal with. Those five outside look ready to jump out of their skins if someone farts at them.'

McGrath grinned. 'OK, but we don't know if they have any of the hostages inside,' he argued. 'If we get Jawara's senior wife shot, I don't reckon much on your chances of promotion.'

Mansa laughed. 'He'd probably make me head of the Field Force. It's the young wife he takes everywhere these days. But . . .' He turned to McGrath. 'How are you thinking we should do this?'

'Send a small party in the back,' McGrath said without hesitation. 'At a given time you call on the ones out front to surrender, which should flush out the ones inside.'

'I take it you would like to be the "small party" at the back,' Mansa said wryly.

'I'll take Kiti,' McGrath said, indicating another of the Field Force men, who grinned back at him.

'OK,' Mansa agreed. 'How long?' he asked.

'Give us fifteen minutes,' McGrath decided.

'Right.'

McGrath and Kiti left the school the way they had come in, over the back wall, and worked their way around in a large circle, crossing Buckle Street a hundred yards down from the station, and ending up in front of the building in Leman Street that backed onto it. They advanced carefully down the side of this structure, until the back windows of the radio station building came into view. Though they were partly hidden by a large mango tree, no one seemed to be keeping a watch from the windows. A back door looked similarly unguarded.

The two men stealthily crossed the intervening space, on the alert for any sign of danger, and McGrath gingerly tried the door handle. It was locked. But the window next to it was not. The shutters opened with only a slight creak, and a judicious insertion of McGrath's knife released the catch on the windows. He climbed in and stood motionless for a moment, listening for any relevant sounds, then gestured Kiti to follow.

Twelve minutes had passed. McGrath signalled Kiti to stay where he was, and went on a short tour of investigation. The next door led into a short corridor, which ended in a lobby. From this another open door led into a large empty room, and carpeted stairs led upwards. He went up them two at a time. The next floor was also unoccupied, though all three rooms seemed in regular use. One was full of records and tapes, one a kitchen, the third a bathroom. On the floor

140

above McGrath thought he could hear voices. Then he did hear the sound of someone beginning to pace up and down.

Almost fourteen minutes. He swiftly descended the stairs, crooked a finger at Kiti, and led him back up to the first floor. He put the Field Force man behind the bathroom door and himself behind the corner of the opening into the music library.

A loud voice suddenly boomed out: Mansa must have found a megaphone somewhere. Almost instantly guns opened up in the street below, though from inside the building it was impossible to tell whose they were. Nor did McGrath have time to think about it. A man came hurtling down the stairs from the floor above, tripped over the Englishman's extended foot, and smashed his head into the kitchen door jamb with a satisfying thud.

McGrath was halfway up the next flight of stairs when a face appeared briefly in the doorway above. By the time McGrath had reached the threshold of the studio, the man it belonged to was backing away, one hand gripping another African around the throat, the other holding a Luger to his head.

'I will kill him, I will kill him,' the man said, but his victim apparently had other ideas. With a look on his face that suggested the end of his tether had finally been reached, he kicked back like a mule at the rebel's shin.

The rebel shrieked, let go his grip and fired the gun, all in the same moment. As his prisoner fell away he tried in vain to re-aim it in McGrath's direction. Two bullets from the Browning knocked him backwards into the glass partition separating the engineer's room from the studio, and he slid slowly down to the floor with a bemused expression freezing on his face.

On the other side of the studio the other man was getting slowly to his feet.

'Are you OK?' McGrath asked.

'I think so,' Mustapha Diop said. It looked like his career as a radio star was over.

The three SAS men sat in the back of the London cab, Franklin and Caskey facing forward, Wynwood perched uneasily on one of the dicky seats facing back. He might be uncomfortable, but the long ride to Heathrow also offered him the first chance he had had to relax since his drink with Stanley in Armagh the previous night. It had been quite a day.

His arm was sore from the typhoid and yellow-fever jabs, his backside sore from the gamma-globulin jab against hepatitis. They had not had an immunization against being shot by African rebels, so at least he had been spared being sore somewhere else.

It was sunny outside, a lovely summer afternoon. London looked almost attractive. Wynwood had always felt vaguely intimidated by the British capital – its sense of . . . smugness was the word. Londoners thought they were the centre of the world, all of them, from the rich, chinless bastards in Kensington to the pink-haired punks in Camden Town.

Maybe they were right. He thought about Pontardulais and its people, living in their small goldfish-bowl world. He thought about Armagh, where everyone seemed to know everyone else, and even kneecappers seemed on first-name terms with the kneecapped. Maybe London was a network of villages like that, which strangers like him could not differentiate, but he doubted it. He would have to ask Franklin sometime. Though maybe it was different for blacks.

Why did he think that? Because he associated black faces with villages? Wynwood realized for the first time that going to Africa would have a very different meaning for Franklin

142

from the one it had for him. For him, the thought of 'Africa' was simply exciting. He had joked that the SAS was 'the glamorous Regiment', but before being badged he had at least half-believed it. Three months in Northern Ireland had cured him of such romanticism, and imbued in him the knowledge that even the most unglamorous jobs could still be well worth doing. But that did not mean he should not enjoy the glamorous assignments when they came. And being part of *the* SAS three-man team to The Gambia was glamorous by any standards. And definitely worth a sore arm and a sore bum.

In the seat opposite, Franklin was having similar thoughts, though in his case the pride in being selected for this job was tempered by the knowledge that the colour of his skin had played an important role in the selection. He had asked Caskey the direct question while Wynwood was receiving his injections, and the Major had not tried to sugar the pill.

'Yes,' was the reply. 'The CO's reasoning was that an all-white team would have less credibility in a black country. But if that upsets you, I can tell you that I would not have agreed to take you if I didn't think you were up to the job. Fair enough?'

'Yes, boss,' Franklin had said, knowing it was the best he could have expected. If it still did not feel quite right – and it did not – then that, he told himself, was too bad. He had to get over it. Whatever the reasons for his selection, he was going. To Africa, where everyone in his family had ultimately come from, and where none of them had ever been. That felt good, and, he had to admit, it also felt good just to be getting out of England. Away from all the problems.

The roads they were travelling down seemed festooned with the litter from the Royal Wedding celebrations, which somehow seemed to sum up the whole country. It was all so fucking inappropriate. All that money spent on a wedding while the cities were going up in flames. And even the unemployed were dancing in the streets for Lady Diana. The briefing on The Gambia had scarcely painted a picture of freedom and prosperity, but it would have to be pretty fucking dire to compete with this. He grunted, causing Wynwood to open his eyes and grin at him. He grinned back.

Next to Franklin, Caskey was still running through all the various tasks they should have completed, and praying that he had not forgotten anything important. Their clothing needs had been met by a combination of what each man had brought with him, a scavenging trip round the Regent's Park barracks and a quick collective trip to Lawrence Corner, the nearby Army and Navy surplus store. The jabs had all been administered, the course of malaria pills started, the water purification tablets procured. Each man had a Browning High Power in his bag, together with a supply of ammo, and a couple of stun grenades. They had some idea of where they were going and why.

He could understand Franklin's questioning of his selection, and hoped it was not the beginning of a problem. In all other respects both he and Wynwood seemed like ideal companions for this particular trip. Though he supposed he should have realized that honeymooners tended not to get out and about very much.

It was just past three o'clock, and they were getting close to Heathrow. At the airport he should be able to get the latest score from Edgbaston, though he doubted whether it would be good news. England had lost a couple of wickets before lunch, and there was not much reason to believe they had not lost another couple since. But it would be nice to know all the same. He would have to buy one of those new portable things with the funny name. Walkmans, that was it.

The taxi drew to a halt outside the terminal building. Caskey paid off the driver with MOD petty cash, added a generous tip and led the other two through the crowds milling around the check-ins to a small door marked 'Security'. He knocked and walked straight in, greeting the surprised uniformed men inside with: 'SAS – we're expected.'

Behind him Wynwood was thinking: a bit over the top, but impressive anyway.

The uniforms certainly jumped to attention, one of them standing nervously in front of them while the other went to get their superior. He was not so easily impressed. 'Major Caskey?' he asked, and on receiving verbal confirmation demanded to see their passports and order papers.

Once satisfied, the security man led them through a series of rooms and corridors, finally emerging through a door on the travelling side of the boarding gate. Wynwood had a brief glimpse of less privileged passengers waiting to board before he was ushered down the flexible loading corridor and into the first-class section of an empty plane. After exchanging a few words with the crew their guide departed. Their bags, and the weaponry they contained, were stowed in the overhead compartments.

A few minutes later the rest of the passengers began to board, and within twenty minutes the plane was airborne. They were over the Channel before Caskey remembered that he had forgotten to find out the test match score.

At Charles de Gaulle they were allowed off the plane before the other passengers and led by a French security official through a labyrinth of corridors and steps to a private lounge overlooking the airport. Here they were offered drinks while they waited for their French Army contact, Major Jules Mathieu.

He arrived about half an hour later, just as Wynwood and Franklin were starting on their second Pils. He looked liked anyone's idea of a French officer, thin-faced and dark, with a pencil moustache and meticulously pressed uniform. His English put their French to shame.

'*Bonjour, messieurs*', he began. 'I have just checked your flight details for tonight. There seems to be no problem with the Dakar flight, despite all the activity down there.' He rubbed his hands together as if they were cold. 'And you will be escorted aboard, without the . . . er, inconvenience of customs clearance or an X-ray check. Yes? *Bon*. And in Dakar you will be met by people from your own embassy. So, I understand you require the latest information about the situation of the Senegalese forces in The Gambia?'

Caskey nodded.

Mathieu spread his arms in an unmistakably Gallic gesture. 'The Senegalese do not tell us everything,' he said, 'but . . . what they have told us . . .' He reached into his briefcase and extracted a photocopy of part of a 1:250,000 map of The Gambia. Someone had already drawn on it with a red felt-tipped pen.

He held it in front of him, so that all three SAS men could see it. 'They say they have secured the road from the airport here at Yundum all the way to Banjul, and placed a strong force here at the Denton Bridge. They claim to have cleared the rebels out of both Banjul and Serekunda during today, and they probably have, though whether that amounts to restoring order or simply retaking the main boulevards I don't know. You know the rebels emptied the prison two nights ago?'

'No. We hadn't heard that.'

'Ah. Well, they did. So there are also many armed criminals on the loose, which must be making the military job more

146

difficult. And then there is the question of the hostages.' He paused to rub his moustache with the outside of his thumb. 'The rebels have made several threats to kill the President's family and the Senegalese envoy and his family – he was released today, by the way – but so far, we think they have not killed anyone. Still, the Senegalese are being very careful . . . You understand – Jawara is Diop's partner in making the confederation between the two countries, and he will be telling his commanders not to take any actions that might trigger off a desperate response. They would like to catch the rebels *and* free the hostages, but now that the coup is, how do you say? – fucked? – the big priority is getting the hostages back alive. And of course, your SAS is famous for the Iran Embassy siege . . .'

'Do you know what weaponry the rebels have?' Caskey asked.

'Kalashnikovs, *c'est tout.* Jawara says they got them from Libya and the Senegalese are saying they came from the Soviets.' He laughed. 'And Tass says the Gambian Government bought them years ago, which sounds the most likely.'

'Do you know any of the Senegalese commanders personally?' Caskey asked.

'Not the C-in-C, General N'Dor. But I was at St Cyr at the same time as his second in command, Aboubakar Ka. He is a good soldier.' Mathieu smiled at some memory. 'And good company,' he added.

There was a silence while Caskey tried to remember if there was anything else he needed to ask.

'If you have no more questions,' Mathieu said, 'perhaps you would enjoy a meal, yes? Because I can assure you the dinner on Air Afrique flights is nothing to look forward to.'

'I could eat a nice French dinner,' Caskey conceded.

'*Bon*. Then follow me.'

They walked down a few more empty corridors, through a security check on Mathieu's say-so, and up to what looked like an extremely expensive restaurant. Mathieu disappeared from view for a few moments, before returning to tell them their meal was on the French Army. 'And *bon appétit*', he told them.

Caskey went off to phone the test match scorecard and came back looking depressed. 'The bloody Aussies have got two days to score a hundred and forty-two,' he said gloomily. 'With nine wickets left on a batsman's pitch.'

But the food did something to restore his spirits, and the wine something more. When Wynwood, glass of Burgundy in one hand and forkful of succulent steak in the other, happily exclaimed that this was indeed the life, Caskey could hardly find it in himself to disagree.

9

Sibou Cham lay stretched out on the camp-bed in her office. She felt weary to the bone but sleep would not come – it was as if her mind had parted company with her body, the one racing madly along, the other abandoned for dead hours ago.

How many people had she treated in the last forty-eight hours? Eighty? A hundred? A hundred and fifty? She had no clear idea any more. The faces and the bodies were all jumbled up. This man's face went with this shattered thigh, that woman's face with that lacerated ear. Or vice versa. They all had red blood and fear-filled eyes and they were all praying to her, the goddess of healing.

Lying there, she felt more alone than ever. She wanted someone to share who she was, she wanted a body beside her that was not broken or bleeding, that needed no help to function but only love to make it feel whole. She wanted someone reaching out to her whom she could reach out to in return.

It was getting light outside, which did not seem right. Maybe she had slept for a couple of hours after all. She got up, walked to the window, and pulled the lever which opened the sheets of slatted glass. Outside two small grey lizards with yellow heads were chasing each other around a tree stump. On one of the mats which had been left to dry in the sun a small boy was curled up asleep, his bare legs caked with dust.

Africa, she thought. Who would care for Africa? It had nothing anyone wanted. Nothing to sell, nothing to bargain with. Only more and more people fighting over the same amount of land, more and more people angry at their inability to grab a foothold in that wonderful world of cars and TVs and hi-fi which the tourists parade before their eyes. African rulers had no power to transform the continent's fate: all they could do – even the cleverest and the most well-meaning ones – was to try to soften the blow. No wonder there were coups. And no wonder they amounted to nothing more than a game of musical chairs. Except of course for those whose blood had been given to the dust.

In medieval times they had tried to cure patients by bleeding them; nowadays it was countries.

The Field Force depot in Bakau had always reminded Junaidi Taal of the prisoner-of-war camps depicted in Hollywood films. It was partly a matter of illusion: the watch-tower, which contributed so much to the effect, was actually part of the fire station next door, but the large trees which were scattered around the two compounds and overhung the wall between them, made visual separation difficult. From the road all that was visible was an impression of one-storey offices and barracks receding into the foliage, and the single, blue-painted tower rising above it.

It had rained heavily throughout the night, and as dawn broke on Sunday heavy drops were still falling from the trees, beating a sporadic tattoo on the corrugated roofs. This sound was mingled with the swelling dawn chorus of the birds and, rather more incongruously, the measured tones of a Bush House announcer reading the World Service News.

Taal looked at his watch, sighed wearily, and climbed laboriously from his bunk. He was getting too old for this sort of life, he thought. The sort which involved only about four hours' sleep in each twenty-four.

He pulled on a shirt, draped a blanket round his shoulders against the chill of the dawn air, and walked out onto the verandah where, as he had expected, Mamadou Jabang was listening to the radio. One hundred and fifty yards away to the left the sentries at the gates seemed awake and reasonably alert. To the right a man was carrying what looked like a pail of eggs towards the kitchen.

Jabang looked up at Taal with what could charitably be described as a wry smile. 'We didn't even make the news this morning,' he said. 'As far as the world is concerned it's all over.'

'The BBC is not the world,' Taal said shortly, and sat down on the chair beside Jabang's.

'I know, I know.' Jabang gestured towards the map which had been spread across the table. 'Tell me the situation,' he said.

Taal got up again and leaned over the map. 'At midnight,' he began, 'we controlled the whole of this road, from the Sunwing Hotel north of Bakau to the Bakotu Hotel in Fajara. On these two roads' – he indicated the highways from Serekunda to Fajara and Banjul to Bakau, which made three sides of a square with the Bakau-Fajara road – 'we have positions about a mile inland which the Senegalese have not really tried to shift.'

'Why not?' Jabang asked, more for confirmation than because he did not know.

151

'Two reasons. One, they have been busy taking and securing Banjul. Two – and this is only guesswork – they haven't made up their minds whether or not to risk us killing the hostages. And I said midnight but I'm assuming that this is still the situation. No one woke me with bad news.'

'I heard no gunfire during the night,' Jabang agreed. 'What about our radio van?'

'Let's find out,' Taal suggested, reaching for the radio. A few seconds later Jabang's own voice was coming out of the speaker. It was the original proclamation of the new government, now somewhat outdated.

'Where are they?' Jabang asked.

'Somewhere in Banjul. With the Senegalese holding the Denton Bridge there's no way they can get out.'

'I'd love to have seen the Senegalese commander's face,' Jabang said. 'They take the radio station, think that's the last the people will hear from us, and like witch doctors there we are again. I don't suppose we can reach them with a new tape?'

Taal smiled. 'We would have to find them first . . .'

'If we could find someone with a recorder in Banjul then I could talk into it down the telephone.'

'Maybe . . .'

'No, you're right, it's not worth it.' He turned back to the map. 'Can we hold the position we have for a few days?'

Taal shrugged. 'We can try, but . . .'

'If they are hesitating because of the hostages, then perhaps we should encourage them to think the worst,' Jabang said, as much to himself as to Taal.

'More threats?'

'Why not? They . . .'

'But what happens when we fail to carry them out again?'

'They will think we don't know what we are doing.' Jabang smiled. 'You have read the books, Junaidi. The hardest thing for the authorities to cope with in a situation like this is not knowing how far the opposition is prepared to go.'

'That is true,' Taal agreed. It was significant, he thought, that Jabang was now calling the other side 'the authorities' again. Even in the leader's mind they had recrossed the divide which separated government from rebellion. 'But, I must ask you, Mamadou: what can we hope for in the few days such threats might buy us?'

Jabang's mouth seemed to set in an obstinate line, the way Taal remembered it had done when he was a child. 'I still believe Libya may send us some assistance,' he said. 'They sent troops into Chad,' he added, almost belligerently, as if defying Taal to argue.

'Have you heard anything new?' Taal asked.

'No. But our friends in New York will still be working for us.'

Taal scratched his eyebrow and stared out across the wakening camp.

'I know it is not likely,' Jabang admitted.

'It will serve no purpose for any of us – for you, in particular, Mamadou – to be put on trial and hanged by Jawara.'

'I know. I have not lost my reason, Junaidi. When it really is hopeless . . .' He waved a hand in the air. 'But that hour has not arrived. This morning I shall talk to the Senegalese commander, and give a good impersonation of a deranged terrorist who thinks nothing of killing Jawara's family and a hundred white tourists. Then maybe we can negotiate some sort of amnesty for our people. Yes?'

* * *

153

The SAS men's Air Afrique plane landed in Dakar soon after dawn. It seemed to taxi for ever before pulling up a good two hundred yards from the terminal building. Just like the old days, Caskey thought, as he walked bleary-eyed down the steps to the ground. Nowadays only the Pope ever touched the tarmac in modern airports, and that was just because he wanted to kiss it.

As it happened, the three of them were the only passengers who did not have to take the long walk. A man from the Gambian High Commission – resplendent in a Hawaiian shirt – was waiting for them at the bottom of the steps, his Renault parked a few yards away. After making sure they had no luggage other than what they were carrying, he ushered the SAS men inside the car and set off at a breakneck pace across the tarmac.

As at Heathrow and Charles de Gaulle the formalities were not so much dispensed with as trampled on. Here at Dakar's Yoff Airport, there was no need even to enter the building. The Renault was stopped at one gate, as much, Caskey reckoned, for the sake of Senegalese pride as anything else. A uniformed officer looked at all three of them in turn, as if checking their faces with the passports he had not seen, and waved them through.

Franklin, watching the exchange between him and their Gambian escort, felt suddenly aware that he was somewhere he had never been before in his adult life – in a country run by black men.

They roared out of the airport, past a scrum of orange taxis and a crowd of people scrambling to board a bus, and out onto a dual carriageway. In the distance, down at the end of long side-roads lined with rough-looking, one-storey dwellings, they could see the ocean. The sky was clear of clouds, but the blue was tainted with brown, and a patina of dust already seemed to hang in the morning air.

'How far is it?' Caskey asked the driver. Unlike the other two, he had found sleep hard to come by on the plane. It was a matter of age, he supposed.

'Twenty minutes, maybe,' the Gambian said.

From the back seats Franklin and Wynwood were getting their first impressions of Senegal. A large sports stadium loomed into view, bare concrete rising out of the yellow earth, its ugliness turned into something else by the profusion of brilliantly coloured bougainvillaea clinging to its lower walls. Elsewhere the ubiquitous concrete was unadorned, fashioned into block houses, turning the landscape into a sandpit for giants. In front of the houses old car tyres had been half-buried in the sand to provide seats.

They raced down an open stretch of highway, with electricity pylons marching overhead, sand verges littered with rubbish, sand hills spotted with scrub receding into the distance. Giant cigarette advertisements loomed out of the dust, as if on a mission to leave no lung unscathed.

'Pretty, it ain't,' Wynwood murmured.

They entered the inner suburbs, where large blocks of flats and relatively modern-looking shops lined the road, then turned down a long, tree-lined avenue between what looked like government buildings of one sort or another. At its end they had a glimpse of a market that sprawled down several narrow streets as far as the eye could see, but the Renault honked its way down another tree-lined avenue. This section looked like Paris, Caskey thought; a seedy, half-finished, tropical Paris.

The car pulled to a halt outside a nondescript building in a nondescript street. 'We are there,' the driver said, climbing out and gesturing them to follow. He seemed determined to do everything at a hundred miles an hour.

Caskey walked slowly after him, shouldering the blue holdall. A brass plaque by the doorway announced the Gambian High Commission. Inside a flight of steps led upwards to a desk area. It reminded Caskey of the Inland Revenue offices in Hereford.

'Please,' the driver said, indicating a waiting area in which comfortable chairs surrounded a large conference table. Seated in the chairs the table's surface was at eye-level, which meant that holding a conversation with someone on the other side of the room required the talkers to either sit bolt upright or slouch.

Caskey closed his eyes. 'Wake me if anything happens,' he told the other two.

'The President will see you now,' a voice said from behind him.

It was a different Gambian from their chauffeur, this time one more formally attired, in a beige suit, white shirt and red tie. He escorted them down a short corridor and into a well-lit, pleasantly furnished room. A large African rug lay in the centre of the floor, and around it had been arranged several armchairs and two sofas. The President was sitting on one of the latter, a pile of papers by his side. He was not a large man, and although he was not particularly good-looking there was a friendliness in his expression which was appealing. He got swiftly to his feet and walked across to greet them, his right arm outstretched. After he had shaken each man's hand, and they had introduced themselves by name, he invited them to take a seat.

'I am very grateful to the British Government for sending you,' he began, smiling at each of them in turn. 'And of course to each of you for accepting such a mission.' He paused as if expecting a response.

Caskey nodded.

'I'm happy to say,' the President continued, 'that the situation in my country is improving by the hour. Our Senegalese friends have secured the airport and the capital and the road between them. In fact, all the rebels now hold is a small strip of land along the coast.' He grimaced. 'Unfortunately they also hold a number of hostages, including my own wife and several of my children, so bringing the whole business to a successful conclusion will not be a straightforward matter. Which is where I hope your expertise will come into play. Tell me, did any of you take part in the Iranian Embassy business last year?'

'Yes, sir,' Caskey lied. He was afraid Jawara might feel he had been fobbed off with duds if he found out that none of them had been at Princes Gate.

'A wonderful piece of work,' the President said. 'But of course I hope we can resolve our problem less . . . less dramatically.' He paused again. 'What I really wanted to make clear to you – the main reason for wanting to see you before we all fly to my country – is that you are my personal advisers, and that you carry my authority. The Senegalese – how shall I say this? – they may be – I think "touchy" is the English word . . . I am sure their commanders will be more than willing to listen to any advice you may have, but they will not want to appear as if they are taking orders . . . You understand? It is one of the legacies of colonialism. In the old days a white man's orders were obeyed no matter how stupid, and to compensate for this there is a tendency nowadays to ignore a white man's advice, no matter how sensible.' He smiled at Franklin. 'And I'm afraid in this matter you will be seen as an honorary white man,' he said.

Franklin smiled politely back, but said nothing.

'Very well,' the President said. 'We can deal with any particular problem if and when one arises. Now, unless something extraordinary happens in the meantime, I plan to fly to Banjul this afternoon. There is room for you on the same plane. We shall leave here at around four o'clock, and until then you can either rest in one of the rooms here or go sightseeing, whichever you wish.'

'I'd like some sleep,' Caskey said, getting up.

The President got up too, and shook each man's hand again. 'Until this afternoon,' he said.

The man in the beige suit was waiting outside to escort them to the next floor, where a large double bed shared a room with a single. Caskey annexed the latter, claiming privilege of rank.

'I'd like to go out for a look round, boss,' Franklin said.

'Me too,' Wynwood agreed.

Caskey looked at them. 'Bloody youngsters,' he said with a sigh. He reached inside his pocket for the CFAs Mathieu had given them at Charles de Gaulle. 'OK. But don't spend it all. And don't get lost and don't start a war. And don't touch anything. Particularly the women.'

'Did you get all that?' Wynwood asked Franklin.

'Yeah. We're not to spend it all on women.'

They left Caskey groaning and went downstairs.

'Any idea which way?' Wynwood asked Franklin as they emerged into the street.

'To where?' Franklin asked.

'To where we want to go' Wynwood said.

'Where do we want to go?'

'How the fuck should I know?'

Franklin decided. 'Well, let's try this way then,' he said, pointing east.

'Suits me.' Outside in the street the temperature was on the rise. Still, it was not as hot as Wynwood had expected – perhaps Dakar's situation on the coast kept things cool. It would have been nice to have had some time to find out something about the country before they arrived. 'Hey, Frankie,' he said, struggling to keep up with the other man's long stride, 'do you know anything about this place?'

'Not a thing. Used to be French, that's about it.'

'You mean they speak French here?'

'Yeah.'

Wynwood looked round. 'Who would have guessed?'

'The word "Aéroport" in letters twenty feet high was a clue,' Franklin told him.

'I thought they were just bad spellers,' Wynwood said.

They walked on, conscious of the stares they were getting from the locals. Franklin wondered whether he would have been as noticeable on his own, and decided he probably would have. His clothes were different, for one thing. The Senegalese seemed undecided whether to wear African robes or European suits, but none of them seemed to be wearing jeans and T-shirts.

The street they were on debouched into a large rectangular space surrounded by multi-storey buildings.

'The Place de l'Indépendance,' Wynwood read off a sign. 'You reckon this is the centre of town?'

'No idea,' Franklin admitted.

'Hello, hello,' a Senegalese greeted them.

'Hello, hello,' echoed Wynwood.

'You are American?' the Senegalese asked them both.

'English,' Franklin said.

'Welsh,' Wynwood corrected him.

'You are in Dakar how many days?'

'One hour.'

More questions followed, and somehow it came up that the Senegalese had a naming ceremony for his son the next day, and that it was customary for a man in such a situation to find a foreigner and offer him a gift. As chance would have it he had on his person such a gift, and here were two foreigners! What luck! He insisted that Wynwood accept the gift, a miniature drum on a thong. The Welshman took it reluctantly, thinking there must be a catch. There was. It turned out that it was also customary for the foreigner to give the baby a gift. Wynwood regretted that he had no gift to hand, but it then transpired that cash was the most appropriate gift of all. The two SAS men looked at each other and burst out laughing.

'You're a real pro,' Wynwood said, and got out the money Caskey had handed him. 'What are these worth?' he asked Franklin, who shrugged.

'Well, a thousand seems a lot to me,' Wynwood said, and handed the man one.

It did not seem a lot to him. 'More, more,' he said.

'You want the drum back?' Wynwood asked.

'No, I want more CFAs.'

'Tough shit. Be seeing you, chum,' Wynwood said, and walked off. Both Franklin and the Senegalese followed, the one feeling vaguely disturbed by the whole episode, the other more than vaguely annoyed.

He stayed with them halfway round the square, and several blocks up Avenue Pompidou, which looked as close to a main street as any they had seen. Trees lined both sides, and many of the buildings were French in style, creating anew the impression of an African Paris. There were cafés as well, and of two distinct types: those with a primarily African clientele and those which seemed to cater mostly to the expatriate French population. The latter looked cleaner, more expensive

160

and more likely to rid them of their Senegalese shadow.

Wynwood chose one, walked in and took a window seat. A beautiful Senegalese girl took their order of omelettes and coffee, but the Frenchwoman behind the bar was obviously in charge. It felt strange to both men. If they looked one way they could have been anywhere in the developed world. The customers' faces, with one exception, were white, and the fittings were modern, right down to an Elvis Presley clock on one wall, his hips swinging out the passing seconds. But if they looked out through the window there was no mistaking which continent it was. A group of men in long robes were crowded on a bench, smoking cigarettes and passing the time. A boy with two stunted legs was parked under a tree, hand extended with a cup to each passer-by. Buses packed beyond the worst nightmares of a sardine rumbled by, blowing dense black smoke from their exhausts into the dusty air.

Franklin sat there, savouring the delicious coffee, watching and wondering.

Wynwood asked a youngish-looking man at a nearby table if he spoke English.

'A little, yes,' the man said.

Wynwood explained that they had only a few hours in Dakar and no idea what might be worth seeing. Could the man suggest anything?

He shrugged. There was nothing special. The Île de Gorée, perhaps, but that was half an hour's ferry ride away, and they might have to wait an hour for the boat.

'What is it?' Franklin asked, feeling he had heard the name somewhere before.

'It's an island, two or three kilometres from the city. It's very pretty, with the old colonial houses and the fort. And of course the Maison des Esclaves, the Slave House.'

161

Now Franklin remembered. It was the place from where most of the West African slaves had been shipped. Maybe even his own ancestors.

Wynwood asked whether there were any beautiful buildings to see in the city.

'Maybe the railway station,' the Frenchman said dubiously. 'Dakar is not a beautiful city,' he added, somewhat superfluously.

Wynwood thanked him. 'Let's just walk around,' he suggested to Franklin.

For a couple of hours they simply wandered the streets together, soaking up the atmosphere, stopping for the occasional drink, and fending off the extraordinary number of men whose sons were being named the following day.

They did stumble across the railway station, which pleased Wynwood. He had always been drawn to the atmosphere they evoked, and this one, with its magical blend of French and Islamic architecture, seemed no exception. A train was in the platform, packed and apparently about to depart. He asked someone where it was going, and was told Bamako, the capital of Mali. The journey was supposed to take twenty-four hours, the man said with a knowing smile. Wynwood asked him how long it really took. Thirty-six, he said, and cackled.

A few minutes later the diesel blew its horn, and the train jerked its way out of the station along the uneven tracks. Franklin watched it disappear, thinking that here in Dakar they were simply standing on the edge of Africa, but that this train was headed out towards the continent's heart. A part of him wished he was on board.

'This is General N'Dor,' a voice said on the other end of the telephone line.

'At last,' Jabang said. He had needed to threaten the immediate killing of a hostage to get the Senegalese commander-in-chief to the phone, and it had made him angry.

'What is it you have such need to tell me?' N'Dor asked, wishing his English was better.

'Would you rather speak in Wollof?' Jabang asked in that language, as if he had read the General's mind.

'It would seem sensible to be sure we understand what each other is saying,' N'Dor replied in the same tongue. 'I understood you were Mandinka.'

'I am.' Jabang wondered whether the General would be impressed by the fact that he had taken the trouble to learn his country's other indigenous languages, and decided that it did not matter a jot.

'So what do you have to tell me?' N'Dor asked again.

'I have to tell you that unless your forces on the Banjul-Bakau road return to the positions they occupied this morning we shall be forced to begin executing the prisoners.'

There was silence at the other end for almost a minute, but Jabang resisted the temptation to speak again.

'The forces you speak of have only moved a few metres since this morning,' N'Dor said.

'We know that. Moving back those few metres would seem a small price to pay for a hostage's life.' Don't ask for much, Junaidi Taal had advised him, but make sure you get it. Somehow they had to establish a pattern whereby the enemy was prepared to reward them for not carrying out threats.

At the other end of the line General N'Dor was in an impossible position. His Government had warned him to take no risks with the hostages' lives, and the Gambian President would not be on hand to remove the restrictions until later that evening. The rebel leader might be bluffing, and N'Dor thought he probably was, but not with enough certainty to risk calling him on it. There was really nothing he could do for the moment other than concede what was being asked. It was only a few metres, after all.

'Very well,' he said finally. 'My men will be withdrawn to the position they occupied this morning. But no further. This is not an ongoing process. You understand that?'

'Perfectly,' Jabang said. 'Thank you, General. Now, I have here a list of the prisoners we currently hold, which I thought you might find useful. I am sure the families of the prisoners would like to know that they are safe.'

'I will bring someone in to write them down,' N'Dor agreed.

'Excellent. Before you do that, can we arrange to talk again tomorrow morning, say at eleven o'clock? I think it must be in everyone's interests that we keep talking.'

Certainly in yours, N'Dor thought. And until someone told him he could take the gloves off, it was probably in his as well. 'Very well,' he agreed. 'Eleven o'clock.'

Jabang passed the phone to Sallah, who was waiting with the list, and with a wide smile on his face turned to Taal. 'We're not finished yet,' he said exultantly.

The flight from Dakar to Yundum in the forty-four-seater took under an hour. There were only eleven passengers on board; the President and seven assorted advisers in the front seats, the three SAS men in the back. Most of the President's men seemed to be chain-smoking, and by the time the plane touched down at Yundum a thin fog separated the two parties.

Two Senegalese officers were waiting on the tarmac beside a line of four vehicles: the presidential limousine and three taxis. Without much preamble everyone climbed in, the SAS men in the rear taxi, and the convoy took off, sweeping out through the airport gates past arms-saluting soldiers and onto an empty highway.

And into Africa, Franklin thought, staring out through the windscreen. There was nothing European about this landscape. On either side of the road flat savannah stretched into the distance, dotted with trees that bore the continent's distinctive style: tapering down from a flat wide top. A little further on a host of palms shaped like giant thistles rose from a stretch of cultivated land on the outskirts of a village. Here the dwellings were all white and of one storey, including the impressive police station with its colonnaded patio.

Dirt tracks led away from the road, and down these, in the distance, Franklin could see people walking. But the main street seemed strangely deserted, as if the President's path had been swept clear of those he claimed to serve. One group of three women did emerge from a house just as they went by, each with a large plastic bowl balanced on the head, but they turned only blank stares to the swishing cars, as if they were looking into the blind side of a two-way mirror.

After ten minutes or so they entered a large town, which the driver told them was Serekunda. Here there were groups of Senegalese soldiers at the two main crossroads, but few civilians on the streets. Franklin asked the driver if that was because it was Sunday. He received a disbelieving smile in return.

'Not exactly coming out in droves to welcome the man home, are they?' Wynwood commented from the back seat.

The driver chortled, and said something under his breath.

'This town is 'coming like a ghost town' ran through Franklin's head.

Beyond Serekunda they traversed another couple of miles of open country, before motoring across the heavily guarded Denton Bridge and entering the outskirts of Banjul. 'That must be the prison they emptied,' Caskey said, pointing out a white building on the right. The words 'Female Wing' had been painted on one wall in huge letters. 'I wonder if they let the women out too,' he said.

'No,' the driver volunteered.

'More discrimination,' Wynwood murmured. Susan's friends would have something to say about that.

The convoy drove down Independence Drive, passing a line of Senegalese armoured cars parked outside the Legislative Assembly, before turning left and then right through the gates of what looked, in the distance, like a miniature Buckingham Palace. A long drive ran straight to the doors through grounds bursting with luxuriant tropical vegetation.

'Nice garden,' Wynwood said, 'shame about the house.'

'Enough,' Caskey told him, but the grin on his face rather weakened the reprimand.

The four cars drew up in the gravelled forecourt and disgorged their cargo. The SAS men followed the President's party in through the front doors, where a posse of servants were doing their best to appear overjoyed by their master's return. One of his aides came over to Caskey and asked the SAS men to take a seat in the first reception room.

They sat there for ten minutes, sweating with the heat, wondering why ninety per cent of life in the Army was spent waiting for some wanker to get his finger out.

The aide returned and escorted them through to another room, where the President was sitting on a sofa with a Senegalese officer. The latter, whom Jawara introduced as General Hassan N'Dor, did not, Caskey thought, seem particularly pleased to see them. In fact, he seemed reluctant to even shake their hands.

Jawara was trying hard to be genial enough for both of them. 'I have been telling the General,' he said, 'that you have been loaned to my country by the British Government to serve as my personal military advisers until the present problem regarding the prisoners has been resolved. He is of course aware of your Regiment's experience and expertise in the matter of hostage situations.'

'We will be happy to offer any assistance,' Caskey told N'Dor diplomatically, 'but of course we don't want to tread on anyone's toes.'

N'Dor gave him a slight nod, as if in appreciation of the sentiment. 'My English is not so good,' he said, which made Caskey wonder if he had understood the sentiment.

'I have suggested,' the President said, 'that we set up a group to oversee the hostage situation. It would include someone to represent the Gambian Government – probably the Vice-President – General N'Dor and his second in command Colonel Ka, and you, Major Caskey. General N'Dor has offered a room at the Senegalese Embassy for the group's headquarters.'

I bet he has, Caskey thought. 'That sounds like an excellent idea,' he said. 'Of course,' he added, 'the first thing we shall need is some current intelligence of the situation on the ground in Bakau. And for that we shall need some form of written authority from both yourself and the General, which will give us the freedom to pass through the lines.'

'Of course,' the President said. 'I'm sure the General will have no objection to that.'

N'Dor's face said he had, but he acquiesced nevertheless. An aide was sent to type out appropriate papers for him and Jawara to both sign. While they waited Caskey asked the General for his opinion of the current situation.

'There is nothing difficult about it,' N'Dor said. 'We could destroy the rebels in a few hours . . .'

'The General spoke to the rebel leader on the telephone this morning,' Jawara volunteered.

N'Dor scowled at the memory. 'He threatened to kill a hostage if I did not withdraw my men to a position further in the rear. I have orders not to risk hostage lives, so I agree.' He shrugged. 'That is all.'

'What kind of man do you think this Jabang is?' Caskey asked, thinking that the General's English was not much worse than his own.

'Not right in the head,' N'Dor answered without hesitation.

It was not the sort of analysis Caskey had in mind, but it would probably have to do.

The aide returned with the written authorities, and a reminder to the President that he was scheduled to make a radio broadcast within the next half an hour. 'I am coming,' Jawara told him, before turning to the SAS men. 'Rooms have been made ready for you here,' he told them. 'Please ask Saiboa here' – he indicated the aide in question – 'for anything you need.'

He left, accompanied by the Senegalese commander.

'Ever get the feeling you're not wanted?' Wynwood asked.

'Yes,' Caskey said. He had also just realized that no time had been set for the first meeting of the new hostage crisis group. 'I think we're going to have to write our own agenda on this one, lads. Which is why I wanted these pieces of paper. Let's find out what's going on and make a plan. Then we can decide which part of the General's anatomy to shove it up.'

'Sounds good to me, boss,' Franklin agreed.

'You know, I've never lived in a palace,' Wynwood said.

10

'My fellow Gambians . . .'

The President's voice, never impressive at the best of times, sounded positively squeaky emerging from Lamin Konko's tiny transistor radio. Konko himself was snoring noisily in the upper bunk, which made it even harder for Moussa Diba to follow what the President was saying.

One thing seemed certain – he was not offering anyone anything. 'It's all over – get back to work' seemed to be the gist of his message. No mention of leniency for anyone who offered helpful information or switched sides, no mention of amnesty at all. Diba was not surprised, but he did feel vaguely disappointed. He really was going to have to leave the country. And probably for good.

Jawara was making a final plea for the rebels to surrender, but still not offering them any incentive to do so. It was just window-dressing, Diba thought. Just propaganda.

He wondered what he would do if he was in Jabang's shoes. Just empty out the bank in Bakau and run for it, probably. What else could they do – they could not make the hostage thing last for ever, and what else did they have to bargain with?

Diba turned the radio off and sat there listening to the snoring Konko, aware that time was running out.

It was an hour or more before Caskey got through to the British High Commission on the telephone. He asked for Bill Myers, whose name he had been given in London.

'You've arrived,' Myers said enthusiastically. 'I was beginning to think McGrath would have it all sorted out before you got here.'

'Why, what's he been doing?' Caskey asked, feeling distinctly envious.

'Oh, shooting his way through roadblocks, capturing radio stations, you know the sort of thing.'

Caskey laughed. 'So why wasn't he at the airport to meet us? Where is he?'

'No idea. He knows you're coming – I told him yesterday. He was staying at the Carlton Hotel. Probably still is.'

'Where's that?'

'Independence Drive. Where have they put you?'

'Where else? The Presidential Palace.'

Myers grunted. 'Jawara probably wants you on hand in case he suddenly needs some bodyguards,' he said. 'Has he given you any instructions?'

'We're supposed to be liaising with the Senegalese, but their CO doesn't seem any too keen on letting us in on the act. I don't think he's a glory-hogger. He's either someone who likes to keep command lines simple or he's one of those Africans with a chip on his shoulder when it comes to accepting any kind of help from the old colonial powers.'

'Bit of both, I'd say,' Myers observed. 'I met him at some reception or other. He seemed to improve with each glass of wine.'

'Your glasses or his?'

'Both, I think. It's hard to remember.'

Caskey laughed again. He was already growing fond of Bill Myers. 'How are things out there with you?' he asked. 'Aren't you only about half a mile from the Field Force depot?'

'Bit more. But yes, we're behind enemy lines all right. There's usually a group of them outside the gate, and we often see lorry-loads going past. But they haven't knocked on the door yet. Or rather they haven't knocked again, since the first morning, when they warned us to keep inside the compound.'

'Have you? What about food?'

'We're OK. But no, we haven't stayed indoors. Several of us have tested the water, literally in fact. We've taken to using the beach instead of the road – they run more or less parallel, and only about fifty yards apart. That way we've been able to keep tabs on the situation in the hotels.'

'Which is?'

'Hunky-dory. Well, almost. The Sunwing seems to have run out of tinned sauerkraut, so the Germans are desperate, but generally speaking everyone has just been sitting round the pool and reading pulp fiction, like they always do. The only difference is that they don't know when they'll be allowed home.'

'And what do you make of the rebels?'

'Mmm. Hard to say. I mean, you'd think any intelligent group of revolutionaries would make sure they were in control of all the relevant communications, right? But the telephone has been operating more or less normally – erratically, in other words – throughout. You could probably phone up the Field Force depot now and talk to Jabang.' He paused. 'But having said that, there's clearly some intelligence at work. They slowed the Senegalese down long enough to secure their

171

hostages, and now they've managed to force a temporary stalemate. There's even a mobile radio transmitter somewhere in Banjul which is irritating the hell out of the Senegalese. They were in the middle of patting themselves on the back for capturing the radio station – which in any case was down to McGrath and some loyal Gambians – when Jabang's voice comes jumping out of the ether at them. Bit of a slap in the face for your friend the General.'

'So we're not dealing with fools here?'

'Not in the usual sense of the word. Irresponsible, yes. Emptying the prison was a stupid thing to do. From what I've heard most of the killing in Banjul was done by ex-prisoners settling scores.'

'Any idea of casualties?'

'Not really. Ask N'Dor. Less than a thousand, I'd say, but it's only a rough guess.'

'OK. I'll keep you up to date with what we're doing . . .'

'Uh-huh. I know what that means – we'll be the first to know what you're planning, some time after the event. I've had dealings with the SAS before.'

Caskey smiled to himself. 'We understand each other then. Ah, one other thing,' he said hurriedly before Myers could hang up, 'you wouldn't know the test score by any chance?'

'Of course we know it,' Myers said. 'What's the diplomatic service for if not to keep Brits up to date with the cricket?'

'Well?'

'Well what?'

'What's the score?!?'

'Oh that. We won of course.'

'Won? They only had about a hundred to make on a pitch like a pudding!'

'You're forgetting Botham.'

'Again?'

'Again. He took five for one in twenty-six balls. They were all out for a hundred and twenty-one.

Caskey could hardly believe it. Lightning obviously did strike twice in the same place. 'Amazing,' he murmured, as much to himself as Myers.

'You said it.'

'We'll be in touch,' Caskey said, still shaking his head in disbelief.

'Good luck,' Myers said, and hung up.

Caskey went back upstairs to where Franklin and Wynwood had established camp, in a suite usually reserved for visiting royalty. Prince Charles had apparently used it once, a piece of information which had caused Wynwood to wonder out loud whether the royal honeymoon was proving a success. 'I mean, tell me, boyo,' he had asked Franklin, 'can you actually imagine the two of them at it? Can you?'

Franklin had tried and failed and gone to have a bath. He was just emerging as Caskey arrived back upstairs. 'Would you believe we won the test match?' he asked the two of them.

'Just about,' Franklin said.

'You know,' Wynwood confided in the West Indian, 'I had this dream that the three of us had been flown out to Africa on some mission or other . . .'

'All right, all right,' Caskey said with a grin. 'Business.' He told the other two the gist of his conversation with Myers.

'So what now, boss?' Wynwood asked.

Caskey looked across at the window, which showed a rapidly darkening sky. 'I think we should talk to McGrath before we decide anything,' he said, 'and I wouldn't object to some food. Or a drink.'

173

'Good thinking, boss,' Wynwood said encouragingly.

'I take it we're going armed,' Franklin said, replacing the Browning in the holster on his belt.

'You bet,' Caskey said.

Downstairs the aide who had been detailed to look after them had bad news. There was no food in the palace, for the rebels had stripped the storeroom before departing on the previous day. He recommended the Atlantic Hotel, which was just up the road. They could use the jeep which had been sent by the Senegalese for their use.

Caskey offered a mental apology to General N'Dor and asked the aide for directions to Independence Drive and the hotel. This was also apparently a short drive away, and, as it happened, an unnecessary one. Caskey had no sooner turned the jeep out of the gate than two figures were caught in the arc of its headlights. One was a black woman, the other the white man he had last seen in an SAS photograph.

Caskey pulled the jeep to a halt. 'Simon McGrath, I presume,' he said with a smile.

'And you must be the Three Musketeers,' McGrath replied.

They shook hands, and Caskey introduced the other two. McGrath ushered Sibou forward. 'This is Dr Cham,' he said. 'She would be The Gambia's Florence Nightingale, but Florence was only a nurse.'

She ignored him. 'My name is Sibou,' she said, offering her hand. Franklin could not remember ever meeting such a lovely woman.

'Where are you headed?' McGrath asked.

'To look for you, and then the Atlantic Hotel for dinner.'

'Which is where we're going,' McGrath said, offering a hand to help Sibou up into the back of the jeep.

Five minutes later they were entering a sparsely populated

dining room, and being ushered to a large table by an army of waiters.

'The tourists from here went home today,' McGrath explained, 'and the next batch have been cancelled because of the situation. Which is why our friends here' – he indicated the hovering waiters – 'all look like they're suffering from withdrawal symptoms.'

Once they had ordered two bottles of wine and several beers Caskey invited McGrath to tell the story of the last couple of days. 'And don't make too much up,' he added with a grin, 'I've already talked to Bill Myers.'

McGrath went through what had happened, leaving nothing out, not even the shooting on the Denton Bridge. He caught Sibou's eye as he recounted those moments, and found he could not read what she was thinking from her expression. Maybe she was not sure herself, he decided.

Franklin, who was sitting between Sibou and McGrath, thought he could feel the tension in her as McGrath told of shooting the rebel, but maybe he was imagining it. He found himself admiring this cynical white Englishman, but not sure whether he liked him very much. He wondered what the relationship between him and the doctor was.

As they ate he managed to share a few words with her, asking whether she was a Gambian and how long she had worked at the hospital. She seemed not to mind being asked, but offered only monosyllabic answers to his questions, and looked genuinely interested only once, when he told her that his mother was a ward sister in a London hospital. It gradually dawned on Franklin that she was tired. Really tired. Tired beyond tired.

Immediately they had finished eating Sibou announced that she had to get back to the hospital.

'You need to go home,' McGrath told her.

'I need . . . you're right, I need to go home,' she agreed.

'I'll take you,' McGrath said, getting up.

'Go and see if there's a taxi,' she said. 'If there is I'll take it. And you can stay and talk to your friends.'

'I . . .'

'I'm not arguing with you,' she said.

McGrath was back a couple of minutes later. 'It's waiting for you,' he said.

'It was good to meet you all,' Sibou said. 'And don't let this idiot talk you into anything. I don't want our next meeting to be at the hospital. Unless you'd like to see what one looks like around here,' she added, looking at Franklin.

He watched her thread her away out through the tables, balanced like a dancer.

'Now,' McGrath said, 'how do you lads feel like a little exercise?'

In the Field Force depot's main office the Revolutionary Council was once again in session. One of the twelve members was sick and confined to his bunk, but the other eleven were all there, and, Taal noted, all looking reasonably smart. It was impressive, he thought. Ludicrous perhaps, but still impressive.

Outside the crickets were making their infernal noise, and tonight there was no sign of a downpour to shut them up. Taal wiped his brow with a saturated handkerchief and wondered how many of those present were going to end up hanging from the gibbet in Banjul Prison.

Snap out of it, he told himself. That was what the English said. 'Snap out of it.' What a strange expression.

He tried to keep his attention on what Mamadou Jabang was telling the Council, but it was hard to concentrate on something you already knew off by heart. He and Jabang had spent most of the afternoon and evening thinking through the new policy, and he did not really care what the rest of the Council thought of it. There was, after all, no alternative.

'We will keep what we have,' Jabang was saying, 'and negotiate from that position. We have the hostages as one bargaining card, and we have the prisoners as another.'

A murmur of surprise greeted this statement.

'I am prepared to admit that releasing them was an error,' Jabang said. 'An offer on our part to deliver them back into custody will show that we are negotiating in good faith.'

'Are we in any position to do that?' one man asked. 'They are all armed now . . .'

'There are only about eighty of them here,' Taal said. 'And more than four hundred of us. It will simply take some organization, that's all. And with any luck it will not be necessary. All that we must do is keep them here, which means trebling the security around the depot. No one should be going in or out without written authorization from this Council.'

There were a few moments of silence while everyone digested this. 'OK,' one man said eventually, 'but what do we want? What are we negotiating *for*'

'Our freedom,' Jabang replied. 'Free passage out of the country.'

'To where?'

'That will depend on which countries are prepared to accept us,' Taal interjected. 'But in any case, first we have to establish the principle.'

'That is true,' Jabang conceded. 'And to establish that principle we must make Jawara fear the consequences of refusal.'

* * *

Diba stood in the shadows under the depot's water tower and watched the two men stop for a few words with the sentries on the gate, before starting another lap along the inside of the wall. A few moments earlier another patrol had passed by on the outside of the gate. They were presumably circling the outer wall.

And then there was the searchlight which had been installed in the fire-station tower that evening. Its operator was either minus a brain or very well instructed, because the search pattern was decidedly random, the wide beam slipping this way and that across the depot compound, spilling out onto the road in front and into the trees behind. A man could get across the wall and away, but he would need to be lucky. There was no way to be certain, and Diba was not yet desperate enough to chance his life on such a throw of the dice.

Besides, he thought, as he walked back towards his barracks, the leaders had promised women the following evening. There was no hurry. If the Senegalese attacked the depot there was no way they could capture all three hundred men – some were bound to escape. He just had to be sure that when the time came he was one of them. And that should not be a problem, because most of the rebels would be too busy playing the hero, and most of the ex-prisoners were too slow on the uptake to think of running.

McGrath brought the jeep to a halt on the side of the open road. 'We'd better walk from here,' he said. 'No point in giving the enemy the idea that anything's happening.'

The other three got out. A cool breeze seemed to be blowing in from the ocean, which by Caskey's reckoning was a mile or so ahead of them. The sky was clear, the stars of the summer triangle bright in the northern sky. To the west, the reddish Arcturus hung balefully above the horizon.

They were on the Serekunda-Fajara road, about a quarter of a mile inland from the Senegalese front line. All four men had spent several minutes in front of the mirror with the make-up kit, and their faces and hands were artistically streaked with camouflage cream.

The soldiers at both the Senegalese checkpoints they had passed through – one at the Denton Bridge, the other at the crossroads in Serekunda – had eyed them with a mixture of suspicion, awe and, it had to be admitted, amusement. Still, the authorizations signed by Jawara and N'Dor had granted them free passage, and after a certain amount of head-scratching they had been allowed just that. The Gambia was their oyster, as McGrath announced. 'Pity there's no pearl,' he had murmured to himself.

'Ready?' Caskey asked. He had made it clear to McGrath, in as friendly a manner as he could manage, that the SAS group in The Gambia had only one boss – himself. He was the one who was responsible to Bryan Weighell, and ultimately to the British Government. As long as McGrath understood and accepted that he was more than welcome to join the party.

'You're the boss,' McGrath had agreed, and only time would tell if he meant it.

'You take lead scout, Simon,' Caskey said, organizing the four men along standard SAS lines. 'Joss, Tail-end Charlie.' As leader he would take up the second position, with responsibility for the left flank. Franklin would come third, and cover the right. For the moment, while they were still supposedly in friendly territory, there was unlikely to be any danger, but it paid to be careful. He could tell from the dark silhouettes of the palms that this was hardly the Brecon Beacons.

They started off, walking at a reasonable pace, but not so fast that they lost their sensitivity to the rest of the world. On either side of the road open countryside dotted with trees and the occasional low building stretched away into the distance. Behind them a dim glow in the sky over Serekunda announced the imminent moonrise.

After about ten minutes McGrath slowly moved his right arm up and down to signal a slow-down. Caskey caught him up, and took a look through his binoculars. Two hundred yards ahead of them, where several buildings were clustered under a group of palms close to the road, a number of vehicles were parked. Between them Caskey could make out a neatly sandbagged emplacement, which probably contained a machine-gun. Some way off the road, and shielded by a house from the enemy's view, four men were sitting round a fire. As Caskey looked one of them dragged on his cigarette, turning it into a miniature flare.

He passed the binoculars to McGrath, who took a look. 'They're Senegalese, all right,' he whispered. 'Not much of a war zone, is it?'

'No point in spoiling their rest,' Caskey observed. 'Right or left, do you reckon?' he asked, looking first to one side, then the other.

McGrath tried to remember what the area looked like in daylight. 'Left,' he said finally. 'I don't know this area well, but I think they've put in a golf course just up ahead, and on the other side of that we should find the approach road to the Bakotu Hotel. From the back of the hotel there's a path leading down to the beach. If we go to the right it'll cut down the distance, but we'll probably end up scrambling over garden walls in Fajara.'

'Left it is. Lead on, MacDuff.'

They crossed an expanse of difficult broken ground. The huge orange moon now looming behind them offered little help, but did manage to throw an almost malevolent sheen over the landscape. In some areas the surface was decidedly swamp-like, and Wynwood found himself imagining strange creatures lurking in the ominous ooze.

It was with some relief that they emerged onto a beautifully cut green, complete with a flag announcing that it was the third hole.

'Fancy a quick round?' McGrath asked Caskey.

'On the way back, maybe.'

Wynwood and Franklin rolled their eyes up at each other. There was only one thing crazier than an SAS trooper, and that was an SAS officer. Or, as in McGrath's case, an ex-SAS officer.

They traversed the third fairway, crossed the low fence which separated the tee from a narrow road, and waited for a moment, ears straining to pick up any sounds not made by nature. There were none. In the distance they could now hear the murmur of the ocean.

A quarter of a mile or so away several pinpoints of light suggested habitation. 'The Bakotu,' McGrath said. 'It has its own generator.'

They followed the road in that direction, still strung out in a line some fifty yards from head to tail, and then closed up on McGrath's hand signal. The hotel was now about a hundred yards distant, and with the aid of the binoculars Caskey picked out two men with rifles on sentry duty. They were standing facing the main entrance, obviously considering it their job to keep the tourists in rather than anyone else out. Caskey forced himself to wait five minutes in case there were others patrolling the grounds, but none appeared. He nodded to McGrath to continue.

They skirted the outer edge of the hotel car park, all the time keeping an eye on the backs of the sentries. Even if they had turned round it was doubtful whether they could have seen the SAS patrol, but they did not. McGrath led the way through a gap between two outbuildings, cautiously opened a squeaky gate, and found himself skirting a swimming pool. A discarded bikini top was floating on the water – clearly someone was still enjoying their holiday.

An arched doorway at the rear led out onto the footpath he remembered, which wound steeply down through trees to the beach. Checking to see that the others were still with him, he started off down the slope.

The tide was out, which was fortunate. If it had been in, the beach would have been impassable in several places between there and their destination. McGrath felt momentarily disappointed in himself for not remembering such an important element at the planning stage, then brought his mind back to the job in hand.

The beach seemed empty in both directions. The half beneath the low cliffs was still in shadow, but the flat sands stretching down to the sea were bathed in moonlight. Walking would be easier down there, McGrath thought, but they would also be plainly visible to anyone watching from above. They would have to trudge through the shadows.

All four men hunkered down in a circle.

'We're about a mile and a half from the nearest point on the beach to the rebel HQ,' McGrath said.

'And how far from the beach is that?' Wynwood asked.

'Only a hundred yards or so. There's a line of buildings – hotels, restaurants, embassies – between the beach and the road, and then the Field Force depot is on the other side. It looks like an American children's camp – all cabins and trees

– except that it's also surrounded by a high wall. There's a fire station next door with a high tower.'

'Any questions?' Caskey asked.

'Yes, boss,' Wynwood said. 'If we run into someone what's the policy?'

'Avoidance if possible,' Caskey said. 'We don't want anyone knowing that we've recced this route if we can help it.' He looked round at the others. 'Anything else?'

There were no questions. McGrath led off along the sand, using any firm ground at the foot of the cliffs he could find, and the rest of the patrol followed, making sure that the spaces between them were both wide enough and irregular.

As Tail-end Charlie, Wynwood would occasionally spin round on his heel to check the area behind them, but no one came into view. This beach was as empty as his own favourite stretch of sand would be in the depths of winter. Nearly every summer of his childhood Wynwood's family had taken their annual holiday in one of the caravan parks around Tremadoc Bay, and at least once each trip they had all walked the six miles across the sands from Criccieth to Portmadoc, getting up such an appetite that the fish-and-chip supper which invariably followed tasted as good as anything on earth.

He sighed at the memory. Somehow he was finding this trip hard to take seriously. They had been whisked away from Britain to live in a palace, had been served a sumptuous dinner by more attendants than Lady Di had had at the Wedding, and had then been treated to an exposition of McGrath's *Boy's Own* exploits. Now here they were walking down a moonlit beach with palms waving overhead. Wynwood half expected to see Biggles roar by in a bi-plane. It felt as if he had come a hell of a long way from Armagh in not much more than forty-eight hours.

Up ahead of him Franklin was keeping his eyes peeled on the clifftops to his right, thinking about Sibou Cham, and asking himself the same questions most people must have asked after meeting her. Like – what was a beautiful, talented girl like her doing in a place like this? He smiled to himself. He already knew the answer – she was making the best use of her talent. Not in terms of her own material gain, and probably not when it came to her own development as a doctor, but undeniably the best in terms of other people's needs. She had simply put herself where she could make a real difference to the largest number of lives.

He wondered whether she had a political axe to grind and decided probably not. She just wanted to do her job and do it well. Like he did. Race never got in the way of doing your best. He realized he wanted to talk to her about these things, that she might . . . not have an answer for him, exactly, but maybe some clues. Just a little wisdom, as his grandmother used to say whenever she was asked what she wanted for Christmas. Just a little wisdom.

Some twenty yards further forward the moonlit sands were also bringing out the philosopher in Caskey. Nights like this were the reason he had loved his military career – the sense of freedom, the sense of being on the edge, the overwhelming sense of being utterly alive. Nothing compared with it, nothing at all, not even the day's news that Botham had done it again. Certainly not sex, which always came with such distressing side-effects – like having to deal with someone else's emotions. The only downside of nights like this was that they cast everything else into their shadow. He would go back to England, continue his military career for a few more years, hang around in pubs reminiscing about old times, watch the cricket. There were many enjoyable ways to pass the time.

The trouble was, that was all they did, just pass it. On a night like this, with life and death at stake, every moment had to matter. And did.

As lead scout, McGrath's responsibilities included picking out their route and keeping an alert eye for any rebel presence up ahead. He was enjoying himself every bit as much as Caskey, and sharing in the same realization that for him this much-loved way of life would soon be over. He would be forty in a couple of months, and though he was as fit as he had ever been, he knew that time was running out for his legs and his reflexes alike. In this job anything less than the best was not good enough.

He was also feeling the pull of home, and knew that the arrival of the three men behind him had done something to make that pull real again. He missed his wife and children, but then he always had – this was something else, a feeling of being tired of places where he felt alone. Sure, he had made friends in The Gambia – he had made friends wherever he had been in the world – but no matter how much he liked people like Sibou Cham or the Camaras he knew a gulf lay between them, a gulf that prevented him or them from ever growing close enough to . . .

The fire leapt into view as he rounded the small headland, causing him to stop in his tracks and inch his way back over those few feet of sand which inertia had carried him across. No shout came after him, no bullets. He signalled Caskey to stop, and walked back to meet him, his mind recreating a picture of the scene around the corner.

The four men gathered in a circle once more, this time deep in the writhing shadows of trees which swayed on the cliff edge above them. 'There are two men – I think they're both in uniform – sitting by a fire in the middle of the beach.

185

Sitting on upright chairs, I think.' McGrath held his arms out, palms upwards, in a gesture of apology. 'I only had a split-second glimpse.'

'Weapons?' Caskey asked.

'One was holding something. Something shiny. I'd guess a rifle, but only because that's all I've seen up to now. It could be an SMG.'

'Suggestions?' Caskey asked them all.

'Is there no way past them?' Franklin asked, looking up. The cliff, though only about fifteen feet high, was virtually sheer.

McGrath shook his head. 'Not that I know of. Not unless we go back a ways and risk the road. And they're bound to be patrolling that.'

'Frankie, how do you feel about impersonating a local?' Caskey asked. 'You could probably get close enough to get the drop on them.'

'He doesn't look like a local,' Wynwood said. 'He's too damn tall, for one thing. And the clothes are all wrong.'

'And if they ask me anything in Mandinka I'm finished,' Franklin said, trying to keep his voice level. He did not want to turn down Caskey's request, but there was something about it that he really resented.

'How about two of us impersonating a couple of tourists?' McGrath suggested. 'Drunken English tourists.'

'I do a convincing drunken Welsh tourist,' Wynwood said.

'No kidding,' McGrath said wryly.

'Why not three?' Caskey wanted to know.

'Two's better,' McGrath insisted. 'Three will look too threatening. We want to look friendly. Very friendly.'

'OK,' Caskey said, looking at him and Wynwood. 'The parts are yours.'

'Who dares wins,' McGrath murmured.

They made sure to start singing some way before they turned the corner. Wynwood opened with a heartfelt chorus of 'Land of My Fathers', but soon decided to join in McGrath's spirited rendition of Abba's 'Knowing Me, Knowing You'. They rounded the end of the headland, two arms about each other's shoulders, two waving wildly at the sky. One of the latter contained a bottle which McGrath had found under the cliff.

'Knowing me, knowing you, AHAAAA, there is nothing we can DO! . . . We just have to face it this time – WE'RE THROUGH!' they bellowed in different keys.

The two uniformed Field Force men were on their feet, and yes, McGrath noticed, they had been sitting in the middle of a beach on two upright wooden chairs. One of them started shouting at the two drunken tourists; something about going back to their hotel.

Wynwood and McGrath staggered on, vocally reaching for the sky.

'In these old familiar rooms, children will play . . . Now there's only emptiness, nothing to say . . . KNOWING ME, KNOWING YOU!'

One of the Field Force men was now laughing at them, his Kalashnikov pointing at the ground, while the other continued to shout at them, brandishing his in their general direction.

'Constable!' McGrath boomed, waving the bottle. 'Have a drink!'

They were only a few feet away now. Wynwood disentangled his arm from around McGrath and put it over his face, as if suddenly stricken by a dizzy spell. Then he opened his mouth as if to yawn, all the time watching McGrath, who had the man with the upraised gun to deal with.

The Englishman did not bother with subtlety. One minute he seemed to be offering the bottle, the next it was crashing down on the African's head. The other Field Force man's eyes were still bulging with surprise when the edge of Wynwood's hand came down on the side of his neck. The eyes could apparently bulge no wider, and he slid to the ground.

'May the Field Force be with you,' Wynwood murmured.

'Nice work,' McGrath said, examining the two men. 'They'll both be out for a while,' he added. 'But let's ice the cake a little . . .' He took a hip-flask from his pocket and began easing small amounts of whisky down the unconscious men's throats. 'No one'll believe their story if they smell of booze,' he explained to the other three.

'Good one,' Caskey said. 'And then . . .'

A shout from behind turned all their heads round, and there, coming down a flight of steps that had been cut in the cliffs was a third Field Force man. He seemed to realize his mistake at almost the same instant, and for what felt like several seconds appeared to hang motionless, like a cartoon character who had just run off the edge of a cliff.

Then he managed to put himself in reverse, and started scooting back up the steps.

'Frankie,' Caskey said, turning to where the black trooper had been standing, but Franklin was already off, racing across the sand and leaping the bottom three steps in one bound before the Field Force man had regained the top. And as he hurled himself up the steps Franklin's mind seemed to be on automatic, asking and answering questions like a computer talking to itself. Did the man he was chasing have a gun? Yes, he did. What had the man seen on the beach? Three white men and himself standing over his two comrades. Looking sober. Looking like they knew what they were doing. Conclusion: this man should not be allowed to report what he had seen.

Franklin reached the top of the steps, from where a pathway led up through a grove of trees towards the road. The man was fifteen yards ahead, and not a good runner. Franklin knew he would catch him within fifty yards.

The African must have known it too from the swelling sound of Franklin's boots behind him. He stopped suddenly and turned, raising the Kalashnikov to his eye and firing wildly. Bullets seemed to zip past Franklin's face, and as one part of his mind was registering disbelief at the fact that he had not been hit, the other was pulling the Browning from his holster, making sure his legs were slightly bent, locking his arms, and pulling the trigger.

The man's knees buckled, and he sank to the ground without making a sound.

Franklin walked forward to where he was lying, suddenly hyper-aware of the sounds around him: the waves rippling on the beach below, the breeze in the palm fronds above, the footsteps behind him.

It was Wynwood, who looked down at the corpse thinking, this is real all right. This man is as dead as the men in that lane in Armagh.

'We'd better get him back down to the beach,' Franklin said. 'I can manage,' he added, and used a fireman's lift to get the body across his shoulder.

'I'll keep watch up here for five minutes,' Wynwood suggested, 'just in case somebody comes to investigate.' It was hard to believe that the burst of automatic fire had not alerted someone, but he had no clear idea how far they were from the rebel HQ. And the breeze now seemed to be blowing offshore, which could only help.

Down on the beach Caskey and McGrath were waiting. 'Nice work,' Caskey told Franklin grimly. 'I wonder . . .'

'The tide's out almost as far as it goes,' McGrath said. 'If we take him out another twenty feet, and weigh him down with a rock or two . . . He only needs to stay hidden for a couple of days.'

They did as he suggested, completing the task just as Wynwood came back down from the clifftop. 'Nothing,' he said.

Caskey breathed out noisily. 'Then let's get moving again,' he said.

They left the two unconscious Field Force men by their glowing fire. Caskey had wondered whether they should be killed as well, but decided against. It might not be the right decision in military terms, but killing men who were already unconscious did not seem like cricket. Even the way the Australians played it.

Ten minutes later they reached a point which McGrath judged was level with the rebel HQ, and he scrambled up the sloping cliff to check his bearings. Away above the trees in the distance a bright light could be seen shining. There was only one place it could be – in the fire-station tower. They were in the right place. He signalled the others to join him.

They found a narrow passage between walls which led in the direction of the road, and cautiously advanced along it. A pile of crates containing empty Coca-Cola bottles suggested they were outside a restaurant or a hotel, and when they were no more than twenty yards from the road an archway led off the passage into a thatch-covered area full of seats and tables. The wall between this and the road was composed of blocks arranged in a geometric pattern, through which the moonlight cast a chequer-board of shadows.

Through the spaces they could see the front gates of the Field Force depot, across the road and some twenty yards to their left. As far as outside movements were concerned it was an ideal observation spot, and for the next hour they used it to log the frequency of both the perimeter patrol and the jeep which seemed to be tracking backwards and forwards between the Sunwing and Bakotu ends of the road.

There was no need to spy out the layout inside the depot – there were loyal Field Force officers to provide such details, and probably architectural plans somewhere or other – but it would be more than useful to know in which particular building or buildings the hostages were located. Such information could only be obtained by either surreptitiously seizing control of the fire-station tower – which would probably prove impossible – or sending someone over the wall. Without any clear idea of the layout within, and with the two men on the beach liable to wake up within a few hours, Caskey reluctantly ruled out the latter option as far as this particular night was concerned.

They went back the way they had come, down to the beach and back along it, passing the unconscious men beside the dying fire. The tide had turned and the moon was now high in the sky, dimming the stars.

They met no one on the path up from the beach, heard nothing as they went past the sleeping Bakotu Hotel, and decided sleep was a more pressing priority than a round of nocturnal golf. The jeep was waiting where they had left it, the Senegalese checkpoints manned by the same soldiers, who seemed to have no curiosity as to where they had been.

Shortly before two in the morning they dropped McGrath off outside the Carlton Hotel and roared back down Independence Drive to their palace.

11

It was scarcely seven o'clock when Franklin woke up, and far from fully light outside. Wynwood was snoring contentedly in the other bed. Franklin turned over and tried to get back to sleep, but the dawn chorus of birds in the Palace grounds was even louder than Wynwood.

Make the most of it, a voice inside his head told him. He would probably only be in Africa for a few days.

By the time he had bathed, dressed and got himself downstairs, the new day had established itself. There was only a single uniformed guard beside the doors in the wide entrance hall. One of the benefits of a coup like this one, Franklin guessed, was that you knew where your enemies were. For a while, anyway.

The guard smiled at him but said nothing. Franklin walked out into the morning, and shielded his eyes against the sun piercing through the trees almost directly ahead of him. Where should he walk to? Did it really matter?

He strolled down the drive to the gates, where two Field Force men did bother to examine his authorization before offering friendly smiles. He asked them which way to the centre of town, was pointed in a vaguely southerly direction, and set off.

The hospital where Sibou worked already seemed open for business, and he thought of dropping in to see her as she had suggested, but on reflection decided that this probably was not the ideal time. He kept going, turning left onto Independence Drive and walking past a small building which claimed to house the National Museum and a medium-sized Christian church proclaiming itself a cathedral. Several people were on the street already, either just walking to work or busying themselves outside their premises on the other side of the street. It felt more normal than the day before, less like a ghost town.

For the first time that morning he let himself think about the man he had killed the night before. The man who was now rotting in the Atlantic surf. He had had no choice. None at all. Saying it, he felt like a character in a Western, but it really had been a case of 'him or me'.

He found himself wondering if the man had a wife or children, and then stood there for a moment, unclenching his fists, telling himself that he was being stupid. This was the sort of thing that happened in wars and revolutions. The dead man had put his own life on the line the moment he picked up the Kalashnikov.

Franklin sighed, and became aware of the world around him again. Two boys, neither of whom could have been more than six years old, were staring at him.

'Have you got a pen?' one of them asked.

Franklin's hand went automatically to his pocket, although he knew he did not have one. 'Sorry, no,' he said. 'What did you want to write?'

The child who had asked looked up at him as if he was mad. 'For school,' he said. 'A pen?'

Franklin held out his arms to indicate he had none.

'Give me something,' the other child asked.

The only thing Franklin had was money, and that only in notes that were worth a pound or more each. Why not, he thought. It was Her Majesty's money; or Jawara's – he was not sure which. He gave them both a note, and watched their faces go through a bewildering range of expressions, of which disbelief, contempt and joy seemed the most dominant.

They did not stop around for him to change his mind. He watched them hurry back across the street and into the grassy area beyond, both clutching their notes for dear life. For all he knew he had launched two children on a lifelong career as beggars. Or maybe he had given their families food for a week. Who knew? Maybe the doctor could tell him.

He retraced his steps, walking slowly to savour the strange sights and sounds, and purchased a bag of what looked like pastries from a roadside vendor. Back at the Palace he found that Caskey and Wynwood were no longer in their suite. The guard in the entrance hall pointed him towards a plain door underneath the palatial stairs, from which a narrower staircase led down to the staff quarters.

He was standing at the bottom, wondering which way to go, when the sound of Wynwood's laugh provided him with the necessary directions. Three rooms down he found the Welshman and Major Caskey sitting on one side of a huge wooden table, talking with a large African woman in a gorgeous blue and white robe.

'Coffee?' she asked Franklin.

He nodded and produced his pastries.

'I think he'll do,' Wynwood said to Caskey.

'He brought the buns,' Caskey admitted, 'but it was us who found the coffee.'

'True.'

'The Morecambe and Wise of the SAS,' Franklin said, sitting down. 'I can hardly see the join,' he added, staring at Wynwood's hairline.

'This hair has been in my family for generations,' Wynwood said indignantly.

'Who was the last owner to comb it?' Caskey asked with interest.

Wynwood spluttered into his coffee.

'You are supposed to drink it,' the African woman told him sternly, as she placed a steaming cup in front of Franklin.

'To business,' Caskey said, once she had gone. 'The first thing to say is that we don't seem to have received our invitations to the Senegalese Embassy. I have a feeling this is one of those parties we're going to have to crash.' He smiled. 'Fortunately, it may also be one of those where the host will be too embarrassed to throw us out once we've got our feet inside the front door. So I suggest we just turn up at the Embassy in . . .' – he looked at his watch – 'in an hour or so. Sound OK?'

'We all like parties, boss,' Wynwood said.

'Right. The next question is deciding what we want from the Senegalese. I did some thinking last night, while we were coming back from our stroll, and it seems to me that one of our squadrons could wrap this all up in an hour or so.'

The other two tried not to eye him too warily. Both troopers knew that Caskey had a reputation for taking big risks. Usually with considerable success.

'We don't have a squadron with us, boss,' Franklin observed.

'No, so we'll have to create one on the spot. Look, the route we took last night – it seems to me that there's no reason why sixty men couldn't arrive opposite that depot the same way we did. And if they kept going straight through the gates, then, provided we knew exactly where the hostages were, we could have them out of there while most of the bad guys were still wondering what woke them up.'

'Where do we get sixty men, boss?'

'We borrow them from the Senegalese.'

Wynwood and Franklin both looked doubtful. 'They're not . . .' Wynwood started to say.

Caskey had anticipated the objection. 'We'd have to give them a rush training course,' he admitted, 'but they are professional soldiers. A few hours' instruction from ours truly, and . . .' He shrugged. 'We're not dealing with a professional enemy here. Think about it.'

The other two did just that. Caskey was the one with the experience, and he was probably right. There was no doubt his plan went to the heart of the matter.

'Will the Senegalese buy it?' Wynwood wondered out loud.

'Will Jawara?' Franklin asked. 'It's his family that's under the gun.'

'Let's ask them,' Caskey suggested.

It turned out that a meeting was scheduled for ten a.m., though whether they would have received any notification of it before the afternoon remained a moot point. As it was, the SAS men's arrival could have been taken as evidence of their possessing a thought-reading capability.

But if General N'Dor was surprised to see them he did not show it. He introduced the SAS men to his second in command, Colonel Aboubakar Ka. The younger man seemed happier to see the British soldiers, offering his hand to each of them with a wide smile. 'I have heard much about your Regiment,' he told Caskey.

Five minutes later Jawara's Vice-President arrived, and the meeting got under way. Colonel Ka confirmed that there had been no substantial change in the overnight situation, and the General then asked Caskey for any thoughts he might have.

'We have come up with a possible course of action,' Caskey said. He recounted the story of their reconnaissance mission the previous night, notably omitting any mention of their unexpected encounters on the beach, and then went through the plan he had already outlined to Wynwood and Franklin.

General N'Dor's face remained mask-like throughout, but Colonel Ka's seemed torn between enthusiasm and something less sympathetic. The Vice-President showed no sign that he was even listening.

'Let me understand this,' N'Dor said in his awkward English, and then aimed several sentences in French at Ka, who replied in kind. 'You wish to train sixty of my soldiers?'

Caskey was nodding, but Franklin saw what had happened, and jumped in. 'We wish to give them special training for this special operation,' he said.

The General looked at Ka, who again told him something in French. This seemed to mollify N'Dor somewhat.

Caskey had also caught on. 'This is not a comment on your troops, General. If they were regular British soldiers we would still want to give them special instruction for an operation like this.'

'*Alors*,' N'Dor said. 'Good.' He looked at them for a moment, then at the table, then at Ka. 'I think there is no problem with this,' he said at last. 'But you understand, the negotiations are Number One. If they fail, or if there is no progress for many days, then we will consider the action you suggest.' He turned to the Vice-President. 'This is acceptable?' he asked.

'The President does not want any action taken which will unnecessarily put the hostages at risk,' he said, as if reciting a line he had learned off by heart.

It was what N'Dor wanted to hear, at least in so far as the three Englishmen were concerned. If anyone was going to take decisive action he wanted it to be his own men, led by his own officers.

He looked at his watch. 'I shall be talking to the terrorist leader in ten minutes,' he said. 'He may have something new to offer.'

In the Field Force depot's command room Jabang was receiving a report from Taal.

'They made no attempt to advance during the night,' Taal said. 'And there is no sign of any this morning.'

Jabang's eyes lit up. 'Stalemate,' he said contentedly. 'So.' He got up and started pacing to and fro across the bare wooden floor. 'Do we try and force them back?'

'Not unless you want to start killing the prisoners,' Taal said.

'Not unless I have to,' Jabang muttered, as if to himself. 'So what do I tell this General? And how do we know that Jawara will accept any deal the Senegalese make?'

Taal shrugged. 'We get him to make a public announcement. And we've already agreed what to ask them for . . .'

'No deadline?' Jabang asked.

'No.'

'OK.' He took a deep breath and picked up the phone. 'Get me the number now,' he told their man at the Bakau exchange.

It rang almost immediately – once, twice, three times. Jabang was beginning to think the idiot had got him a wrong number when someone at the other end answered, and the gruff tones of General N'Dor barked 'yes!?' in Wollof – '*waaw*!?'

'*Jamanga fanaan*, General,' Jabang said.

'Good morning,' N'Dor echoed, with an equal lack of sincerity.

'I would like to commend you on moving your troops back as we requested,' Jabang said.

N'Dor said nothing.

'Let me be completely honest with you, General,' Jabang continued. 'Our coup has failed. Not because the people of The Gambia wanted it to fail, but because the leader they do not want had already arranged to have a foreign army on hand to put him back in power. I . . .'

'I am not interested in political speeches,' N'Dor interrupted him.

'Of course not,' Jabang agreed sardonically. 'What soldier can afford to be? The point I am making is that we are realists here, not starry-eyed idealists who wish to die in a blaze of glory. We accept that this time we have failed.'

'We can agree on that much.'

Jabang ignored the sarcasm. 'We would like transport for three hundred men,' he said. 'However many planes that requires. And of course free passage to the airport. If this is arranged then we will release all the hostages – with the exception of Lady Jawara and the wife of the Senegalese envoy – at the airport. Lady Jawara and Madame Diop will be released when we reach our destination.'

'Which is?'

'That has not yet been finalized. But the planes must carry enough fuel for a four-thousand-mile journey.'

Cuba rather than Libya, N'Dor thought. 'Is that all?' he asked.

'That is all,' Jabang agreed.

'Then I will pass on your demands to my government, and to the government of The Gambia. I would guess they will have decided their reply by this time tomorrow.'

Jabang said nothing for a moment, wondering whether to challenge the length of time. No, he decided. 'We shall be waiting,' he said, but could not resist adding: 'and the hostages too.'

There was a click at the other end as N'Dor hung up.

'When?' Taal wanted to know.

'This time tomorrow. Do you think they will buy it, Junaidi? Surely the man wants his children alive more than he wants us dead?'

Taal shook his head. 'I don't know,' he said. 'I don't know.'

Some six miles to the west N'Dor was recounting the conversation to Ka, the Vice-President and the three SAS men. Caskey had originally asked if he could listen in on the other line, so as to get some idea of what sort of man they were dealing with, but N'Dor had refused, ostensibly because there was no point in an Englishman listening in to a conversation in Wollof.

'There were no new threats?' Caskey asked.

'They still threaten to kill the hostages,' N'Dor said.

'But there are no new deadlines?'

'No.'

'And no deadline for providing them with their planes?'

'No.'

'They are bluffing,' Caskey said.

'Why do you say so?' Ka wanted to know.

'If they had any intention of really killing the hostages then they would be tying themselves to deadlines, and killing one each time we failed to deliver. They are deliberately not putting themselves into a corner where they have to kill somebody. Because they don't want to.'

'You are not suggesting these are model citizens?' Ka asked with a smile, translating his remark into French for the General.

'Of course not. They may have just worked out that a dead hostage is no use to anyone, including them. As long as they don't do anything too barbaric,' he went on, 'they are giving us the chance to say – well, they're not so bad, why not let them go?'

'You may be right,' N'Dor interjected. 'And if you are, then it seems less risky for the hostages to continue the negotiation, *n'est-ce pas?* If we follow your plan to attack the depot they may start killing in the panic.'

'I think we could have the hostages safe before there was any chance of that,' Caskey insisted.

'Maybe,' N'Dor said in a tone that implied the opposite. He stood up to indicate the meeting was over. 'Colonel Ka will give you the men you need for this special training,' he said. '*Pour l'éventualité.* But I do not think we will need this operation.'

An hour later four lorries containing sixty-four Senegalese troops rolled up outside the Victoria Sports Ground, which Caskey had chosen as the only available piece of open ground in the immediate neighbourhood. While waiting for the Senegalese to arrive, however, he had become more aware of its primary disadvantage – openness to the public eye. Too many people seemed to be hanging around its edges wondering what the Englishmen were doing.

'You're a runner, Frankie,' Caskey said as the Senegalese disembarked. 'How about taking this lot for a run while Joss and I find somewhere more private for the training? We need some idea of how fit they are.'

'OK, boss. A couple of miles enough?'

'Perfect. Take them on a tour of sunny Banjul.'

Caskey gathered together the NCOs, explained what was happening, and handed them over to Franklin. He led them off at a jogging pace, down Leman Street towards the centre of the town. The streets still seemed half-deserted, but those Gambians who were up and about all stopped to stare at the sight of a man in civilian clothes leading sixty-four African soldiers down the middle of the road.

He took them down about three-quarters of a mile, cut through to the river, and led them back up Wellington Street. Several men were breathing pretty heavily, but it was a hot and humid morning. No one had collapsed with exhaustion or fallen far behind. They were fitter than Franklin had expected.

Back at the Sports Ground, Caskey had disappeared and Wynwood was busy loading two tins of paint, one red and one orange, into the cab of one of the lorries. 'Let's get them all aboard,' he told Franklin. 'It's prison for them,' he added with a straight face.

Caskey returned, and they set off in convoy for Banjul Prison, which he had managed to borrow from the authorities for their training ground. On the way he explained what he had in mind. 'This has to be a belt-and-braces op,' he began, 'because that's about all we've got. Guns and half a dozen stun grenades. We didn't bring anything fancy with us, and there's sod-all chance of finding anything around here. So . . . that's the bad news. The good news is that the enemy is probably no better off. We're not likely to be worrying about remote detonations or anything like that. It'll just be in and at 'em.' He paused for breath. 'Now as you two youngsters probably know, the most likely way to get shot in these situations is by your own side. And that goes for the hostages too – they're more likely to get shot by one of their rescuers than they are by the terrorists. So what we need to do with this lot is just concentrate on making them aware of what they should be shooting at and how. With the aid of those tins of paint we can turn one of the cell blocks here into a rough copy of the Killing House back home. No fancy mirrors of course, and no live targets either, but it should give them an idea. OK?'

'Yes, boss,' the other two said in unison. Both were secretly impressed.

They arrived at the prison, met and overcame the warden's expected resistance to their plans – 'but who will pay to have the cells redecorated?' – temporarily transferred the two murderers to the female wing, and lined up the Senegalese for Caskey to explain the morning's activities. He had to do this twice, since none of the Senegalese admitted to not understanding his French until after he had finished. The second time round one of the NCOs translated, although exactly how well no one was sure.

In the meantime Franklin and Wynwood had been busy painting figure outlines on cell walls in both red and orange, the idea being that the red ones represented the enemy, while the orange ones stood for the hostages. The Senegalese would be expected to fire bullets into the trunk of each rebel without injuring any of their captives. Since the two colours were not that dissimilar, particularly in light conditions which varied from cell to cell, it would not be an easy task.

The Senegalese seemed to enjoy it though, and by the afternoon had shown a substantial improvement. The morning's training had decimated the hostages, but in the session after lunch – which arrived by Senegalese mess lorry, and which proved considerably less tasty than the meals-on-wheels Wynwood's grandmother received – only two were killed.

Shortly after lunch the architectural plans Caskey had been waiting for arrived by motorcycle, and he used one cell wall and the remainder of the paint to copy out a large diagram of the Field Force depot layout. Through the afternoon groups of Senegalese were brought in to familiarize themselves with the basic layout, so that when more detailed information became available it would be easier to assimilate.

By five o'clock Caskey was well satisfied with the day's work. He reckoned that these men were capable of doing the job that was required of them, and was pleased to find that both Wynwood and Franklin agreed with him. The problem, he already knew, would be persuading General N'Dor to let them try.

Night had almost fallen by the time Franklin had washed all the dust out of his body and hair. He stood at the palace window rubbing himself with a large towel, watching the last vestiges of the tropical sunset being consumed by the darkness. Having put on his last set of clean clothes, he looked around the bathroom for something to wash the others with, thinking that in a palace there should be someone to do the laundry for him. 'And just who did you have in mind, boy?' he could hear his mother say.

He smiled to himself and used the hand soap to wash out some underwear, socks and a T-shirt.

Caskey had gone off to fill in McGrath on the day's events, and God only knew what the two of them would be getting up to. Franklin would not put it past them to invade Senegal, replace the Government, and have the new lot recall N'Dor, just so they could lead the charge on the Field Force depot.

And why not? Franklin asked himself.

As for Wynwood, he had gone off to the Atlantic Hotel to try and ring his wife. An exercise which would probably take up all of his evening and half the night.

Franklin rinsed out the washed clothes, hung them on the shower rail and went back to the window, wondering what to do. Who was he kidding? He had spoken to only two other people in The Gambia, and he had no desire to drop in on General N'Dor. Still, the thought of visiting the doctor made him unusually nervous.

She probably would not be there, he decided, as he walked out through the palace gates and across the road to the hospital entrance. But she was, and even flashed him a quick smile over the heads of the half-dozen or so patients waiting for her attention. He settled down in the reception area to wait – something for which the Army had trained him well.

After about fifteen minutes she suddenly appeared at his shoulder, and sat down beside him, smelling faintly of disinfectant. 'I can't talk for more than a moment,' she said. 'We seem to be having a busy evening, though . . .'

'Can I help at all?' he asked.

She gave him a doubtful glance.

'We each have an area of expertise,' he said. 'Mine's medicine. I mean, I'm not a doctor, or anything, but I can do basic tasks . . .'

'I never turn down offers of help,' she said. 'If you're sure . . .?'

'A soldier's life is nine-tenths boredom,' he said. 'I'd be happy to.'

'You can read vital signs?'

'Yep.'

'Then follow me.'

For the next two hours he took temperatures, read pulses and checked blood pressures on all the new arrivals, and when required helped with the application of dressings. Most of the patients had the sort of complaints that a GP might have dealt with in England, but there were also several real emergency cases, like a woman who had just bloodily miscarried and a man who seemed to have had a mild stroke. The only evidence of the political emergency still in progress came from a man with a three-day-old bullet wound that had become infected.

While he worked Franklin observed the way Sibou dealt with the patients, watched her rummage for drugs in an impossibly disorganized cupboard, and listened in on her end of conversations with other parts of the hospital. One of the latter would long stick in his mind: she was saying that yes, she knew there were no beds available, but that this new patient – the woman who had miscarried – had to have one, and that so-and-so, who was going to be released on the following day in any case, would just to have to spend the night in 'the chair with arms'.

It was gone nine o'clock when the last patient had been dealt with, and the concertina door pulled shut.

'What happens between now and morning?' Franklin asked. 'If there's an emergency?'

'You mean, if an ambulance brings someone in from one of the villages?' she asked.

'Yes . . . oh, I see what you mean.'

'If someone rich cuts his finger off by accident then he takes a taxi to his private doctor. He'd never use this hospital anyway. And in a country with no ambulances and not many telephones someone poor who can manage to get himself to this hospital in the middle of the night either lives just round the corner or probably doesn't need treatment that badly. There are people here who can deal with the exceptions, but it only happens about twice a year.'

'Like the last few days.'

'Fortunately we don't have that many coups,' she said, taking off her white coat and hanging it on the back of her office door. Underneath it she was wearing brightly tie-dyed African trousers and a dark-blue shirt.

'I haven't eaten,' Franklin said. 'Would you like . . .?'

'I have my supper,' she said, indicating a plastic box. But she did not feel like dispensing with his company, not for a while anyway. 'I'll share it with you,' she said.

'What, here?'

'We can take it to the beach. It's only a five-minute walk.'

It took even less. The moon had not yet risen, and the horizon between sea and sky was black meeting black. The only light came from the stars, with the Milky Way hanging directly above them like a dim but particularly beautiful fluorescent tube.

'Do you often come out here?' he asked, as they sat down side by side in the sand, facing in the direction of the dark sea.

'In the daytime. I bring my lunch out here when I can. After dark it's not so safe any more.'

'Was it ever?'

'Oh yes,' she said, surprised that he should ask. She handed him something which was similar in size and consistency to a vegetable samosa. 'This was an incredibly peaceful country until recently,' she said. 'There was hardly any crime at all.'

'What changed it?' Franklin asked between bites. Whatever it was, it tasted good.

'Who knows? Most of the world seems to be going the same way. Maybe it's just that more people are aware of what they haven't got, and can see no good reason why other people have. I don't know . . . Frankie is your name, isn't it?'

'That's just a nickname. Worrell is my real name.'

'Where do you come from, Worrell?'

'Brixton. In south London.'

'I know it. I was a medical student at Guy's, near London Bridge.' As she said it, she wondered what had made this man want to be a soldier. He seemed too gentle in some ways – in fact, if his work that evening was anything to go by, he would have made a fine doctor. She found herself wondering what his touch would be like, and scolded herself. This was just loneliness talking, a voice in her head said. Then let it talk, another replied.

He broke the silence. 'I want to ask why you came back here,' he said, 'but I think I know the answer.'

'You do?' She flashed a challenging smile in the darkness.

'You can do more good here.'

'Maybe that's part of it,' she said. 'Maybe a big part. I guess I'd like to think so. But it's not everything. I am a Gambian, an African. This is my home. It may not be a very rich or rewarding home in some ways, but it still feels like one. And in any case we can't all be born in London or Paris.'

'I was born in Jamaica,' Franklin said.

'Do you want to go back there?' she asked.

'I left it when I was three. England is my home.'

'You don't sound very enthusiastic.'

'You've lived there – you know what it's like.'

'You mean the racism? I guess I've forgotten. Or maybe I was lucky. Medical students live in a world of their own, and they come in all colours. What about the Army? You seem to get on all right with the others . . .'

'I only just met them, but yes, the Army's OK, most of the time. How long have you known Simon McGrath?'

'A couple of months. He saved me from an attack. Do you know the story?'

'No.'

'I was in the hospital one evening, and this man came in with a knife. He came to steal drugs, but he was high on something and he made a spur-of-the-moment decision that he wanted me too.' Her voice was almost playful, but Franklin could hear the tension beneath. 'Well, he hit me a couple of times in the face, and started tearing off my clothes . . . there were patients watching, but he told them if they interfered he'd cut my throat. And he enjoyed the fact that they were watching. Simon came in at just the right moment, and simply took the knife away from the man. It was miraculous really. He just made it look so easy.'

'What happened to the man?'

'He was given five years in prison. But . . .'

'Was he one of the men the rebels released?'

'They released everyone, I think. Yes, he's out there somewhere. And I can't say it makes me feel very good,' she added, grasping both arms around her knees and hugging herself.

He thought about putting an arm around her, but decided not to. 'I'm not surprised,' he murmured, and tried to think of another subject.

'Shall we walk for a bit?' she asked.

'Yeah, why not.'

She led the way down to the water's edge, and they walked along beside it in the direction of the Atlantic Hotel beach. The two boys from that morning came into his mind, and he told her the history of the entire encounter, right up to his over-generous donation. 'I thought afterwards it was a bad thing to do, but . . .'

'A pen is better,' she said, but the look on her face seemed to say that he had done the right thing.

'Do you have a boyfriend?' he asked.

'No,' she said. 'I . . .'

'Could I kiss you?' he asked suddenly, surprising even himself.

'I don't see why not,' she said, and turned into his arms, laying both of hers across his shoulders and turning her face up to his. In the dim light her loveliness almost took his breath away, and as they kissed the absurd notion went through his mind that he had finally come home.

The kiss stretched out, feeding their mutual hunger for company, sex, love, each other. Franklin felt himself hardening, and for the first time since he was sixteen felt embarrassed by it. He tried to pull himself gently away, but she dropped her hands to his haunches and pulled him back.

And then they were kneeling in front of each other and removing their shirts, kissing some more, and finally sinking onto the sand and kicking their trousers away.

12

General N'Dor arrived fifteen minutes early at the Senegalese Embassy in Cameron Street, lit a cigarette and began pacing up and down the carpeted room. He never seemed to get a moment to himself at the military HQ in Serekunda, and he felt the need of some space to think in. The Embassy staff, unlike his own, seemed prepared to leave him alone.

He was not looking forward to another conversation with Comrade Jabang. 'Never take responsibility for something without first securing the necessary control,' he recited to himself. Where had his memory dragged that up from?

It was certainly pertinent. Here he was, with the responsibility for bringing these negotiations to a successful conclusion, but none of the necessary control. On the contrary, he was being given contradictory 'advice' from all over the place. The Gambian President, not surprisingly, wanted him to be patient, to take no risks with the hostages. Meanwhile his own Government was being pressured by the French, who in turn were probably being urged on by the British, to do something. The European tourists had been deprived of their European comforts for a few more days than they had expected, and wanted to go home. After all he had the famous

SAS at his disposal, so why not use them? They had got the hostages out at the Iranian Embassy in London. All but one of them, anyway.

N'Dor asked himself whether he was being unreasonable. The thought of two white men leading sixty black Senegalese into battle seemed so redolent of the past, such an insult to his country, that he found it hard to consider the matter in a purely practical manner. But there were other, less emotional reasons for opposing the Englishmen's plan. This was not London, there had not been three hundred armed men in the Iranian Embassy, and one of them had not been the Prime Minister's wife. Such an assault simply left too much to chance.

He told himself he had to keep an open mind. There probably was no course of action which did not carry serious risks. He simply had to keep a cool head, listen and evaluate.

N'Dor stubbed out his cigarette with a feeling of having reached some sort of conclusion.

The illusion lasted through the arrival of Caskey and the Vice-President, and almost a minute into their meeting. Then the Vice-President announced that he had brought with him the President's counter-offer to the terrorists. Provided that they laid down their arms and returned the hostages unharmed, the President promised a maximum of five years in prison for all former members of the Field Force. He was also prepared to agree a secret deal whereby the twelve members of the Revolutionary Council would be flown into permanent exile.

'Divide and rule,' Caskey murmured to himself. Jawara must have been educated in England.

'What is your opinion, Major?' N'Dor asked him.

'It's hard to say without more information about who we're dealing with. As I said yesterday, my instinct is that they're bluffing. In which case, offering them less makes sense. But,

214

General, your people must have talked to the envoy who was rescued at the radio station – I forget his name. What were his opinions of the rebels?'

'His name is Mustapha Diop,' N'Dor said. 'And it was Colonel Ka who spoke to him.'

'Monsieur Diop seems unable to make up his mind about them,' Ka said drily. 'They took him on a ride around Banjul to show him how much support their revolution had, and there was no one on the streets. He laughed when he told me the story. But it was not happy laughter, you understand. I think they frightened him a lot. Not so much with their threats, but because he never knew what they would do next. He seems to think they didn't know themselves, but from what we've seen I'm not sure he is correct in that. He is very concerned about his wife and children, of course.'

'Not much help there,' Caskey said. 'There is one thing we should ask for,' he went on, 'an expression of good faith on their part. The release of the children would seem a reasonable request in the circumstances.'

'I am sure the President would wish such a request to be made,' the Vice-President agreed.

'A good idea,' N'Dor said, thinking of his own children back in Dakar.

'It is almost eleven o'clock,' Ka said, looking at his watch.

N'Dor reached for the telephone, thinking that Jawara's offer had at least removed some of the responsibility from his own shoulders. If the rebels responded by shooting the Gambian President's wife, then no one could blame the Senegalese Army.

The phone rang several times before Jabang picked it up. 'You are early,' he said in response to N'Dor's good morning.

'I will call again,' N'Dor said shortly.

'No, it doesn't matter.' There was a momentary pause. 'Do you have the President's answer to our ultimatum?'

'We were not aware that it was an ultimatum,' N'Dor said. Jabang sounded on edge this morning, which was hardly a good sign. 'We consider this a negotiating process,' he added, 'a bargaining process without a fixed time limit.'

'We are in no hurry,' Jabang said, more coolly. 'Call it what you like. What is the answer?'

'The answer to the first demand is no, as it always is in a bargaining process,' N'Dor said calmly. 'But . . .'

'We are not discussing the purchase of a piece of cloth,' Jabang interjected coldly.

'Of course not. There are many lives at stake – those of the hostages you hold, yourselves and your men, my own men. I am not treating this matter lightly, Mr Jabang.'

There was silence at the other end.

N'Dor decided to continue. 'President Jawara is prepared to allow the twelve members of your Council free passage out of the country, and a maximum term of five years' imprisonment for all former members of the Field Force. All this depends on the unconditional surrender of all weapons and the absolute safety of the hostages. We would also like you to demonstrate your good faith by releasing all the children under the age of fourteen.'

The silence at the other end continued for what seemed an age, but was probably no more than fifteen seconds. 'I will call you back in an hour,' Jabang said, and hung up.

McGrath had spent the morning nursing a hangover and continuing his reluctant readjustment to civilian life. On the previous day, while the three current members of the SAS had been introducing the Senegalese to the joys of continuation training, he had been trying to gather information on how much damage had been wreaked on The Gambia's infrastructure by a week of political turmoil.

Not a lot, apparently. There might be well over a thousand dead according to the latest unofficial reckoning, but only two bridges and one electricity line were down. Another triumph for underdevelopment, he thought sourly.

His thoughts slipped back to two nights before, and the reconnaissance mission behind the rebel lines. It might have been a thousand times as dangerous as sitting behind a desk, but it had not felt half so much like work. He shook his head, which turned out to be a mistake.

'More coffee,' he muttered to himself, and was busy spooning Nescafé into a chipped mug when Jobo Camara came through the office door.

'Wasn't expecting you until next week,' McGrath said.

'I'm not here to work,' Jobo said with a grin. 'But my shoulder is OK, and I will be in tomorrow. Today is just a social visit – I came to see how the English hero of the radio station is doing.'

'I've become a legend in my own time, have I?' McGrath asked wryly.

'Don't worry about it,' Jobo told him, 'there are no plans for a statue. Not yet, anyway.'

McGrath laughed. 'They should put up one of that Senegalese with the wicked back-heel. It would make an interesting tableau.'

'My uncle told me about that. I'm going to see him now, at the police station. Want to come along?'

McGrath looked down. Whatever Mansa Camara was doing, it was bound to be more interesting than the stuff lying on the desk in front of him. 'Sure,' he said, 'I'll give you a lift.'

During the two-minute drive Jobo filled in McGrath on his uncle's sudden elevation to the position of Field Force commander in the capital. 'It must have been the radio station capture,' Jobo said, 'though I guess my uncle had a good reputation before the coup. Anyway, the President just promoted him on the spot.'

It was unlikely to be a long-lasting position though, as Mansa himself explained over coffee in his new office. 'That is the worst of this business,' he said. 'The Gambia has never had an army, but now we will have one. So that the next time this happens the President will be able to use his own troops rather than the Senegalese.' He grimaced. 'Always assuming that next time it is not his own army mounting the coup.'

'Uncle!' Jobo protested.

'What, boy?' Mansa asked. 'You expect me to forget about truth because the President gives me a good job? I'd rather go back to the village.'

'The Gambia will still need a police force,' McGrath interjected diplomatically.

'Yes, of course. But something good has ended. Maybe . . .'

There was a knock on the door, and a Field Force officer burst in, excitedly clenching his fists in front of him. 'It has been seen,' he cried. 'Sir,' he added as an afterthought.

Mansa was halfway out of his seat. 'Where?' he asked.

'In the Albert Market.'

Mansa was reaching for his uniform jacket.

'What has been seen?' McGrath asked.

'The mobile radio van that the rebels have been broadcasting from. We have been looking for it since Saturday.' He was on his way out of the door. 'Mr McGrath, I'm sorry to leave so suddenly but . . .'

They followed him down the stairs to where five men were waiting, all carrying Kalashnikovs. Mansa strode out through the door, beckoning the three men after him.

McGrath followed at a more leisurely pace, sorry to be missing out on whatever excitement was about to take place. He need not have worried – this was obviously the week for his guardian angel to keep him in the thick of things.

On the other side of the door he found Mansa waiting patiently for someone to bring a vehicle round. A few seconds later an officer emerged at a run from around the building. 'All the cars are out,' he told Mansa, who stood there looking like he could not believe it for a good ten seconds.

'You can borrow the Ministry jeep,' McGrath offered, 'provided you also borrow the driver.'

Mansa rolled his eyes at the sky. 'Yes, yes,' he said.

A minute later they were careering north along Wellington Street, McGrath and Mansa in front, three men in the back, and two more clinging to the sides.

'What does it look like?' McGrath shouted.

'Just a small Leyland truck. It has Radio Gambia written on the side, or at least used to have. If it's transmitting there will be an aerial . . .'

McGrath took the left fork onto Russell Street on two wheels, narrowly missing a lorry going in the opposite direc-tion. There was no aerial, no Radio Gambia on the side, but it did look as though it had been recently painted, and it was a Leyland. He slowed sufficiently to make a U-turn without losing his passengers.

'What are you doing?' Mansa asked in surprise.

McGrath pointed at the truck, which was now about a hundred yards ahead of them. 'That's them,' he said, hoping to God he was right.

'Are you sure?'

'Ninety per cent,' he said, 'but there's one easy way to find out.' He rammed his foot on the accelerator and simultaneously sounded the jeep's horn. The driver in front took a sudden right turn, and then left at the next crossroads, before accelerating up Buckle Street past the fire station.

McGrath was now only fifty yards adrift. Both vehicles were doing about sixty, which was quite a speed for a main street that was only about half a mile long.

The van slowed dramatically to turn, shrinking the distance between them and giving McGrath a glimpse of two worried African faces in its back windows, then accelerated away. A rifle went off almost in McGrath's ear – one of the Field Force men had got overexcited and shot out a shop window. Mansa shouted at the man to sit down, and McGrath had a mental memory of Keystone Kops films he had seen as a child.

The van turned again, and again. This chase could go on indefinitely, McGrath thought, or at least until one of them ran out of petrol or misjudged a corner. And sooner or later some hapless civilian was going to step out onto the wrong street at the wrong time.

And then the driver in front made his mistake. Maybe he did not know Banjul as well as he thought he did, or maybe he just lost concentration at the wrong moment, but what he expected to be an open street turned out to be full of market stalls, with only a narrow, tunnel-like space between them. He negotiated this with aplomb, scattering pedestrians and bringing down at least two stalls in his wake, but the lack of an obvious path out of the area was his undoing. Reaching open ground he instinctively accelerated, only to find that the street in question ended about twenty yards later, on the ramp that led onto the River Gambia ferry.

Since, by order of the Senegalese authorities, the ferry was still anchored in midstream, the driver of the Leyland van had only his brakes to stop him. These squealed furiously but in vain, and the van skidded over the edge of the ramp and into the water with a mighty splash.

McGrath pulled the jeep up some ten feet short of the edge, and its occupants leapt out to scan the river for the van's occupants. Three at least had managed to get out, and were swimming sheepishly towards the waiting arms of the law.

The van itself was no longer visible, unless one counted the series of large bubbles it was sending to the surface.

Rebel Radio had gone off the air with a vengeance.

In the command room of the Field Force depot the atmosphere was a strange mixture of the electric and the funereal. Eleven men were sitting round the room while the twelfth kept guard at the door. No doubt some of their men could have been trusted to overhear the Council debate Jawara's latest offer, but no one could be certain of knowing which they were.

Jabang had decided to hear the opinions of the other Council members before expressing his own, a decision which he now realized had been a mistake. Three men had so far spoken, and all of them were for at least considering the offer, subject to various safeguards. As one of them said: if they handed back the hostages and laid down their arms, what was to stop the President simply having them all shot? He wanted the children as a token of faith, but what was he offering in return?

For the first time since the business had started Jabang felt a sense of despair gnawing at his heart. 'Junaidi,' he broke in, before a fourth man could counsel surrender, 'what do you think?'

Taal sighed and ran a hand through his thinning hair. 'We cannot accept such an offer,' he said straightforwardly, 'and retain any dignity. Or any political credibility.'

'What choice do we have?' Sallah asked him.

'We have several,' Taal answered him. 'We can fight and die for what we believe. We can attempt to escape without first betraying the men under our command. Or we can continue negotiating – I do not believe they can expect us to accept a deal like this.'

'Is there . . .' Jabang began.

'One last thing,' Taal said. 'We should keep all our people informed as to what the other side is offering. Because the other side may tell them anyway.'

'How could they?' Jabang asked, surprised.

'There are radios in the camp,' Taal said. Sometimes he wondered how someone as clever as Jabang could also be so obtuse. 'Of course, we could confiscate them, but that would look like we don't trust our own men.'

'We don't,' someone pointed out. 'Not all of them. And certainly not the prisoners.'

'We should never have released the prisoners,' Taal said quietly. 'I am not blaming anyone,' he added, 'I agreed to the decision at the time.' He paused. 'I have a suggestion. Let us accept the offer of free passage for ourselves, but only on condition that a general amnesty is granted for all those who have been involved. Except for the prisoners. Look at it from Jawara's point of view – he'll have us in exile, and the prisoners to take out his rage on. Which is hardly unjust, for they were responsible for ninety-nine per cent of the killing in Banjul.'

'And if he agrees we can immediately release the children,' Jabang added.

Twenty minutes later only he and Taal remained in the command room for the call to General N'Dor.

'As in any bargaining process,' Jabang began ironically, 'the first counter-offer is also refused. We are prepared to accept the offer of free passage, provided that a full amnesty is granted to all members of the Socialist and Revolutionary Labour Party. In return, we will release all our hostages and take all the former inmates of Banjul Prison back into custody. If you wish to accept these terms, then have the offers of free passage and amnesty announced on the radio at ten a.m. tomorrow, and we will release all the children at midday.'

'You don't wish us to mention the rearrest of the prisoners?' N'Dor asked, managing to keep most of the sarcasm out of his tone.

'That would not be in our interest or yours,' Jabang said coldly. 'Do you have any questions?'

'No, that seems clear,' N'Dor said. He did not suppose for a moment that Jawara would accept such terms, but they were certainly clear.

'Ten a.m. tomorrow,' Jabang repeated, and hung up.

After the unsatisfactory discussion with N'Dor, Caskey had returned to the prison, where Wynwood and Franklin were still attempting to hone the skills of the Senegalese. Some had taken to the course like fish to water, while others had proved more resistant to developing a capacity for instant decision-making. Rank seemed to play little part in this, and the two SAS troopers were busy trying to gather together their best students in the first assault teams without ruffling any feathers.

'No joy?' Wynwood asked, seeing the look on Caskey's face.

'No. I have a feeling the bastard would rather have all the hostages shot than accept any help from us.'

'He hasn't called it off?'

'No,' Caskey admitted. 'But he might as well. How are they doing?' he asked, meaning the Senegalese.

OK, Wynwood thought. 'If the General gave them the chance I think he'd probably end up feeling proud of them.'

Caskey sighed. 'Well, let's keep them at it. We've got nothing better to do.'

For the next two hours they continued with the simulated assaults, noting a steady improvement in their trainees' reflexes when it came to distinguishing hostages from jailers. Caskey was about to call it a day, and wondering whether to try using praise of his troops to change N'Dor's mind, when one of the prison guards – all of whom had greatly enjoyed watching the exercises – came up to tell him that an Englishman was at the gate asking for him.

Not surprisingly it was McGrath. 'Thought you'd like to know,' McGrath started without preamble, 'one of the rebel leaders has been arrested. Apparently just walked across no man's land and gave himself up.'

'Where is he?'

'At N'Dor's HQ in Serekunda. I imagine he's spilling a lot of useful information about his comrades' state of mind, not to mention the layout inside the Bakau depot and the exact location of the hostages.'

'You're not kidding,' Caskey agreed. 'How on earth did you find out – have you got spies everywhere?'

'I have,' McGrath said modestly. 'No, his name's Sharif Sallah, and he used to be number two in the Banjul Field Force unit, so someone at Serekunda must have phoned the Banjul police station with the news. That's where I heard about it.'

'And what were you doing in the Banjul Police Station?'

'Oh, just coming back from fishing Radio Gambia out of the river.'

'What?'

'It's a long story. And I've got to get back. I'll tell you later.'

He disappeared back through the gate. Caskey called over Wynwood and Franklin, told them the news, and announced that he was off to pay General N'Dor a visit.

'Good luck,' Franklin said.

'Be tactful,' Wynwood advised.

Caskey considered this advice as he drove the jeep across the Denton Bridge, and decided to hell with it. If the defector, whatever his name was, had any information which made it either easier or more imperative to launch their operation then he was going to tell General N'Dor so. And if the General did not like it, he could stick it up his Senegalese arse. And Caskey would take it straight to Jawara.

Diplomacy was for the diplomats.

At the Serekunda HQ General N'Dor was less than pleased to see Caskey, and angry that someone should have informed the Englishmen of the rebel defection without express sanction from himself, but he remained as politely dour as ever.

'Colonel Ka is interrogating him now,' he told Caskey, who immediately asked if he could join the interrogation team.

The General could think of no good reason for saying no, and a minute later Caskey was being escorted by an NCO out into the yard behind the building, where Colonel Ka was sitting behind a collapsible table in the shadow of a huge baobab tree. A few yards in front of him, and sweating profusely in the fierce sun, the defector perched uneasily on an upright wooden chair.

Things were not going quite the way Sharif Sallah had wanted. He realized now that he had acted somewhat

225

precipitately, but sitting there in the Field Force depot command room, listening to Jabang and Taal throw away what seemed like their last chance of escaping retribution, he had inwardly succumbed to panic. If they would not accept Jawara's offer, he had reasoned to himself, then that was their affair. There was no reason why he should have to pay for their determination to martyr themselves. Why should he not simply accept the offer for himself?

He had waited half an hour and then simply asked one of the drivers to take him to the front line. The man had not thought to question him, for he was, after all, one of the leaders. And the rebel soldiers at the front had accepted his story that he was delivering a message to the enemy under a flag of truce. He had marched down the road with the white shirt held over his head and surrendered himself.

Once he had been driven to Serekunda, Sallah was told in no uncertain terms that no deal had been struck, and in rather vaguer ones that an unpleasant choice between jail and the noose was still his to make. If he cooperated fully, it was hinted, he might live to enjoy a life in Banjul Prison.

Sallah had not been prepared for this, and, rather than think things through, he had found himself entangled in the coils of self-justification. Since he could not admit to betraying his friends merely to save his own skin, he found it necessary to paint a highly exaggerated picture of his fellow Council members as confused, dangerous and unpredictable. If the negotiations failed, he said, they would undoubtedly kill both the hostages and themselves. He could not be part of such actions, he said. He was and ever had been a revolutionary, he emphasized, but history had always shown that revolutionary change could not be bought at the price of killing women and children.

He was going through this story again when Caskey arrived, and by the second time it had gained something in the telling. Caskey realized Sallah was trying to save his own hide, and thought him despicable on account of it, but he had no reason to doubt the traitor's description of the rebels' state of mind as a mixture of the desperate and the resigned.

'There's no knowing when they'll blow a fuse,' Caskey told N'Dor.

The General did not understand Caskey's meaning, but he had a shrewd idea of what was being said from the Englishman's red face and aggressive tone.

'We have finished the training programme,' Caskey went on. 'They are excellent soldiers,' he added diplomatically. 'All we need to mount the operation tonight is your say-so.'

'That is not possible,' N'Dor said.

'Why not, for Christ's sake?' Caskey asked, rapidly losing the battle to keep his temper in check.

N'Dor eyed him coldly. 'For one reason, *I* am not convinced that yours is the best plan for the situation. And *I* am the man responsible for the conduct of operations, for the lives of my troops and the lives of the hostages.'

Caskey stared back at him. 'Did you ever have any intention of allowing this operation?' he asked.

'It is one of the options,' N'Dor said. 'And that is all.'

Caskey drove back to the prison, where Wynwood and Franklin had ordered a break in the training programme. 'They've had enough,' Wynwood told Caskey.

'Then send 'em back,' Caskey said. 'It doesn't look like we'll be needing them.' He told them what Sharif Sallah had said, and what N'Dor's reaction had been.

'He wants to do it his way,' Wynwood muttered.

'You can see his point,' Franklin said. 'Even if he's wrong,' he added in response to a glare from Caskey.

Wynwood and Franklin informed the Senegalese NCOs that the day's training was over, and watched them load their charges into the three lorries for the trip back to their camp near the airport. Then they joined Caskey, who was sitting motionless in the jeep's driving seat, apparently watching the sun go down across the distant sea.

'So what now, boss?' Wynwood asked.

'That's what I've been wondering,' Caskey said, making no attempt to start the engine. 'Any ideas?'

The three men sat in silence for a minute or more, each going over the situation in his mind.

'There's no way we could get any of the hostages out without raising the alarm,' Wynwood said. 'Especially children.'

'I have an idea,' Franklin said.

'Go on,' Caskey encouraged him.

'I was talking to Sibou – to Dr Cham . . .'

'I should think a lot of people have had that idea,' Wynwood commented.

Franklin ignored him. 'She told me there's another hospital about a quarter of a mile up the road from the Field Force depot. It's called the Medical Research Centre, and it's part-research establishment, part-hospital. It's run with British Government money, and there are about five doctors from England working there. If we could get some of the hostages – say, Lady Chilel and her children – to pretend they were sick enough to need a doctor, then maybe the rebels would take them to the hospital . . .'

'Why would they not just bring the doctor to the depot?' Caskey asked.

'The doctors could refuse. They'd have to be in on it.'

'If they're English doctors they probably drink like fish,' Caskey conceded, 'in which case Simon will probably know them all.'

'Why would the rebels take the risk, though?' Wynwood wanted to know.

'It won't seem like a risk,' Franklin said. 'This place is behind their lines, so they won't be expecting any trouble.'

'Makes sense,' Wynwood agreed. 'So all we've got to do is call Lady Chilel on the phone and get her to poison her children.'

'All we have to do,' Franklin explained patiently, 'is get to within whispering distance of her and pass over a few laxatives.'

'You mean someone will have to go over the wall?' Caskey said. It was not really a question. 'And the ideal candidate is you, Frankie,' he said. 'You'll be less conspicuous than either of us.'

'I thought he looked like an escaped prisoner the first time I saw him,' Wynwood admitted.

'Mr President,' Caskey began. It had taken an hour and a half's wait, but he had finally secured an audience with the man himself. 'I presume you know what has been going on. We have trained sixty Senegalese troops for a surprise attack on the rebel camp, believing that it is the best way to secure the release of the hostages unharmed. But . . . well, not to beat around the bush, General N'Dor refuses to sanction the operation . . .'

'I have no authority over General N'Dor's troops,' Jawara interjected.

'No, I realize that. And we realize that the operation we planned is a no-go. But given that, we still believe that an attempt could and should be made as quickly as possible to free at least some of the hostages, in particular Lady Chilel and your children. We have another plan which we would like you to consider.'

'This plan does not involve the use of Senegalese troops?'

'No.'

Jawara looked interested. 'Then tell me what you intend,' he said.

13

The three men set out at three in the morning, and the moon was already riding high above the ocean as their jeep sped across the Denton Bridge. The men at the Senegalese check-points passed bleary eyes over their authorizations, and wearily waved them on. The walk across the broken ground to the golf course proved a lot easier by the full light of a risen moon.

Down on the beach the sands were being shrunken by the incoming tide, but this time they planned to use the top of the cliffs for at least a part of their journey up the coastline. Phone calls to several of the hotels and embassies which were situated between the road and the sea had confirmed that a broken path did indeed exist, and would offer a way past any sentries on the beach itself.

Predictably enough, there were none. As they skirted the stretch of beach where Wynwood and McGrath had done their Björn and Benny impersonation, only sea and empty sands were visible below. They passed by the foot of the path which led up into the tunnel of foliage where Franklin had shot dead the rebel. He was presumably still anchored beneath the waves, Franklin thought, and blacked out the mental picture which came to mind.

Once installed in the restaurant's covered terrace, the main gate of the Field Force depot filling the view through Caskey's binoculars, the three men set out to construct a timetable for the patrols covering the inner and outer walls. They had an excellent map of the depot's layout, copied from architectural drawings in the Ministry of the Interior's files, and what they hoped was up to the minute information as to who was in which building at that precise time.

Sharif Sallah might have lied to them but Caskey doubted it. The rebel leaders might have decided to move everyone around once they knew of Sallah's defection, but there was only one block of prison cells, and no other obvious place to keep the hostages. With any luck they would still be where Sallah said they were.

Caskey wondered whether General N'Dor had suspected that they were planning something. Probably, he decided. If they had only wanted Sallah's information for the mass assault contingency plan then it could have waited until the next morning, and N'Dor was not stupid. He just did not want white men leading black men into battle.

'There's the inside mob again,' Wynwood whispered. He wrote the time down, made several calculations in the margins of the map, and turned to the other two. 'Not counting the searchlight,' he said, 'there's a four to five-minute window of opportunity along our wall. The next one begins at four-seventeen – which we couldn't make. The one after that should be at four-thirty-one – which we can.'

'Are they that regular?' Caskey asked.

'Within a couple of minutes, so far.'

Caskey turned to Franklin. 'All set?'

'I can hardly wait.'

Wynwood grinned at him. 'At least if you get constipated you'll have some laxatives with you,' he said.

'Yeah,' Franklin said. 'Whose crazy idea was this?' he muttered to himself.

'Good luck,' Caskey said.

'Thanks, boss,' Franklin replied, and was gone, back down the passage to the beach and along behind several buildings to a point where he could approach the road, out of the sight of both the sentries on the gate and the men in the fire-station tower.

He waited a full minute, checking for any movement that might have escaped their attention, and then silently loped across the road and into the shadows of the trees on the other side. He worked his way towards the depot, slipping across the entrance to the fire station, and stopped where he had planned, in the dark niche between the wall and a drunken-looking palm, some thirty yards from the corner of the Field Force depot.

He looked at his watch – another two minutes and the outer patrol should be rounding the corner. The seconds ticked away, past the appointed time by ten, twenty . . . Then he could hear the footfalls above the breeze in the foliage, and the low murmur of conversation. The two men rounded the corner and walked away from him, the down-pointed barrels of their Kalashnikovs gleaming dully in the moonlight.

Franklin moved forward carefully, more intent on silence than speed, and turned away from the road down the side of the outer wall, conscious that for the first time he was in danger of being picked out by the searchlight. Fortunately its current operator seemed intent on drawing lazy patterns across the area, rather than flashing from space to space in the manner of two nights before.

The SAS man counted his paces as he went, and after one hundred and fifteen he stopped, arranged himself behind the trunk of a convenient tree, and waited again. After a minute or so the searchlight beam snaked past him, catching the top of the eight-foot wall, and then swiftly retraced its path, as if the operator had seen something. Franklin tried harder to make himself as thin as the trunk which shielded him, but it proved to be a false alarm. He took a deep breath and carried on waiting.

The patrol on the inner wall were also later than the schedule dictated – almost a minute later. He listened to the sound of their feet grow and fade, gave himself another thirty seconds for luck, and then swung himself athletically up onto the top of the wall. He barely had time to drop down into the depot grounds before the searchlight beam swept past him once more.

The building almost immediately in front of him was, according to the defector, a storeroom. The one behind it should be the barrack block which had been converted into police cells. Sallah had said it did not have exterior guards of its own, but Franklin took no chances, watching and listening from a position behind the corner of the storeroom for a good two minutes.

The patrols apart, the camp seemed to be mostly asleep. He thought he saw a cigarette flare in the distant gloom, and definitely heard someone laugh away to his right, but the cell block seemed devoid of life. Franklin stepped out across the space, hoping that this did not mean the hostages had already been shot.

The cell at the end was supposed to hold Lady Jawara and four of the President's children. Sallah had not known whether it had a window, but the general opinion had been that it should have, and Franklin dearly hoped the general opinion was right.

There was a window, though it was not the one he had imagined. It occurred to him that he had been expecting a space with bars across it, like a jail window in a Western. He had only to pull out a stick of dynamite, light it from his cheroot, throw it through the bars and grin at the camera. Which film was that in? One of Clint Eastwood's . . . He smiled to himself in the gloom and examined the real window. It had horizontal bars across the outside, slatted glass shutters on the inside, and a mosquito screen full of holes in between the two. Inside he could hear someone snoring.

He took out his knife and used it to beat a gentle tattoo on the slatted glass. Thinking he heard someone stir he chanced a loud whisper of 'come to the window', but no one came. He tried a little louder with the knife, praying that anyone outside would think it was something caught in the wind.

'Who is it?' a frightened voice asked. One of the children.

'A friend,' Franklin whispered. 'Come to the window so that I can talk to you,' he went on. 'But be very quiet.'

The child came into view – a little girl of no more than five, her lovely large eyes brimming with apprehension and curiosity.

'I have come from your father,' Franklin said softly, 'to give a message to your mother. Can you wake her up for me?'

The girl examined his face, as if she was searching for honesty. 'My father is the President,' she said.

'I know,' he told her. 'I have a message from him for your mother. Can you wake her up?'

'OK,' she said, and disappeared again.

Franklin could hear the child talking to someone, heard someone else groan and mutter angrily, then a loud 'sssshhhh', followed by 'don't you sssshhhh me, girl!' The child's voice started again, and half a minute later the face of Lady Child Jawara appeared in front of Franklin. 'Who are you and what is all this?' she asked in a haughty whisper.

'I am a British soldier,' Franklin said. 'Here's a letter from your husband to prove that I'm genuine.' He passed it through the window. 'Read it after I'm gone – I don't have much time. First thing tomorrow morning we want you to ask them to let your children see a doctor – Dr Greenwell at the Medical Research Centre up the road. Tell the people in charge here that he's their usual doctor. He will refuse to come here, so then you must demand that yourself and the children be taken up there to see him. Under guard, of course. Then leave the rest to us.' He fished in his pocket for the vial of pills. 'These will give you all diarrhoea and a slight fever,' he said, 'without doing you any permanent harm.'

'After five days of rice and water we already have diarrhoea,' she said, then shook her head as if unable to quite believe what was going on.

'Any questions?' he asked, looking at his watch. He had two minutes to get back across the wall.

She thought for a good ten seconds. 'No,' she said.

'See you in the morning, then,' he said and turned away. The coast seemed to be clear, and he slipped back across the open space between the cell block and the storeroom.

Suddenly a voice called out a challenge. Franklin sank down onto his haunches and searched the darkness for its owner. Whoever it was, he neither repeated the question nor seemed to be moving. He might just be standing there, waiting to see if Franklin would give himself away.

He waited, conscious that seconds were ticking, and that the inside patrol could arrive at any moment.

The voice cursed, and a cigarette end arced across the darkness, landing some six feet from Franklin. Footsteps faded into the distance.

The SAS man moved as fast and as silently as he could to the wall, and was just swinging himself up when he heard the sounds of an approaching patrol. His instinct told him it was the one inside the wall, but he had no sooner reached the top than it became obvious that instinct had played him false. The two men of the outer patrol were ambling towards him, deep in conversation.

Franklin lay stretched out along the top of the wall, wishing he could become as thin as one of those cartoon characters who had just been run over by a steamroller.

At some punchline the guards snorted with laughter, almost directly under Franklin's perch, stopping momentarily before walking on towards the road. The SAS man found himself offering heartfelt thanks to whatever it was that had amused them. And then, incongruously, he remembered making love on the beach with Sibou Cham. Not now, boy, he told himself. He lowered himself quietly to the ground and followed the patrol towards the road. Ten minutes later he was rejoining Wynwood and Caskey, and giving a mute thumbs-up to the latter's raised eyebrow.

Two hours later Jabang was sitting outside his room, staring blankly up at the mosaic of foliage above his head, dimly aware of the birds singing around him. He had not slept well, and the thought of Sallah's betrayal was still like an ache in his heart. I'd like to wake up now, he told himself, and discover that this has all been a bad dream.

Mansa Nouma, one of the younger men whom he had once thought of as his disciple, suddenly appeared beside him on the verandah. 'Lady Jawara is demanding to see you,' Nouma said apologetically.

Jabang looked at his watch. 'At this hour?' he asked disbelievingly.

'She says her children are dying, and need a doctor.'

Jabang grunted in amusement. 'A likely story.'

'I thought, since the Council may decide on releasing the children . . .' the young man said hesitantly.

'What's this?' Taal said, coming onto the verandah.

Nouma repeated himself.

'Let's go and see,' Taal suggested.

They threaded their way between the various barracks to the cell block, and in through the open front doors. At the end of the central corridor a shouting match was already in progress, between two men in Field Force uniform and the redoubtable figure of Lady Jawara.

'My children could be dying,' she shouted, catching sight of Jabang and turning the full force of her wrath on him, 'and these idiots who call you leader say they cannot see a doctor. What kind of men are you that take out your hatred on children? What kind of a revolution did you think you were going to have here, eh? I thought better of you, Mamadou Jabang. Not much better, but better than this. Using children as a shield.' The last words she spat out contemptuously.

Jabang refused to take the bait. 'So you think your children are dying,' he said unsympathetically. 'A third of the children born in the villages don't live to see their fifth birthday. But I don't suppose that comes up very often in palace conversation.'

'Is that a reason to punish my children?' she asked.

Jabang stood there looking at the ground, torn between his lifelong anger and his better self.

'Come in and see them,' Lady Jawara said simply. 'Please.'

The two leaders followed her into the cell, and were immediately set back on their heels by the stench. Two pails seemed almost brimful of diarrhoea. On the floor, two to each mattress, four pale children were laid out.

'Is this how you want your revolution to be remembered?' she asked them quietly.

Jabang turned on his heel and walked back out of the cell.

Taal caught up with him. 'We can't bargain with dead children,' he said.

'No,' Jabang agreed. 'We've got a doctor here, haven't we?'

'Not at the moment,' Nouma told them. 'Two were brought here from the tourist hotels when we had all the casualties, but they've both disappeared since. In any case she wants to see their usual doctor at the Medical Research Centre up the road. An Englishman. She says either he can come here or she will carry the children up to the Centre herself.'

Jabang sighed. 'An Englishman,' he murmured to himself. 'I suppose an outsider might be preferable. Call the Centre and tell – what's his name?' he asked her.

'Dr Greenwell.'

'Tell him . . . no . . . let me think.' Did they want outside eyes inside the camp? Did they have anything to hide? No . . . And then it suddenly occurred to him that it might all be a trick to get someone in, to spy out the land for a possible assault.

He turned to Nouma once more. 'You can escort Lady Jawara and the children to the Research Centre,' he said. 'Take a couple of men with you,' he added. 'And be sure to have everyone back here by eleven.' That was when he was due to speak to the Senegalese commander again.

'Thank you,' Lady Jawara said quietly.

He gave her an ironic bow.

Some four hundred yards to the south, on the Fajara road, the Medical Research Centre had roughly the same number of buildings as the Field Force depot, but in an area about five times as large. Modern one-storey cream and white buildings were arranged around large areas of open grass, with cultivated flowerbeds marking the boundaries between them. It made Franklin think of the TV series *The Jewel in the Crown*. This, he thought, was what the British Empire had looked like.

He was sitting out in front of the building which housed the two wards comprising the hospital section of the research centre. He was wearing a doctor's white coat and stethoscope, listening to a flock of crows cawing in the trees around him, and keeping watch on the distant entrance for any sign of the expected visitors.

He was also thinking that maybe less British money should be going into places like this, and more into places like the Royal Victoria. But what did he know?

The large lizard which had been clinging motionless to the nearby tree stump suddenly scuttled away across the grass, almost making him jump. And at that moment a taxi emerged from the trees around the entrance and headed down the road to his right.

The driver turned left and came to a halt in front of the hospital doors, a few yards from Franklin. Two men climbed out of the front seats, both of them carrying Kalashnikovs. One wore a red T-shirt and black trousers, the other, Mansa Nouma, was dressed in an ordinary blue shirt and jeans. Franklin thought they both looked about twenty.

'Is this the place for Dr Greenwell?' Nouma asked Franklin. He nodded.

Red Shirt opened one of the taxi's back doors to let out Lady Jawara and the four children.

'Go and find him for us,' Nouma asked Franklin, airily waving the gun's barrel to reinforce his request.

Franklin walked past them and through the doors into the entrance lobby. From there doors to left and right led into the two wards, while straight ahead there was a single large office for the sisters in charge. Dr Greenwell, as Franklin well knew, was waiting in that office. He knocked, went in and gave the doctor the prearranged signal.

By this time the two rebels had brought Lady Jawara and the four children into the lobby. Red Shirt was checking the window onto the men's ward, while Nouma was looking back through the open doors at the grounds outside.

'What can I do for you?' Dr Greenwell asked cheerily.

'She will tell you,' Nouma told him, gesturing with the gun towards Lady Jawara.

'I'm sorry,' Dr Greenwell said, 'but exactly who is it who is sick?'

'All my children. And myself,' Lady Jawara said.

'Then you must come this way,' the doctor said smoothly, gesturing them towards the women's ward.

The two rebels started to follow.

'No, no,' he said firmly. 'You cannot bring weapons through here. You will frighten the patients to death.'

'These are our prisoners,' Nouma said angrily.

'They will still be your prisoners,' the doctor said. 'We are only going to walk through a room full of sick women. Please, either wait here with your guns, or come with us and leave your guns behind. They will still be here when you get back.'

Nouma hesitated, then shrugged his acquiescence. It had been a masterful performance by the doctor, Franklin thought, but maybe they were also getting some help from a lack of confidence in the rebel camp.

The party walked down through the women's ward, Dr Greenwell in the lead, Lady Jawara behind carrying one child, the three other children and finally Nouma and Red Shirt, who seemed unsure of what to do with the hands that no longer held the Kalashnikovs.

At the end of the ward, twin doors led through to another corridor, which ran between a series of offices and a line of curtained cubicles. Dr Greenwell opened one of the office doors and ushered in Lady Jawara and the children. Nouma was about to follow when the door closed gently in his face.

'Surprise, surprise,' Wynwood said, as he and Caskey emerged from behind the curtains, Brownings in hand. The two rebels looked round for escape, and found Franklin's Browning also pointed their way.

The day had started badly for Mamadou Jabang, and it did not seem to get any better. He ate the breakfast that was placed in front of him, but not because he had any appetite – his mind was too busy racing through unpleasant possibilities to consider his body's needs. The thought that Jawara might refuse their terms gnawed at him mercilessly, because he could think of no other solution which gave him the chance of life with honour. They could certainly fight and die, as Taal had said, but it seemed such a waste. They could kill the hostages as they had threatened, but he had no real appetite for that either.

After two hours of chasing the same unwelcome thoughts around his brain it suddenly occurred to Jabang that no one had notified him of Lady Jawara's return. With a sinking feeling in his stomach he sent someone to the gates to find out if Nouma and the hostages had indeed come back.

The answer was no. He sat there for a moment, palms together across his nose, wondering how he could have been so stupid. 'Get me the Medical Research Centre on the phone,' he told the messenger.

Making the connection proved easy enough, but Jabang had to threaten sending an armed unit before anyone would admit to knowing anything. Finally a doctor told him that, yes, they had been expecting Lady Jawara and her children for several hours – where were they?

'Are you telling me they never arrived?' Jabang asked coldly.

'That is correct,' the doctor said, with the kind of patronizing English accent that made Jabang want to throttle him.

Instead he simply hung up, and spent an angry few seconds wondering whether to send a lorry-load of men to search the Centre. It would be a waste of time, he knew that. They would not find Lady Jawara. The fat bitch had escaped.

The sound of distant gunfire startled him out of his unpleasant reverie. It seemed to be coming from the direction of Fajara, though it was hard to tell. Another burst seemed to come from the opposite direction, and closer. What the fuck was happening?

Right on cue, Taal appeared through the screen door, buckling the holster over the Field Force uniform he still insisted on wearing.

'What is it?' Jabang asked.

'No idea,' Taal replied, 'and no one seems to be reporting in. I'm going to find out. Why don't you come along? The men would appreciate seeing you.'

That made Jabang smile, partly with genuine pleasure, partly at the irony of it. 'I have to talk to General N'Dor,' he said.

'OK,' Taal said. He nodded his head in the direction of the latest gunfire. 'Though that may be N'Dor talking to us now.'

It was, albeit with a certain lack of eloquence. After being informed, soon after eight a.m., of the successful SAS swoop to release Lady Jawara and the four children, the General had spent half an hour letting his rage gradually subside. How dare they mount such an operation without his approval? Who knew what might happen to the other hostages in retribution for Lady Jawara's escape?

He knew he was overreacting, and guessed that President Jawara must have sanctioned the operation in person. It was his country, after all, and he had the right to employ whatever foreign help he felt he needed. That, N'Dor realized, was what really hurt – that Jawara had felt he needed more than the Senegalese. And the General knew that this resentment was also irrational. The English had centuries of military tradition, money to burn on training and weaponry, and far more experience of this sort of thing than his own troops could ever hope to have. Even so . . .

The General lit a cigarette and walked outside into the yard, where the giant baobab tree loomed over him like Africa incarnate. It was time to do something, he thought, and the English had at least removed the main obstacle to military action. There might still be thirty or so hostages in the depot, but none as prominent as Lady Jawara. It was time to take a small risk, to give the rebels a push and see what happened. They might fight back one way or another, in which case he could stop pushing. Or they might simply collapse, in which case his Senegalese troops would be the heroes of the hour. Africans sorting out an African problem.

He walked inside to his office, telephoned Colonel Ka, and issued the code-word to activate the contingency plan. Senegalese units would advance on and around the two major roadblocks, and into the area behind them. Flanking forces would liberate the Sunwing and Bakotu hotels at either end of the Bakau-Fajara road, where over a hundred Europeans had been luxuriously trapped for almost a week.

He went back out to sit in the shadow of the baobab and lit another cigarette. Almost immediately the first sounds of battle drifted in from the north on the warm breeze.

He had been there about half an hour when an aide emerged from the doorway to tell him that the terrorist leader was on the line. N'Dor looked at his watch as he walked in – it was only ten-thirty-five.

'Good morning,' he said in Wollof.

'Who is firing those guns?' Jabang half-shouted at him.

'I don't know,' N'Dor lied. 'Whoever it is sounds nearer to you than to me,' he added disingenuously.

'If it is your troops it will mean an end to all negotiation.'

'If it is my troops, they will be firing in self-defence,' N'Dor said. 'Or without my sanction. You will have no reason to withdraw from the negotiations.'

'I already have one,' Jabang said. 'Lady Jawara was taken to the Medical Research Centre under a flag of truce, and this was violated. What more reason do I need?'

N'Dor resisted the temptation to blame the English. 'Your soldiers drove her straight to an embassy,' he said, 'where they released Lady Jawara and then asked for political asylum for themselves.'

'I don't believe you,' Jabang said automatically. He did find it hard to believe that Nouma would betray him, but then he had felt the same about Sallah. 'Which embassy did they drive to?'

245

'I can't tell you that,' N'Dor said. 'For obvious reasons. You could simply march in and take Lady Jawara back.'

'I could march into all the embassies,' Jabang retorted.

'You could. But that would damn you in the eyes of the entire international community, so you won't.'

There was a silence at the other end, in which the sound of several muffled voices could be heard.

'Can you please wait a minute?' Jabang suddenly asked with a courtesy that N'Dor found utterly incongruous. He lit another cigarette and waited.

In the Field Force depot command room Jabang, his hand over the mouthpiece, was hearing a report from Taal. 'It's impossible to tell if it was a coordinated attack,' Taal was saying, his eyes shining with excitement, 'but if it was they made an utter balls-up of it. At both roadblocks our men fired a few shots at the Senegalese, more to slow them down than stop them, but on the Fajara road the Senegalese simply retreated to their original positions and on the Banjul road they just turned tail and ran. Another unit which tried to outflank us on the Banjul road was attacked by a pack of dogs. I tell you, Mamadou, it's a farce out there.'

'But why?' Jabang wanted to know. He had never dreamed of news this good.

'They're just disorganized, that's all.'

'So it won't last. You're not saying we have any chance of victory?'

'Oh, no, none at all,' Taal said, crushing the hope that Jabang already knew was ridiculous. 'But it must improve our negotiating position.'

'Yes,' Jabang agreed. He took his hand away from the mouthpiece. 'General,' he said, 'your attack on our positions has apparently failed. You have obviously not been negotiating in good faith, but I am prepared to give you one last chance. I would have asked you to remove your troops to their previous positions, but my fighters seem to have done that for you.'

'I have not . . .'

'Just listen, General,' Jabang said contemptuously. 'I expect to hear President Jawara publicly accept our terms on the radio at ten o'clock tomorrow morning. If this happens, then all the children will be released immediately. If it does not, I shall begin executing the hostages until it does. Have I made myself clear, General?'

'Very,' General N'Dor said. 'But I . . .'

There was a click as the line went dead.

After having delivered Lady Jawara and the children to the British High Commission, the three SAS men had shared a celebratory drink with Bill Myers on the back verandah, and then retraced their path southwards along the beach. They had arrived at the back door of the Bakotu Hotel just as the Senegalese troops arrived at the front. The rebel guards had already vanished. Seventy tourists who had spent a nerve-racking week around the swimming pool reading thrillers were informed that they would soon be able to go home.

All three SAS men were dog-tired, but from what Lady Jawara had told them Caskey thought it more important than ever that General N'Dor sanction the much-postponed assault on the depot. The rebels were disorganized enough for it to work, and maybe desperate enough to do something stupid if left to their own devices.

Caskey was also keen to find out exactly what it was the Senegalese were doing. The officer in charge of liberating the

Bakotu seemed oblivious to any other operations taking place, but the sound of gunfire to the north told a different story. Caskey only hoped that N'Dor had not decided simply to storm the depot with troops who had no clear idea of what they were doing.

'I've got a lift with the Senegalese to Serekunda,' he told the other two. 'You two stay here, get a couple of hours' sleep if you can. I'm going to try and persuade N'Dor to give us a green light for tonight.'

'Good luck,' Wynwood said drily.

Colonel Ka arrived back at General N'Dor's HQ with all the enthusiasm of a Spanish Armada admiral returning to Spain. On the ride over from the outskirts of Bakau his memory had served up just about every childhood and adult humiliation it contained, and now, standing on the threshold of the General's operations room, he had to muster up all his courage to simply walk on in.

N'Dor looked up, sighed, and gestured Ka to a chair.

He took it, wondering why the tongue-lashing had not yet begun. A scene from one of those absurd James Bond films came to mind – the one in which the head villain dispatched one of his underlings, chair and all, into a pool full of piranhas. The Colonel found himself involuntarily searching the floor for signs of a trapdoor.

'What happened?' N'Dor asked, his voice more resigned than angry.

'We have taken the Bakotu and the Sunwing,' Ka said. 'So most of the Europeans who were in the rebel-held zone have now been released. But the advance in the centre was frustrated.' He paused, wondering how to explain it.

'By the rebels or ourselves?' N'Dor asked.

'Both,' Ka said. 'But mostly ourselves,' he admitted. 'Either the instructions given were not clear enough, or individual officers failed to follow them correctly. There seems to have been hardly any attempt on the ground to coordinate the various moves.' He sat up straighter in the seat. 'But whatever the reason, the responsibility is mine, and I . . .'

'No, it isn't,' N'Dor snapped. 'It's mine. And if we don't take immediate steps to improve the situation, I shall no doubt pay the price of failure.'

Ka decided it was wisest to say nothing.

'Time also seems to be running out as far as the hostages are concerned,' the General added, and gave Ka a blow-by-blow account of his conversation with Jabang.

'Then we will have to move before ten o'clock tomorrow morning,' Ka said. He hesitated for a moment. 'May I offer a suggestion?' he asked eventually.

N'Dor nodded.

'Our unit which was detailed to take the Sunwing ran into some resistance just outside the hotel. In the forecourt and among the gardens to one side. There was an exchange of fire which lasted something like ten minutes before the rebels made a run for it towards the beach . . .'

'The point?'

'About halfway through this fire-fight two tourists carrying tennis rackets suddenly appeared in the middle of the no man's land between the two forces. I've no idea how or why, but that's not important. The point is that everyone stopped firing, just like that. Our men and the rebels. These two white men walked calmly across the forecourt and two groups of Africans waited until they had gone before restarting their battle.'

'I am sorry, Colonel,' N'Dor said, 'but this does not surprise me.'

249

'No, sir, but that is not my point. It seems likely to me that the rebel soldiers, like our own, are under strict instructions to avoid any European casualties . . .'

'Probably.'

'General, if we let the three SAS men lead the assault on the Field Force depot it will probably prove successful. If it isn't, it's their failure. But if it is, we can say that we allowed white men to lead our attack because we knew that the presence of their white faces was likely to reduce casualties among our own soldiers.'

The General looked at him for several seconds with what could only be described as an inscrutable smile, and then suddenly burst out laughing.

N'Dor was still smiling twenty minutes later when Caskey arrived. 'As you no doubt know,' he told the Englishman, 'our offensive has run into some difficulties. I believe the time has come to launch the operation for which you trained my men.'

'Wonderful,' Caskey said, as pleased as he was surprised.

'One request,' N'Dor said, in a tone which made it clear that he was not asking. 'I should like the operation to take place soon after dawn tomorrow – in daylight, that is – as part of a general offensive against all the rebel positions. My regular troops are not equipped for night fighting,' he added in explanation.

'Very well,' Caskey agreed, not wishing to push his luck. In any case, he thought, there were also advantages in conducting their operation in daylight. It would certainly make it easier to tell friend from foe once they were inside the depot.

It did not occur to him that daylight would also make it easier to distinguish black faces from white.

14

Wynwood stopped suddenly, thinking he had heard a sound off to their right. 'Hear anything?' he asked in a whisper.

Franklin shook his head. The twelve Senegalese behind him were bumping into each other like trucks on a braking goods train.

It had probably been a representative of the local wildlife. Wynwood started forward again, moving their line of march in a long arc towards the rear of the enemy position. They had not seen anyone moving for some time, around either the barricade in the road or the houses the rebels were using as their camp, but that did not necessarily mean a thing. For all Wynwood knew the bastards were watching them through binoculars right now, and just waiting until they came into SMG range.

It was not likely though. It had rained for an hour or so in the middle of the night, the ground was soft, the moonlight dulled by high cloud cover. Conditions for a silent approach were almost perfect. And as far as they had been able to tell from observation the rebels had no binoculars.

Wynwood was twenty yards from the first building now, with the rest of the party strung out across the open ground behind him. He passed through the deep shadow of a mango tree, savouring its sweet scent but hoping that a ripe fruit would not drop onto his head.

As planned, the last two Senegalese in line were left by the door of the first building, and the two then bringing up the rear at the next. By the time they reached the back of the house which was being used by the officer in charge of the road-block, only Wynwood, Franklin and four of the Senegalese remained. Two were left at the back door.

Wynwood reached the front corner of the house and put an eye around it. Four men were sitting round a smoky fire, two in uniform and two not, each with a gun within reach. Two of these were Kalashnikovs, the other two Sterling sub-machine-guns. The Welshman withdrew his head and used a finger to spell out SMGs on the wall. Franklin nodded in understanding. Silence might be a priority but not if it involved looking down the barrel of an SMG. The rebels would not be given any second chances.

'OK?' Wynwood mouthed silently. Franklin nodded again, the two Senegalese simply looked nervous.

The four men walked out into the open space, so naturally that it took the rebels a full three seconds to realize that they were not on the same side. And by that time they had also become aware of the four guns aimed in their direction.

'Stand up and put your hands above your heads,' Franklin said softly but with deliberate clarity, hoping that all four spoke English. Apparently they did. 'Now walk this way and lie flat on the ground. On your stomachs.' They did as they were told.

Wynwood went to pick up the Sterlings, gave one to Franklin, and indicated to the two Senegalese that they should keep their guns on the four prone rebels. Then the two Englishmen took up position at the front door of the HQ house, and Wynwood shouted 'now!' with all the power in his lungs.

There was the sound of doors being pushed open, shouldered open, kicked open, the sound of surprised voices woken from sleep, one crash of broken glass, one drawn-out groan, but not a single shot was fired. Ten minutes later thirty-five rebels were being led in single file up the road in the direction of Serekunda, with six of the Senegalese soldiers in attendance.

If four of the prisoners looked somewhat underdressed for their night-time stroll it was because Franklin and three of the Senegalese were now sitting around the fire in the clothes they had been wearing. Twenty minutes later, when the four men of the regular rebel road patrol arrived in their jeep, even the growing light of dawn was not enough to expose the deception. All four were arrested without a fight, and sent on down the road after their comrades. As the first glow of the sun emerged from the distant ocean horizon one route to the rebel HQ was wide open.

A mile and a half away, at almost the same moment, Diba awoke with a start. He lay there for a few moments, wondering what had woken him, but could hear only the birds in the tree canopy that covered the depot. His mouth was dry from the booze, and maybe his brain was a little fuzzy from the dope. He could still smell the women on him, which made him feel good. A feeling spread through him, as strong as it was unreasoned, that this would be an important day in his life.

It was time to get away from the depot – even with the sort of entertainment that had been provided on the previous evening, the place was beginning to feel more and more like a prison. There was little doubt that Comrade Jabang and his revolution were doomed, and who knew what the crazy bastards might do with their backs against the wall. This lot might be more interested in looking good and ordering people around than anything else, but Diba had a sneaking suspicion that they *thought* they were trying to help humanity, and anyone who even thought something like that needed their brains washing out.

It was definitely time to put some distance between himself and the comrades, and get started on his own programme. The first thing was to get hold of a decent gun. A Kalashnikov was probably a great weapon for fighting wars, or even hijacking planes, but it did not fit snugly in the waistband of his trousers.

The sun was now clear of the sea, the sky beginning to clear. Caskey, standing up in the turret of the armoured car, looked back along the column of vehicles stretched out on the Serekunda road. Directly behind his vehicle were the four lorries containing their sixty-four Senegalese troopers, and behind them more armoured cars and lorries loaded with several hundred more soldiers. If N'Dor had got his act together a similar force would be launching an attack along the Bakau road in precisely twenty-five minutes.

Feeling a little like Ward Bond in *Wagon Train*, Caskey raised his arm and gestured the column forward. The armoured car jerked forward, almost throwing him off balance, and then settled into a satisfyingly smooth rumble. Caskey grinned to himself. The sun was shining, there was a breeze in his face, gorgeous palm trees waving him by, and he was off to war again. In moments like this he could understand the Sioux going into battle crying out that it was a good day to die.

Not that he expected to die in The Gambia. There would probably be a lot of sound and fury in the next half-hour or so – in fact he was counting on it – but Caskey did not really expect the terrorists to put up much of a show. It would be like sex, he thought – arriving was nice enough but it was the journey which provided most of the excitement.

Two lorries back Franklin was also thinking about sex. Or perhaps love – who could tell? He had not seen Sibou for more than two days, since escorting her home on the night they had made love. On the following afternoon the three SAS men had come across to Bakau for their appointment with Lady Jawara, and they had not been back to Banjul since. He wondered whether she was angry that he had not made contact. Or pleased. Maybe she would rather forget the whole business. After all, what could come of it – with him a soldier in Hereford and her a doctor in The Gambia?

He tried to put it all out of his mind. The Senegalese soldiers packed alongside him were mostly sitting in silence, some of them nervously chewing their lower lips or breathing deeply. A couple of the men who had taken part in the pre-dawn capture of the roadblock unit were in his lorry, and they seemed more relaxed than the others. It was all about confidence, as his athletics coach had told him over and over again.

They had been travelling for several minutes now; they had to be near the disembarkation point. Right on cue, the lorry started slowing down, and then turned right through the familiar gates of the Medical Research Centre. If the rebels had heard the approaching vehicles, then with any luck they would assume that they were on hospital business.

The Senegalese troops dismounted, and formed up in a column of pairs behind Caskey, Franklin and Wynwood. There was a lot of nervous grinning now, a clutching of amulets and the odd bow in what was presumably the direction of Mecca.

At Caskey's signal the column started off, with the Englishman at the front maintaining a steady jogging pace along the stretch of bare earth which adjoined the right-hand side of the road. They had about four hundred yards to go, which at this pace translated into not much more than two minutes.

It felt longer. The trees which leant across their path offered some cover, particularly if the Field Force depot sentries were in their usual position just inside the gates, and the sound of a hundred and thirty-four feet was more muted than Caskey would have believed possible, but sooner or later someone was bound to become aware of their approach.

They were more than halfway now, and he was beginning to feel the pace a little. By this time the armoured cars should be on the move behind them, the plan being that they should become audible at exactly the same moment as the first assault team became visible. 'Hit 'em with everything at once,' was Caskey's motto, and preferably at speed.

The gates were only a hundred yards away now, and the fire-station tower leapt into view above the trees, but still no shots or cries of alarm rose up from the rebel stronghold. And then suddenly one of the sentries ambled out across the road and into view, looking as if he had not a care in the world. For several seconds he seemed engrossed in rolling a cigarette, but either the movement or the sound of the runners must have caught his attention, because his head jerked round and his mouth dropped open. The cigarette slipped from his grasp, he looked around wildly as if in search of somewhere to hide, and then half-ran, half-scrambled his way back towards the gates.

Through the entire pantomime not a sound escaped his lips. It was his fellow-sentry who raised the alarm, letting out a blood-curdling shout at the same time as he opened fire with his Kalashnikov, apparently at the trees across the street.

The moment the alarm went up, Caskey had told his men, make as much noise as an entire fucking army. They now obliged, firing their Kalashnikovs and SMGs into the air with wild abandon, and shrieking like a bunch of hyperactive banshees. The drumming of their feet on the road suddenly seemed three times as loud, as if someone had accidentally knocked the volume control.

The ambling sentry had already disappeared, the one with the gun took one appalled look at what was coming towards him and bolted out of sight through the gates. Caskey was about twenty yards behind him, shooting through the open gateway in a half-crouching run, braced for the impact of whatever it was the rebels had to throw at him.

There seemed to be nothing. Figures were visible in the distance, some already running for cover, some foolishly just standing there, curiosity getting the better of their survival instincts. Thanking their lucky stars, the SAS men and the Senegalese troops spread out in the prearranged pattern, still running, with the leading twenty men heading straight for the last-known location of the hostages.

Jabang had, as usual, been sitting on the command office veran- dah when the first shot rang out. Instinctively, he knew what was happening, even before the sudden, tumultuous outburst of gunfire and shouting which came on the first shot's heels.

He walked quickly inside and picked up the light sub- machine-gun which Taal had got for him, and stood there for a few seconds, holding the gun and staring blankly into space. Then he strode purposefully through the command room and out of the building's front door. About a hundred yards away he could see men in uniform running in what looked like all directions. The Senegalese.

He became conscious that several of his own men were standing around him, all carrying guns, all looking at him and waiting for his orders.

He did not know what to tell them.

There was a loud explosion away to his right, in the direction of the cell block. The hostages were being released! Jabang started off instinctively in that direction, his men dutifully following him, but almost immediately found himself face to face with Taal.

The military commander, who had neither shirt nor shoes on, was carrying only an automatic pistol. 'Get to the back gate,' he told Jabang, 'it's the only way out.'

Jabang looked at him as if he was a creature from Mars.

'Go!' Taal shouted at him.

Jabang went, collecting more and more men as he went. The mad burst of gunfire which had started the attack now seemed reduced to the occasional shot, and at the gate Jabang could see many of his men already hightailing it into the distance across the stretch of mostly open countryside. He took one last look back, wondering where Taal was, and then started running for his life down the dirt lane and through the knee-high grass.

For all his determination to be ready when the time came, Diba had the misfortune to be in the middle of his morning shower when the assault team came through the gates. He struggled back into his clothes, grabbed the rifle which he had had the sense to keep with him, and cautiously poked his head out of the washroom barracks, just in time to see two white men race past him, followed by a bunch of Senegalese soldiers.

He pulled his head quickly back, waited five seconds, and tried again. The soldiers were gone. He stepped out, turned a corner and started running like everyone else towards the rear of the depot, swivelling his eyes to left and right for any sign of immediate danger. The parade ground in the centre seemed empty at first, but as Diba loped across it he saw a man emerge from the command offices on the far side, carefully buttoning his Field Force uniform shirt, as if this was the day of all days for being smartly turned out.

The man was carrying an automatic pistol, Diba realized, and he slowed his pace to a fast walk as Taal came towards him, then pulled up the Kalashnikov and blew a bloody hole in the neatly buttoned shirt. Hardly breaking step, Diba let the rifle drop and stooped to pick up the pistol. Now he had a weapon for the outside world.

Not far away Wynwood and Franklin were taking turns smashing the cell locks, and telling the hostages they were safe. Most of them looked undernourished and generally the worse for wear, but it seemed that none had been tortured or killed. In a world like this one, Wynwood thought, be thankful for such mercies.

Outside Caskey was experiencing a mix of emotions. The operation seemed to have been a complete success when it came to safely rescuing the hostages, but most of the rebels had probably escaped, because it had been planned that they should. The normal procedure for an op like this was to have assault and perimeter teams, the latter mopping up what the former flushed out. But this time Jawara and N'Dor between them had vetoed the encirclement of the depot, on the grounds that the terrorists were more likely to harm the hostages if they had no means of escape. Caskey had argued that the assault team would be moving so fast that the terrorists would have no time to realize they even had such options, but he had been overruled.

Still, he thought, looking round at the Senegalese troops now swarming through the depot grounds, the rebellion was over. They had done what they had come to do. The Gambia belonged to President Jawara once more.

Two hours later General N'Dor gave a press conference under the baobab tree behind his HQ. He confirmed the strong rumour that two British Army advisers had taken part in the attack on the Field Force depot. 'We knew that the rebels did not shoot at white men,' he explained, 'because we had seen white men going and coming even in areas we considered dangerous. The rebels didn't shoot at them because they wouldn't know whether they were diplomats or other personnel, injury to whom could bring down outside intervention on their heads.' The General nodded here, as if he saw the rebels' point. 'Lives have been saved,' he went on, 'and that's what matters. Whether they were saved by white, blue or green men is to us unimportant.'

He offered no explanation as to why the rebels, seeing their last stronghold being overrun, should still be worrying about outside intervention.

By this time the three SAS men had been given a lift by the Senegalese back to the Presidential Palace, where they found the red carpet conspicuous by its absence. The President had apparently removed himself to his bungalow in Bakau, and the SAS men were politely informed that rooms had been reserved for them at the Atlantic Hotel. Their belongings had already been packed and taken across.

'I've heard of overstaying a welcome, but this is ridiculous,' Caskey said.

'At least our bags weren't taken to the airport,' Wynwood said.

Worse was to come for Caskey. From the Atlantic he phoned Bill Myers, who told him that direct communications with London had been established, and that the Foreign Office was less than ecstatic about the SAS unit's elastic interpretation of 'military advice'. They were also wondering why Caskey had not sent back a single report since their departure from London.

'Because we've been too damn busy doing the job we were sent to do,' Caskey said angrily. 'Sorry, Bill,' he added, 'it's not you I should be yelling at.'

'Don't worry about it,' Myers said. 'And your real boss sent you all a "well done".'

'Well, that's something.'

'And he's given you all a week's immediate leave.'

Caskey went back upstairs to tell the others, but both men were stretched out in their rooms, fast asleep. He went to his own room and sat down on the edge of the bed, feeling the familiar flatness of a mission completed.

It was early afternoon before Radio Gambia announced the routing of the terrorists and 'the restoration of democracy and order'. Those few rebels and criminals still at large in the Bakau-Fajara area would soon be captured, the announcer said. All those people who had not yet returned to their work should do so without delay.

Sibou Cham listened to the broadcast in the nurses' common room at the Royal Victoria, and wondered whether Moussa Diba was dead, captured, or one of the 'few still at large'. The odds were on his having been taken, but she had no intention of taking any risks until she knew for certain.

She wondered whether the news on the radio meant she would see Worrell Franklin that evening. It was always possible that she had completely misread him, and that he had no intention of ever making contact with her again, but she did not think so. It had been so wonderful that night on the beach, and she found it hard to believe that he would not be as willing to repeat the experience as she was.

Two hundred or more rebels and ex-prisoners had managed to swarm out through the Field Force depot's back gate, but for most of them it proved to be no more than a temporary reprieve. There were only three ways out of the Bakau area: by sea, across open country, or by road. Few of the rebels had any experience with boats, the open savannah made them sitting targets, and all traffic on the few roads and tracks out of the area was subject to stop and search by the authorities. Not surprisingly, more than half of the escapees had been captured by midday, and a majority of the rest before the daylight faded.

Diba was not one of them. He had immediately realized that the suburbs of Bakau offered a better chance of avoiding detection than open country, and once he had gained the relative safety of populated streets Diba did not make either of the two mistakes most popular with his ex-comrades. Instead of beginning to believe in his own invisibility or instantly seeking out a ride to the haven of the poorer townships, he worked his way across the suburbs and out the other side, to where the mangrove swamps around Cape Creek offered a multitude of hiding places.

Through the rest of the daylight hours he waited, daydreaming of possible futures far from Banjul, and occasionally slipping into sleep for a few blissful minutes. He would wake with hunger gnawing at his stomach, limbs cramped from their confinement within the mangrove roots, and the sun apparently no further across the sky.

At long last night began to fall, and as soon as he judged it dark enough Diba started off on the three-mile walk which would bring him to the Denton Bridge. Working his way along the strip of broken country which lay between the ocean and the road was neither easy nor fast, but this route did keep him clear of checkpoints or patrols, and after less than an hour's walking he found himself looking out over Oyster Creek, the bridge a hundred yards or so away to his right. Beyond it, on the same bank, were the tourist-boat moorings.

He made his way down to the water's edge and began following it towards the bridge, keeping a careful eye on the Senegalese checkpoint at its near end. As luck would have it, a minibus had just arrived, and the soldiers had their work cut out examining the passengers and their luggage. As Diba passed under the bridge he could hear a heated argument start up on the road above – something to do with a chicken, though he had no way of knowing what.

There was no light on the small wooden jetty, and it was difficult to choose between the dozen or so dug-out canoes tied up against it. Diba had never been particularly comfortable in boats, but he was not much of a swimmer, and in Oyster Creek there was always the chance of meeting an undernourished crocodile. He untied the mooring rope of the best-looking craft, climbed gingerly aboard, and managed to sit down without tipping the boat over and himself into the water. Though the argument around the brightly lit bus on the bridge was still filling the evening air, he focused all his concentration on making no sound with the paddle until he was at least halfway across the wide creek.

In midstream he crossed under the bridge, so as to reach the shore on the ocean side of the road. There was no check-point on the Banjul end, and he decided to risk walking straight down the unlit road into town. An hour later he was making a wide loop round a checkpoint outside the Banjul High School, crossing Box Bar Road and ducking into the backstreets of Portuguese Town. Another ten minutes and he was slipping through the gate of Anja's compound.

Her room was in darkness, so Diba simply let himself in, anger rising at the thought of finding her with someone else. But she was not there, and neither were any of her things. The room had been stripped bare of everything but the bedstead.

He went in search of neighbours, and found two young men sharing some ganja in one of the other rooms. They looked at him blankly when he asked about Anja, so he dragged one of them across the yard by the ear to jog his memory. It worked, but not in the way he had wanted. Anja, it seemed, had moved out several days ago. And had not given anyone any idea where she was going. She had been frightened of someone, one of the young men volunteered, before realizing that he was probably talking to the frightener.

Diba gave him a contemptuous look and went back to Anja's old room to think. He had been savouring this moment for days, and now it had all been snatched away from him. He needed a woman, he needed to . . . to show someone who he was.

He told himself to calm down and think. His clothes had survived the day without getting too soiled, which was good. His first need was money – enough of it to get clear of the country.

He knew exactly where to go. Halfway down Jones Street, just by the intersection with Spalding, was the home of a money-changer who went by the name of The Christian. Diba had no idea what his real name was, but he did know the man kept his money at home, because he had once tailed him there from his pitch opposite the tourist market. In those days his ambitions had not extended beyond Banjul, and the fear of being identified had held him back from going ahead with a robbery, but now he was on his way out of the country. And in any case, no one was ever identified by a dead man.

He arrived outside The Christian's house, saw a light burning inside, and knocked on the door. The man himself answered it, his eyes growing rounder as he saw the automatic pointing at his chest.

'Get in,' Diba growled.

The man backed away. 'What do you want?' he pleaded.

'What do you think?' Diba sneered, closing the door behind him and bringing the gun up to within an inch of his terrified face. 'I want all the money you keep here, and it had better be a good sum. Or I'll just blow your head all over the wall.'

The man looked into his eyes, and did not like what he saw. 'OK, OK,' he said, 'it's in here, come, I'll give it to you, all of it.'

The money – a thick wad containing assorted denominations of dalasis, CFAs, English pounds, French francs and US dollars – was in a padlocked metal box under the table.

Diba's mouth watered at the sight. 'How much is there here?' he asked softly.

'About two thousand five hundred dalasis – that's almost a thousand dollars . . .'

It was a fortune. 'Turn round,' said Diba.

The man opened his mouth to speak, but decided not to. He turned round, and Diba swung the automatic against the side of his skull with all the force he could muster. After gathering up the money he put an ear against the man's chest to see if the heart was still beating. It seemed not to be, but just to make sure he hit him again in the same place.

He let himself back out into the night, feeling the adrenalin flowing through his veins, a faint throbbing in his head. A woman cast a doubtful glance in his direction as she walked by, and his smile in return only served to hasten her steps.

He needed a woman, he thought. And soon.

McGrath heard a later airing of the same news broadcast as Sibou, and immediately telephoned Mansa Camara's office to find out whether Diba was on the list of those killed or captured. The Field Force man was not there, but one of his subordinates told McGrath that he would try to get him the information. Ten minutes later he called back with the news that Diba had so far not been found, either alive or dead.

McGrath packed up work for the day and drove the ministry jeep up to the Royal Victoria. The reception area was empty and she was sitting in her office, feet up on the desk, apparently deep in thought. She looked up with a start, and he caught a flash of disappointment where he had expected fear. 'Waiting for someone?' he asked.

'No,' she said. 'How are you?'

'As well as can be expected.' He sat down on the edge of her desk. 'He may still be out there,' he told her bluntly.

'I know.'

'So I've come to take you home.'

She smiled at him. 'That's very kind,' she said, 'but – I don't know – I feel restless this evening . . .'

'Then let's paint the town red – what's left of it.'

'Oh . . . I don't know . . . what have your English friends been doing?'

'I don't know the details, but they've been over in Bakau for the last couple of days. And probably running the whole show, if Caskey had anything to do with it.'

'And now it's over they'll be going back, I suppose?' she said, a little too obviously.

McGrath's face split into a grin. 'I get it,' he said. 'So which one is it? No, don't tell me . . . Wynwood's happily married and Caskey's older than I am. It must be our Mr Franklin.'

She rolled her eyes at the ceiling. 'I like him, OK?'

He laughed. 'It's great,' he said. 'I was beginning to get worried about you.'

'You're impossible,' she said.

'So my wife tells me. Anyway, they're staying at the Atlantic Hotel now . . .'

'Since when?'

'Since this afternoon. I'm meeting Caskey up there in an hour or so. Want to come? Or would you like me to take your boyfriend a message?'

'He's not . . . And I can deliver my own messages, thank you.' She smiled at him. 'But you could drive me home, wait while I have a shower and change, and then drive me over to the hotel.'

'Uh-huh. And what's in it for me.'

'A double whisky?'

'You could have had me for a single.'

'I know.'

Diba could not believe his luck. Not only had the doctor emerged with the Englishman McGrath, but he was able to flag down a passing taxi in time to follow them back to the house in Wellington Street. He saw them enter the front door as his cab went by, and by the time he had paid off the driver and walked back the fifty yards someone had turned on the second-floor lights.

It was an old building from colonial days, and as far as Diba could tell its bottom two floors were occupied by a daytime business. Certainly there was no sign of life through their shuttered windows, and generally speaking this was a commercial rather than a residential area.

He thought about simply knocking on the door and having one of them open it onto his gun. The trouble was, it might be the woman, and then he would have to find a way to deal with the Englishman. He knew from experience that was not likely to be easy. No, this time he had to be certain, and not give the bastard the slightest chance of a comeback.

Fifteen minutes they had been up there now, and the only reason he had for supposing they were coming down again was the slapdash way the Englishman had parked the jeep, slewed halfway across the road. Diba examined the columned porch, and decided that it would be an ideal spot for an ambush if they did come down again.

He went back into the road, looked up at the lights, and wondered if they were fucking at that moment. It made him feel hot thinking about it.

One light went out, and then another. Diba hurried back into the shadows of the porch and waited for the hoped-for sound of feet on the stairs inside. The seconds stretched out until he was almost convinced that they had gone to bed, and then he heard her voice, sounding almost insultingly happy, and the door swung open. She came out first, and he caught a glimpse of her body profile as she walked past him. The Englishman followed, almost too quickly, but in one motion Diba took a single step forward and brought the automatic swinging down on the side of his head. Not as hard as he had hit the money-changer – he wanted this victim alive, at least for a while.

Franklin examined himself in the mirror, took one last admiring look at the batik trousers he had just purchased in the hotel shop, and left the room. 'See you later,' he told Wynwood through the Welshman's open door.

'Not if you're wearing those trousers,' Wynwood said. 'Have fun,' he yelled after him.

Franklin smiled to himself as he walked down the stairs. He could get to really like Wynwood, he thought. The Welshman did not get serious very often, but when he did it counted. He knew where the line was between being real and playing games, and in the work they were in it was a good thing to know.

He left the hotel and briskly walked the few hundred yards which separated it from the entrance to the Royal Victoria emergency department. There he received his first shock – it was in darkness. He looked at his watch, which told him it was half-past eight. Somehow he had assumed she would still be working, as she had been on the other days. Why, he asked himself, had he not thought to phone her earlier?

She must have gone home, he decided. He did not have her home telephone number, and he had no certain knowledge of the address, only a visual memory of where the taxi had stopped that night when he took her home. She had not wanted him to come up, and in the street he had been too busy kissing her goodnight to take much note of the surroundings.

But he did remember the name of the street.

Franklin walked down to Independence Drive, still cursing himself for his stupidity, and managed to find a taxi.

He climbed into the front seat. 'Wellington Street,' he told the driver.

'What number?' the man asked.

'I don't know. Just start at one end and drive slowly down.'

The driver gave him an odd look and pulled away. In not much more than a minute they were at the head of the street in question, and about half a mile down Franklin spotted the tell-tale clue – McGrath's Ministry of Development jeep. It was possible that the Ministry had more than one jeep, but highly unlikely that they employed two men with such indifferent parking skills.

It was now about twenty minutes since Diba had knocked McGrath unconscious and pressed the barrel of his automatic between Sibou's lips. Pulling the Englishman up two long flights of stairs had taken up quite a time – the man was heavy and Diba could only use one hand, since the other was needed for keeping the gun on the doctor.

She was worried that McGrath might be dying, but Diba would not let her examine him. In any case, it probably did not matter, she told herself, because the maniac was going to kill them both anyway. She fought back the rising tide of panic which accompanied this realization, and a second – that Diba had been so humiliated at their first meeting that the likelihood of him making any mistake at all was extremely slim.

But he might, she told herself, he might. And if he did she had to be calm enough to make the most of it.

They finally reached her flat on the second floor. After she had turned on the lights he dragged McGrath to the middle of the carpeted floor and then went back to lock the door, all the time keeping the gun pointed at her.

'Nice place,' he said, walking to the open window and looking out. The sky was full of twinkling stars, and the lights of Barra, two miles away across the river, seemed dead by comparison. Tomorrow he would get a taxi from there to the Senegalese border, and try and find some way round the border post. But that was tomorrow . . . He turned back to her.

'The house belongs to my father,' she said, thinking that any conversation was better than none.

'And where is he?'

'He lives in New York. He used to own the business downstairs.'

'And he gave his little rich-girl daughter all these rooms just for herself.'

'There are only two.'

'Two is a lot,' he muttered. His eyes were darting to and fro, as if looking for something. 'Find something to tie him up with,' he told her.

'I don't have anything.'

'Take off that dress and tear it into strips,' he said, grinning.

'I have another dress,' she said, turning away.

'That one,' he said, 'or I kill him now.'

She gave him a contemptuous look, pushed the straps from her shoulders and stepped out of the dress. She was shaking inside but trying hard not to show it.

'I thought about your body such a lot in prison,' he told her.

'It's only a body,' she said, wondering how long it would be before he asked her to remove her underwear.

He tore the dress up himself, and braided several strips until they were strong enough to hold McGrath's wrists together behind his back. Then he used the Englishman's belt to loop his tied wrists to the leg of a heavy wooden table.

'Now you can take a look at him,' he said. 'And bring him back to life. I want him to be able to see it all.'

She knelt down to examine the head wound. It was not as bad as she'd feared . . .

The bell rang in the hallway outside. Someone had pulled the rope at the front door.

'What's that?' Diba hissed.

'Someone at the door,' she said. She could only think of one person it would be, and the sudden feeling of hope almost overwhelmed her.

He stood there, uncertain what to do.

'They'll have seen the lights,' she said.

'Who is it?' he asked.

'I don't know.'

He slapped her with the back of his hand, almost knocking her off her feet. 'I don't know!' she half-shouted.

'Come with me,' he said, grabbing her by the arm and pulling her alongside him out through the door and down the stairs, just as the bell rang again above them.

He stopped and swung her round at the first-floor landing, intending to say how he expected her to get rid of the caller at the door, and remembered she was almost naked. 'Fuck!' he muttered violently. 'OK, you'll get behind the door,' he hissed. 'And if you make a single sound both you and whoever it is out there are dead.'

Franklin had spent a few minutes wondering what to do. Sibou had told him that McGrath was only a friend, and he had believed her, but standing out there in the street, the man's jeep in front of her house, he had begun to fear the worst.

You're being stupid, he told himself. Go and knock on the door.

He found an old-fashioned bell-pull and tugged on it, causing a bell to ring somewhere high in the house. For what seemed like an age nothing happened, so he pulled again, and then footsteps could be heard, which seemed to stop and start again, bringing all his suspicions back to life.

And then the door opened and an African face appeared, that of a man in his mid or late twenties, with a smile on his face and eyes that seemed not to match it.

Franklin had never seen Diba, never heard him described, but in that moment he knew that this was the man who had attacked her, the man whom McGrath had disarmed, and that he was holding a gun in the hand hidden from view behind the door.

Diba, for his part, had opened the door not only prepared for trouble, but also assuming that it would wear a white face. The sight of a man with a black face and batik trousers instantly eased his mind. 'What do you want?' he asked.

'Taxi,' the Englishman said creatively, making a fair stab at delivering both syllables with a Gambian accent. He looked at Diba, waiting expectantly. 'Woman called,' he added helpfully.

'She changed her mind,' Diba said, digging in his pocket and coming up with a five-dalasi note. 'Take this,' he said, and began to close the door.

The other hand was still out of view, and Franklin could not risk setting off the gun by launching himself forward. The door clicked shut, but no footsteps sounded inside. The man was waiting for him to leave before he moved back upstairs.

Franklin walked back down the steps, and turned left up the street, continuing on until he knew he was out of sight of the house. What should he do? The idea of going for the police was quickly abandoned: it would take hours and Sibou might only have minutes. She might already be dead. The thought cut through his mind like a knife.

There was only one thing for it – he had to get into the house, and now. It would have to be the back. He found a way between the next two houses down and stumbled his way through the dark backyard of the one which stood next to Sibou's building. The ground behind the latter was over-grown, the only back door seemed both locked and rusted shut, and the windows were barred as well as shuttered. The verandah on the first floor looked more promising, but it was fifteen feet up, and the wall seemed to offer no help to a would-be climber.

Inside the house Sibou was holding on to the hope that the man at the door had been Franklin. The voice had not sounded like his, but she could not think who else it could have been. She wondered for a moment if McGrath might have phoned for a taxi while she was in the shower, but there would have been no reason – they had his jeep. And anyway, she suddenly remembered, the man had said it was a woman who called.

It had to be Franklin. He would get help or something. She just had to stay alive long enough for it to arrive.

All these thoughts ran through her head as Diba dragged her back up the stairs. At the top he pushed her into the flat and again locked the door behind him.

Franklin, or whoever he went for, would have to come through that door, she thought. There was no other entrance. She would have to distract Diba somehow, make noises to cover any that her rescuers might make. One thought came into her mind and caused her to shudder. She would sooner die, she thought, and then realized she would rather not.

274

'Wake him up,' Diba said, waving the gun in the direction of McGrath. She dutifully leant over the Englishman and took his pulse, which was surprisingly strong. 'He'll come round in a little while,' she said, and at that moment an almost inaudible groan escaped from his lips.

Franklin had already wasted several minutes looking for something to help him onto the verandah when he discovered the line of iron rungs just round the corner of the building. Silently cursing himself, he started to clamber up as fast as the need for silence would allow, until one rung came half out of the wall and nearly sent him tumbling thirty feet down to the ground.

Moving more cautiously, he reached the level of the top-floor windows. Craning his neck round the corner of the house, he could see dim light coming from both, which suggested that light was filtering through from the room at the front. But he could see no way of reaching the windows from the ladder of iron rungs, and for a few moments he could see no reason whatsoever why the rungs had been placed where they had. Then he realized: the newer bricks to his right were blocking up what had once been a doorway.

He carried on up to the flat roof, pulled himself over the edge and lay still for a second, listening for any sounds that might be coming through from below. There were none. He got carefully to his feet and tiptoed over to the front edge, almost strangling himself on a half-invisible washing line. Here he could hear a voice – the man's – but not what he was saying. And then Sibou, who replied more clearly: 'You'll kill him!'

Putting his head over the edge, Franklin could see the lighted windows below. The shutters were open, and he guessed that the glass windows were too, but there was probably a mosquito screen. The top of the window was about five feet below the level of the roof. He had no harness, but there was little choice.

He went back for the washing line, decided it was strong enough, and spent a few minutes knotting foot and hand holds at one end. Then he tied the other through one of the holes in the parapet where the water drained off the roof.

He stood there for a moment, thinking that he should have called the police, or someone, before coming up to the roof. If he fucked this up then there would be no help for her or McGrath.

But it was too late to think about that. Just don't fuck up, he told himself, and everything will be fine.

He lowered himself over the edge, walking his feet down the wall inch by inch as he let the rope out through his hands. When he was level with the window he paused, and wondered how many years' wages he would give for one stun grenade. Then he took a deep breath, bent at the knees, and pushed himself off the wall and out into space.

Sibou had told Diba that McGrath needed water, and he had accompanied her into the kitchen while she filled a cup from the tap. She noticed he had an erection, and wondered how long his desire for an audience would dampen his desire for her. Back in the living room she applied water to McGrath's lips and forehead, and was just opening the top button on his shirt when her ears, already straining for any sound from beyond the locked door, picked up the slightest of scraping noises from outside the open window.

She managed not to look at Diba, instead rising to her feet as noisily as she could manage. 'He can see now,' she said aggressively, walking away from McGrath. 'Let's get it over with,' she went on, moving towards the couch, pulling Diba's eyes away from the direction of the window. To hold them on her she reached back to unhook her bra, flicking it off her shoulders and letting her breasts fall free, just as Franklin came hurtling feet first through the open window.

Diba whirled around, tried to raise the arm that held the gun, but found both her hands wrapped around it. He slashed out with his other hand, sending her flying, and turned in time for a final glimpse of the taxi driver from downstairs, perched on his knees, both hands around the butt of an automatic that was aimed between his eyes.

Darkness fell swift as a camera shutter, eclipsing his world.

Epilogue

Caskey and Wynwood set foot again on British soil the following Sunday afternoon, having flown from the reopened Yundum Airport to Luton with a plane full of complaining package tourists. Despite assurances to the contrary from the High Commission in Bakau, their passage through customs and immigration was neither smooth nor speedy. No one at Luton had been given any advance warning of two returning SAS men bearing semi-automatic handguns, and the ensuing phone calls took much longer than the process under way in the main hall, that of relieving the tourists of their duty-free excesses.

Caskey had been half-expecting a posse of journalists, but not even a single newshound was waiting to dog their steps, and the two men ended up boarding the bus for the railway station like any pair of returning holiday-makers. A newspaper left lying on one of the seats gave no clue that The Gambia existed, let alone that anything newsworthy had happened there.

They sat on Luton Station, waiting for the delayed train to London, eyeing their fellow travellers as if they were from another planet. 'We've been gone almost exactly eight days,' Wynwood murmured, 'and it seems like a couple of months.'

'It always feels like that,' Caskey said. 'This time next week it'll feel like three months since we came back.'

The train finally arrived, and while Caskey read the paper Wynwood stared out of the window at the darkening countryside and suburbs, mentally comparing the silhouettes of oaks and poplars with palms and mango trees. Caskey was right, he thought, already Africa was turning into a dream.

In London the MOD had arranged for a taxi to whisk them across town in time to catch the last connecting train from Paddington to Hereford. Wynwood had time to call Susan before it left, and found himself, wholly unexpectedly, almost in tears simply from hearing the sound of her voice.

She brought the car to Hereford Station, and they gave Caskey a lift back to his flat in the centre of town. 'It was a pleasure working with you,' the Major told Wynwood as he climbed out of the back seat.

'It was mutual, boss,' Wynwood said.

Caskey walked slowly upstairs, feeling faintly envious of Wynwood's youth, not to mention the Welshman's obvious joy in being in love. He let himself into the flat, poured himself a generous drink, and sat down on the sofa. The previous Saturday's paper was still sitting on the coffee table, its back page headlining the news of England's inevitable defeat.

He leaned back in the chair and smiled. What a summer it had been!

Late that night Mamadou Jabang and three of his young acolytes arrived in the small town of Cacheu on the river of the same name. After a day holed up in a terrified supporter's house in Bakau they had travelled south in the President's speedboat, which Junaidi Taal had used for his escape from the Denton Bridge a week before, and which the Senegalese had not thought to either guard or remove from the beach beneath the African Village Hotel. The fuel had soon run out, but two days of drifting on the prevailing southerly current, the second without water, had brought them, bedraggled but hopefully safe, to this estuary town in the small republic of Guinea-Bissau.

What the next twenty-four hours held in store none of them could know. They had no money, and no way of sending for any. The local authorities might simply return them to The Gambia, or they might agree to give them political asylum. Most likely of all, if Jabang knew anything about his fellow African politicians, they would choose to do neither. Letting revolutionaries stay in one's country invited trouble, and sending them back reminded your own people how oppressive your regime had become. No, the local authorities would simply find some way to pass on the problem to someone else.

Through such means, sooner or later, Jabang hoped to find himself back among friends willing and able to support him in a second attempt at rescuing The Gambia from international capitalism.

Next time, though, he would steel himself to be harder.

Arriving at his office that Monday morning, Cecil Matheson found a full report waiting for him on the events of the past two weeks in The Gambia. The *status quo ante* had been satisfactorily restored, thanks in large part to the efforts of the three SAS military advisers.

By this account – and by most others that Matheson had picked up on the Whitehall grapevine – they had somewhat exceeded their authority. Questions were also being asked about the activities of a fourth man, apparently an ex-SAS officer, who had not even had any authority to exceed.

Still . . . Matheson smiled to himself and closed the folder. Perhaps he should send his American counterpart a copy, he thought. After the farcical mess they had made of trying to rescue their hostages from Iran the previous year, Lubanski and the Pentagon could do with some professional advice.

That same morning McGrath dropped in on Mansa Camara at his home in Serekunda. McGrath still had headaches, but the Medical Research Centre had given him a clean bill of health, provided he agreed to avoid excitement for a fortnight. Chance would be a fine thing, he thought, as he parked the jeep. His SAS friends were gone, and Sibou would not be back for a few days yet.

He found Mansa in cheerful mood, despite the announcement that The Gambia was now to have an official army of its own. 'It's either that or risk the Senegalese Army marching across the border every time there's any trouble,' the ex-Field Force officer said. 'Sooner or later they might just decide it would be easier to keep their troops here on a permanent basis. And if we have to have an army I'd rather it was made up of Gambians. No country deserves an army that speaks another language.'

'So the Field Force is being abolished?'

'Yes.' Mansa grunted. 'Too many officers ended up on the wrong side. Some of them good men,' he added, as if surprised by his own readiness to admit such a thing. 'And there is one good thing about an army. It means the police force can be just that, and not get itself mixed up in politics.'

'Maybe,' McGrath agreed. 'I've been an Army man since I left school, but I was kind of getting used to being in a country where there wasn't one.'

'I noticed,' Mansa said wryly. 'Yes, well . . . Jabang and the comrades wanted to bring about change, and in that at

282

least they were successful – The Gambia will never be the same again.' He shrugged. 'But in the long run I expect all the tourism will change us even more, and not for the better.'

McGrath thought about that as he drove back to Banjul. Mansa was probably right, but there seemed to be very few other ways that the country could earn the money to pay for all those consumer goods which most of its people seemed to want. It was sad, he thought. From what he had seen, the African people deserved better.

It had taken Franklin two days to sum up the courage to talk to Sibou about their relationship, and when he finally did so it came out much more negatively than he intended. 'I know you can't give up what you do,' he said, 'and I can't give up what I do. How can we keep anything alive when we live and work three thousand miles apart?'

She had looked at him for a moment. 'Do you want to keep it alive?'

'Yes, but . . .'

'There are things called planes,' she said. 'If you're coming from England, The Gambia is the cheapest place to get to in Africa. And that works both ways.' She had taken him by the shoulders. 'It won't be easy, and it may be impossible, but we can try. What have we got to lose?'

He had her to lose, he thought that afternoon, as they sat together on a stone wall overlooking the ocean. They had come to the Île de Gorée, the island off Dakar which the man in the French café had recommended to him and Wynwood, and which she had visited and loved several years before. Most tourists came over on the ferry, visited the famous Slave House, shopped for souvenirs, walked along the bougainvillaea-covered lanes, and returned to Dakar a few hours later, but there was one hotel on the island, with three high-ceilinged rooms and shuttered windows that opened onto a view across the beach and jetty.

Now they were sitting at the rear of the red-stoned Slave House, above the cells where hundreds of thousands had waited in suffocating squalor for a voyage to the New World. Here was where their two lives divided. His ancestors had been taken, and hers had not.

'Did you read that report,' she asked, 'the Senegalese General saying that he only let your friends lead the assault because the rebels would not shoot at white faces?'

'Yeah,' Franklin said. 'And all the reports I've seen only mention two SAS men, or two British soldiers.' He laughed. 'I might as well have been invisible.'

'Doesn't that make you angry?' she asked.

'Two weeks ago it would have,' he said. 'And I guess if I think about it then it still does . . .' He looked at her. 'But if I hadn't had a black face when I came to your door that night, Diba would have killed me, and probably you and McGrath as well . . .' He opened his palms in a gesture of resignation, and smiled at her.

'I like *your* face,' she said.